From

Colonel Winston breathed deeply of the air. God, it felt good, and it tasted good. It boosted his spirit and made him thankful that he was alive. He walked taller and with renewed confidence along the carpet of thick grass. He looked at the trees, listened to the sounds, scanned the plants, admired the blooms and the colors of the foliage.

Until he reached the spot where Yamaguchi's body had been found. The crime scene tape had been removed yesterday, but the spot was clearly marked in his mind. He wanted to shy away, but something made him peer into the shadows under the brush where Yamaguchi's body had been found. His eyes widened and he stopped cold. God! There were two shoes sticking out from under the brush . . .

MORE MYSTERIES FROM THE BERKLEY PUBLISHING GROUP . . .

FORREST EVERS MYSTERIES: A former race-car driver solves the high-speed crimes of world-class racing . . . "A Dick Francis on wheels!"
—Jackie Stewart

by Bob Judd
BURN
CURVE
SPIN

THE REVEREND LUCAS HOLT MYSTERIES: They call him "The Rev," a name he earned as pastor of a Texas prison. Now he solves crimes with a group of reformed ex-cons . . .

by Charles Meyer
THE SAINTS OF GOD MURDERS
BLESSED ARE THE MERCILESS

FRED VICKERY MYSTERIES: Senior sleuth Fred Vickery has been around long enough to know where the bodies are buried in the small town of Cutler, Colorado . . .

by Sherry Lewis
NO PLACE FOR SECRETS
NO PLACE FOR DEATH
NO PLACE FOR SIN
NO PLACE LIKE HOME
NO PLACE FOR TEARS

INSPECTOR BANKS MYSTERIES: Award-winning British detective fiction at its finest . . . "Robinson's novels are habit-forming!"
—*West Coast Review of Books*

by Peter Robinson
THE HANGING VALLEY
WEDNESDAY'S CHILD
INNOCENT GRAVES
PAST REASON HATED
FINAL ACCOUNT
GALLOWS VIEW

JACK McMORROW MYSTERIES: The highly acclaimed series set in a Maine mill town and starring a newspaperman with a knack for crime solving . . . "Gerry Boyle is the genuine article." —Robert B. Parker

by Gerry Boyle
DEADLINE
LIFELINE
BORDERLINE
BLOODLINE
POTSHOT

SCOTLAND YARD MYSTERIES: Featuring Detective Superintendent Duncan Kincaid and his partner, Sergeant Gemma James . . . "Charming!"
—*New York Times Book Review*

by Deborah Crombie
A SHARE IN DEATH
LEAVE THE GRAVE GREEN
ALL SHALL BE WELL
MOURN NOT YOUR DEAD

As Crime Goes By

RICHARD F. WEST

BERKLEY PRIME CRIME, NEW YORK

AS CRIME GOES BY

A Berkley Prime Crime Book / published by arrangement with the author

PRINTING HISTORY
Berkley Prime Crime edition / September 1998

For information address: The Berkley Publishing Group, a member of Penguin Putnam Inc., 200 Madison Avenue, New York, NY 10016.

The Putnam Berkley Inc. World Wide Web site address is http://www.penguinputnam.com

ISBN: 0-425-16536-1

Berkley Prime Crime Books are published by The Berkley Publishing Group, a member of Penguin Putnam Inc., 200 Madison Avenue, New York, NY 10016.

PRINTED IN THE UNITED STATES OF AMERICA

10 9 8 7 6 5 4 3 2 1

Special thanks to Henny Youngman
for his cooperation on this work,
and for all the laughs over the years.

For Jeanette with all my love and devotion
"until death do us part."

PREFACE

The following are common abbreviations used in the online chat rooms. There are many abbreviations that are in common use. In this story only these few are used.

lol or LOL—laugh out loud
<g>—grins
< >—encloses an action, ie. <smiles>
{ }—a hug
:*—kiss (on its side it is a face with puckered lips)
c(≡)—mug of beer or any other drink

CHAPTER 1

The shoe was just visible beneath the bushes. The heel run down, the sole thinning, it was a shoe made for work and had seen much of what it was made for. Over time the leather had stretched and softened and formed to fit the foot of the owner like a comfortable extension of the man. Brown dirt had been so often scuffed into the leather that it had become part of the surface, and the leather had changed to the color of the dirt. Where the leather had been repeatedly creased, cracks had formed. The lace was worn and the end was broken off. The frayed ends of what remained were tied into a tight knot below the top eyelets. At the moment the shoe was still, the bushes above it quiet.

The computer screen glowed a soft white. The words appeared in black and slowly scrolled up the screen.

Shy-Guy: It is so nice talking to you. Feel I've known you my whole life.
FineLace: Yes. I'm so glad we met. Nice to find a friend.
Shy-Guy: It's been almost a month. Maybe we should celebrate? <g>
FineLace: A long term relationship. <smiles>
Shy-Guy: We should toast to it becoming longer. c(=) ← Beer is all I have to offer right now. <g>
FineLace: Beer is good. <g> But only one. Not much of a drinker I'm afraid.

Shy-Guy: You mean I can't get you drunk and seduce you? <grins slyly>
FineLace: Afraid not. That wouldn't be much fun anyway, would it? <smiles seductively>
Shy-Guy: To be serious a moment, Mildred, I have to say that I feel we should take this relationship to another step.
FineLace: Now, now. Don't rush things. <smiles>
Shy-Guy: Not like we have a lot of time, you know.
FineLace: ?
Shy-Guy: We aren't getting any younger . . . I . . . I would like to meet you.
FineLace: Well, I don't think that's a good idea.
Shy-Guy: Why?
FineLace: You really know nothing about me.
Shy-Guy: What are you hiding from me?
FineLace: I could be an old bag lady.
Shy-Guy: Old Bag Lady with a computer? Long extension cord on your shopping cart? <g>
FineLace: lol. Well, I am an Old Bag. <g>
Shy-Guy: At our time in life, it's the person, not the age that means anything. I like the person I've come to know. And I'd like to know her more.
FineLace: I don't want to spoil what we have.
Shy-Guy: It's time we took this relationship further. You know it, too. I want to put a face to this person. All I see of her is font Arial 12. How can I put a picture of Arial 12 on my dresser?
FineLace: Silly. <g>
Shy-Guy: Exactly. We aren't fonts. We are people. And people should get to know each other face-to-face.
FineLace: I feel it is too soon, Timothy.
Shy-Guy: When I was young, a month was a small piece of the time pie. At my age, a month is a big piece of the little time left. Let's not waste the rest of it . . . Meet me somewhere? You pick the place. I'll go wherever I have to . . .
Please don't say no.
FineLace: Let me think about it, Timothy. Please. This is not an easy thing for me to decide.
Shy-Guy: Tomorrow night? Will you be able to give me your answer then?

FineLace: Yes. I will tell you tomorrow night.
Shy-Guy: Goodnight, then, Mildred. Until tomorrow night. You have pretty dreams, dear one.
FineLace: Goodnight, Timothy.
Shy-Guy has left the conversation

Mildred stopped scrolling through the chat history and let the screen stay on those last few lines. This was the conversation she'd had with Timothy last night online. She'd promised him she'd give him an answer tonight, and she'd been up half the night struggling with that promise.

She had mixed feelings about meeting with Timothy. She liked him, that went without question. And she truly would like to meet him, to get to know him better. It was not the prospect of romance that prompted her. Romance was a naïve little girl tittering in the background. What she needed more was a friend. Someone to share the remaining fun that life had to offer.

Timothy was right about one thing. Time was racing by, and there wasn't much left in her life. She was seventy-three. What did she have left? Ten years, maybe? Maybe less. Then there was the threat of debilitating illness hanging over those ten years. So there were too few years remaining to taste joy, and share it with someone. Why should she deprive herself? She knew she should meet Timothy and see where things went from there. True, she'd taken worse risks in her life—and most had ended in disaster. But life was an adventure, and there wasn't much adventure left to live. Someone once said that the greatest regrets we have are those risks we never took. Maybe that applied now more than ever.

And, yet, something nagged in the back of her mind. Some small voice kept whispering that this was moving too fast. She truly did not know the man. He was just a string of words appearing on the computer. This was no way for a woman, especially a supposedly respectable old lady, to meet someone. It simply was not done.

Things were never simple. Mildred sighed in frustration. What was she going to tell Timothy?

• • •

The morning sun was draining the coolness from the air, the coolness that came with each night. Soon the day would be warm, then hot, and people would huddle in air-conditioned interiors for relief. Floridians gave up shoveling winter in the North for the ninety-degree summer weather in the South. A trade-off few regretted. But summer was slipping away. Soon the days would become more pleasant.

Benny Ashe walked past the swimming pool and onto the spongy St. Augustine grass, heading toward the gazebo that sat overlooking the lake. Benny was a short, wiry man with a tough-guy disposition. Seventy-three years had not softened the steel core that had been tempered by growing up on the streets of Brooklyn. Benny had only an eighth grade education, but he had a lifetime of common sense. He wore his usual worn sneakers, faded cotton pants, and faded blue shirt with short sleeves. On his head was a dark peaked cap with NY printed on it in letters that were once white, but now were crumbling and gray.

He was looking around him, squinting in the sunlight as he approached the gazebo. In the gazebo sat two old men. By the standards of the residents of the Home these men, in their eighties, were truly old. The residents called them Tweedledee and Tweedledum—though there was no agreement on which was which.

One had fair skin with plenty of wrinkles. His gray hair was long and thin and flew everywhere in the breeze. This didn't bother him. He was beyond trying to impress anyone. He wore an old and colorless sports shirt. His tan cotton pants looked as old as he did, but his sneakers were still quite new. He was thin and tall, and his brown eyes, hidden by brown sunglasses, were muddied with age. He was stretched out in his favorite position. His long legs, reaching far out from the chair, were crossed at the ankles, and his hands were folded on his chest.

The other man was shorter than the first and also very thin. Age had bent his back somewhat. He sat with his legs crossed and his arms up, hands tucked behind his head. His usual position. His skin was nut tough and more wrinkled than the other man. Reflector sunglasses hid clear and alert washed-out blue eyes. On his head he wore a sailor's hat that hung like a limp rag, the life drained from it. Too many washings, too much wear. This man's sneakers and shorts also looked old and worn. The T-shirt he wore was new. Written on the back of the shirt was D.A.D.—DADS AGAINST DIAPERS . . . IT'S NOT A JOB IT'S A DOODIE.

As Benny approached the two men he could hear them talking.

Gray Hair kept looking out at the lake as he spoke. "You ever change a diaper?"

Sailor Hat kept his eyes on the lake, as well. "Why? Is mine smelly?"

Gray Hair said, "I meant when you were young and had kids. If you can remember back that far."

"Got a good memory considering how far back it goes."

"I go back pretty far, too. When I was young all the Us were Vs. Stone and chisel were for taking notes."

"Never changed a diaper. In those days women knew their place—not like today."

"Where did the younger generation go wrong?"

"Guys?" Benny said, coming up behind them. They didn't turn around. "You seen Yamaguchi around?"

"Today?" Sailor Hat asked.

"Yeah. I was supposed to have breakfast with him this morning." As he spoke, Benny kept looking over the grounds, looking for signs of Yamaguchi. "He didn't show up."

"Sorry," Gray Hair said. "Don't pay much attention to gardeners."

"You don't pay for anything," Sailor Hat said. Then to Benny, "Did see The Colonel walk by a little while ago. Might want to check with him. He walks the grounds about every morning."

"He was headed that way." Gray Hair pointed toward the rear of the Home—Coral Sands Assisted Living Retirement Residence to those who didn't live there. It was a large pink stucco building, three stories high and surrounded by landscaped grounds. Plenty of grass and flowering shrubs. A beautiful place to stroll.

"It's called a constitutional," Gray Hair said. "The Colonel was out for his morning constitutional."

"Constitutional is the law of the land," Sailor Hat said.

"You mean I gotta take a walk every morning?"

''It's the law.''

''What about wheelchairs and crutches?''

''Everybody.''

''Is it called a constitutional if you're rolling around or limping?''

Benny sighed. It was impossible to talk to these guys. ''Thanks.'' He turned to walk away but pulled up with a start, face-to-face with Elaine Singleton. ''Jesus!''

Elaine, emaciated to nothing but a skeleton covered in mottled skin, was dressed neatly. Her gray-straw hair was combed back severely. ''Do not use the Lord's name in vain,'' she said, holding her hand up to ward him off, the hand wavering unsteadily. ''The Lord's vengeance is swift and powerful. Woe to the sinner that stands against him!''

Benny's face was inches from hers, and the words came out of her mouth accompanied by breath that was eighty proof. Benny winced from the power of the fumes and turned his head away.

''Morning Elaine.'' Benny nodded and stepped past her. He headed off toward the rear of the building in search of The Colonel.

''The final justice will be the Lord's,'' she shouted at his back. ''You can not escape his wrath!''

''A silver gravy boat.'' Manuel said, his hint of a Spanish accent rounding over the harsh tones. ''Is missing.'' He stood in the doorway of Jessie Cummings's office, leaning against the doorframe. The apron was wrapped all the way around his lean body. Short and dark, with black hair and dark eyes, Manuel had gentle features and always the hint of a knowing smile.

Here we go again, Jessie Cummings thought. *Please, God, give me a rest. Ten years of managing this place, and the surprises never stop. Let this be something simple?* ''Is there anything else missing?''

An attractive woman, Jessie Cummings wore a tailored tan suit that she felt made her look slimmer than she was. Forty was the time when the food a woman ate went to her waist, and Jessie Cummings could see it accumulating there daily. It was also the time when a woman faced the realization that she was aging, and Jessie took to the bottles—magic potions of hair dye, skin lotions, and wrinkle creams—to keep her hair shiny black and youthful-looking, and to give her skin the appearance of being wrinkle-free and flushed with life.

"No. Gravy boat was not in dishes I wash from dinner of last night. Is maybe the beginning, no?"

"Just the gravy boat? Maybe it was an oversight. Did you double check the count?" Once the words were out, she was sorry she said them. She knew Manuel would not have come to her without making sure the silver gravy boat was definitely missing.

"No. No oversight. I check carefully. Is missing. For now I will count the dishes from each of the meals."

"Any of the new people in the kitchen walking out with unusual packages?"

Manuel shrugged. "Who steals gravy boats? Is not something in demand on world market."

Jessie nodded and sighed. "Yeah, well watch them anyway. World markets have a way of changing rapidly. And please keep a running total of the items that turn up missing."

"I will count, also, the tablecloths, napkins, and chairs." He gave her a small knowing grin.

Jessie grinned back at him. "Don't forget the lamps and pots and pans."

Benny Ashe spotted The Colonel with Charlie Aspen standing by the edge of the lake looking out over the water and the palm trees beyond. Benny headed for them. Great day to be out walking, Benny thought, surprised he had noticed. So many great days that they became the norm, and he hardly noticed them anymore.

The Colonel was a tall straight man with the commanding air that surrounds people who were once in authority. He had a full head of neatly trimmed gray hair, and his clothes seemed neatly trimmed as well. A Marine to the bone.

Charlie, on the other hand, was a big burly man going to paunch. He'd been head of the European sales force for some company, and had a salesman's confidence in his voice and manner.

"Seems ironic," Charlie was saying. "You spent all those

years in the Marines living and fighting in the tropics, and here you are—retired among the palm trees. I would think you would want no more to do with this environment.''

''Does seem masochistic in a way, doesn't it,'' The Colonel said. ''I saw a lot of awful things in brush like this.'' He shook his head slowly—not at the irony, more to push away the memories that threatened to come out of the dark. ''But this all gives my life some continuity. Retiring from the service and leaving the surroundings in which I had spent so much of my life was too much of a break with the past, I guess.''

''Excuse me, Colonel,'' Benny said, coming up behind them. The two men turned to him. ''Hi, Charlie.'' Charlie nodded. ''Either of you guys seen Yamaguchi today? I was supposed to have breakfast with him, and he didn't show. Waited in the dining room for over an hour. Finally came out looking for him.''

''I just came outside,'' Charlie said.

''No, Benny,'' The Colonel said, frowning, searching his memory. ''I haven't seen him. Walked all over this place this morning.''

Benny shook his head, ''I don't understand it. Not like the guy to not show up.''

''You sure you have the right day?'' The Colonel asked. ''He only stops by once a week, as I remember. His sons do the lawn mowing and trimming, and I know they're not due until tomorrow.''

''Yep, today. This week he was gonna be here every day in the morning. He was supposed to plant some new ground cover all around.'' Benny smiled. ''That's the part of the business he likes to do himself. He leaves the grunt work for his sons. But he likes to put the plants in the ground and see how the whole scene changes instantly.''

''Wait a minute,'' The Colonel said, his memory revealing a clue. ''I did see a large number of potted plants on the other side of the building. Maybe he's a little late. Let's take a look.''

''It's all right,'' Benny said. ''I don't need an escort.''

The Colonel looked at Charlie as he spoke to Benny. ''It's not like we have any pressing business. Do we, Charlie?''

Charlie shrugged. ''This is the time of my life when I can

move freely on the spur of a moment. Don't deprive me of that joy, Benny.''

Benny smiled. ''C'mon along. I'd enjoy your company.''

The three men walked over the lush lawn around toward the back of the building.

The woman's scream startled everyone in the dining hall. Forks stopped in midair, mouths froze open, eyes widened with fright, and stomachs tightened like hard fists around eggs, bacon, and anything else recently consumed for breakfast. Pacemakers shifted into gear, medications strained as blood pressures took a jump skyward, lungs froze in mid-breath, and in that instant all conversation and idle thought stopped cold. Everyone snapped their heads to look where the scream came from. At the far end of the dining hall Constance Beardsley, a chubby woman in a dress too-tight for her, was standing by a table, her hands locked onto the back of the chair she'd just pulled out from the table. She had fully intended to sit on that chair until she saw what was already on it. She changed her mind in a flash and screamed as loud as she could. She kept screaming, frozen into the position of holding the back of the chair, until one of the waiters rushed over. All eyes watched. At first he peered at the chair, hesitated, then picked up a gray fuzzy critter from her chair by the tail and carefully examined it. Constance stopped screaming and cringed away from the waiter. He grinned in relief, held it up for all to see, and then squeezed the mouse body. It squeaked.

''Rubber mouse!'' he said, loud enough for all to hear.

A sigh of relief mixed with mutterings and smiles swept over the room. Constance's shoulders sagged and her body relaxed. She shook her head in disbelief at the prank.

''The Mad Joker strikes again,'' Walter Innes said. He was a gaunt man with sagging knobby features, long bony hands, and short gray hair that was a bit disheveled. Walter's clothing was color matched so only a color-blind man would appreciate it. The handle of a wood cane poked up between the arm of the chair and his leg. He was a physician who had reluctantly retired when his own physical deterioration made it impossible to continue practicing. Seated at the table with him were three other people.

"He is certainly creative," Peter Benington said, willing himself to calm down after that sudden jolt. He was listening internally to his heart beating like a drunken man falling down a flight of stairs. "And indefatigable." He hoped the beta blocker he'd been taking would keep that heartbeat from getting out of control. Peter was suave in a David Niven sort of way, which included a thin, neatly trimmed white mustache and a similar English accent. His clothing was a neat arrangement of shades of tan.

"Always on the job"—Eleanor said, her voice smooth and confident—"to entertain us." It was clear she was *not* entertained. Eleanor was an attractive woman with superbly colored brown hair that was informally coifed and ended in a soft flow just above her shoulders.

"And give us indigestion," Walter said. He grimaced, pushed away the plate that held the remains of his breakfast, and placed a hand on the knot in his stomach.

"Or a heart attack," Betty said, in a tiny fragile voice. She was a dumpy little woman in a blue dress with a tiny flower pattern, her hair dyed black to match her black button eyes, "It's too bad Benny wasn't here. He'd be rolling in the aisle."

"Yes," Walter said. "Humor, like music has its levels of sophistication. Benny enjoys the simpler forms of humor."

"What makes you think the Mad Joker is a 'he'?" Eleanor asked Peter, her tone a bit defensive. "Don't you think women are capable of bad taste?"

Peter looked at her with a sly grin. "I am sure women are truly capable of more devious things than mere men can imagine. For instance," he said, turning his face to scan the dining room, "the room is filled with so many more women who have outlived their exhausted husbands and are enjoying the money it killed them to earn. Devious." He grinned playfully at Eleanor.

Eleanor returned the grin. "It's not who wins the battles, it's who wins the war."

Peter liked her smile. He liked a lot about this woman. So much so, that for the two months he'd been at Coral Sands, he'd approached her carefully to avoid scaring her away.

"So, Peter," Walter said, "you've been here a couple of months. Has Coral Sands lived up to your expectations?"

"Frankly, I feel it is too early to form a valid judgment, Doctor. You see, I have as yet not been to the beach. Eleanor keeps promising to take me but it never happens."

Eleanor laughed, "We live here, we don't go to the beach."

Betty giggled.

"I'm sure you can do better than that, my boy," Walter said.

"May I say," Peter said, "that I did have a more simple opinion of what retirement would be like in a place such as this."

"Oh, I do love that way he talks. So English," Betty twittered.

Eleanor grinned. "A bunch of quiet, dozing old folks?"

Peter smiled. "A little extreme. But, to a certain degree, yes."

"People stop being interesting when they get old?" Walter added.

Peter said, "Well, it has been a concept I have held since my youth. But"—with a grin—"that has changed since I have joined the ranks."

"Too many interesting things going on for people to become boring," Walter said. Then he added with a smile, "You have to work at it, like I do."

"This from the man who just bought a computer," Eleanor said.

"Bought is the operative word," Walter said. "Georgie Allan is bringing over one of his computer whiz friends this morning, some fourteen-year-old, who's going to help me learn about what I just purchased. It should be interesting. Today everyone has their own web site and E-mail address. It might be fun to know what they are all talking about. Maybe I won't feel . . ."

"Oh, there's Elaine Singleton," Betty interrupted. She had spotted Elaine moving past the windows that looked over the grounds toward the lake. "Poor woman."

"Yes," Eleanor said. "She hasn't been the same since her son took her to the doctor two weeks ago."

"She's got religion," Betty said. "Maybe the doctor told her something terrible?"

"Facing one's own mortality can do strange things to a

person's personality,'' Walter said. ''I'm sure the alcohol isn't helping her any, either. If she's taking any medications she could have peculiar psychological side effects, and especially when enhanced by alcohol. Not to mention the combination could be downright deadly.''

''I'm sure Elaine's doctor must have warned her about all that,'' Betty said.

Walter chuckled, ''It is not the doctor's responsibility. We were clever enough to pass that on to the pharmacist. Patients already had too many grounds for suing us. So we spread some of that liability in the direction of the local druggist. Gives the lawyers more to do.''

''I think lawyers have plenty of mischief to do,'' Betty said. There was anger in her face and in her tone.

''Been talking to Eugene, again?'' Eleanor asked.

''Yes,'' Betty said, merely annoyed now, not angry. ''He doesn't make himself clear sometimes. He toys with me, like he enjoys teasing me.'' She let out a sigh. ''He always was like that—teasing me a lot.''

''You mean death hasn't changed him,'' Walter said, with a hint of amusement.

Eleanor gave Walter a look that said he should not push any further. Then she gave Peter the same warning look.

''I think he's gotten worse at the teasing since he died,'' Betty said, ignoring Walter's tone.

Even though some inexplicable things had happened, Peter still had a hard time accepting the whole scene with Eugene. Two months had not been long enough for his mind to adjust to the eccentricities and eccentrics surrounding him at Coral Sands.

''So, what did he have to say, Betty?'' Eleanor asked.

It was Eleanor's view of this fantasy that fascinated Peter. She was such a levelheaded, insightful person. Yet, she had no trouble accepting Betty's communications with Eugene. Just because it appeared strange, she had said to him, didn't mean it was not possible. He couldn't argue with that logic. But he felt there were some strange things that were just strange, and not possible at all. The trouble was that so many of these things had happened, and he couldn't be sure about Eugene.

"Well, he said I should trust in my investments," Betty said.

"Sounds perfectly clear to me," Walter said.

"Well, it isn't clear to me what that has to do with anything," Betty's tiny voice was strained with her annoyance. "What I asked him about had nothing to do with investments."

"What's the problem, Betty?" Eleanor was genuinely concerned.

Betty shook her head and made a small wave with her hand, indicating that she didn't want to discuss it.

"Maybe Eugene doesn't have the answer?" Eleanor suggested. "Maybe it's something we can help you with?"

"It's too embarrassing," Betty said. "I really don't want to talk about it, Eleanor." Then, as if to settle the matter, "Eugene *always* has the answer."

Peter looked at Walter, who just rolled his eyes. Peter saw Eleanor watching him, and it took all his strength not to make a visual comment to Walter on what he himself was thinking.

The lobby of Coral Sands was like an upscale hotel. Done in muted pink and green pastels, it was furnished with lush plants in brass pots, brass and glass tables, sofas, and stuffed chairs. The ceiling vaulted three stories to an expanse of skylight. At the rear of the lobby was a glass elevator that went to the second and third floors.

The elevator was descending slowly to the lobby floor. When it stopped, Mildred got off and stepped across the lobby toward the clown sitting on a sofa. The clown had on a curly bright red wig, and a bright red-and-white checked outfit complete with big flappy shoes. The clown's face was done up in stark white with a broad red smile and large red nose. But the clown sat quietly, hands covered in white gloves, folded in a red-and-white lap.

Mildred sat down on the sofa next to the clown.

"I hope I'm not keeping you from something," Mildred said.

"You got about five minutes before my ride comes," the clown said in a husky, gravelly voice. "I'll be back in a couple of hours. Just doing a rich kid's birthday party. Then I'm free for the day. We can always continue then, if you want."

"Alice, I really don't want to wait, if you don't mind," Mildred said. "You see, I have a problem that's kept me up half the night, and I don't know what to do. I need your advice."

Alice gave out a big husky laugh. "Coming to a clown for advice already says you have a problem."

Mildred didn't laugh. "This is a woman thing. And I was hoping you could help me. I've been meeting with this man on the computer for a month. Nothing outrageous. Just casual conversation. He's a very nice man."

"Computer, huh?" Alice shook her clown head and little bells rattled. "Don't know anything about them except they are everywhere these days. But I do have some experience in the men department. So, fire away."

"Well, Timothy wants to meet me face-to-face." Mildred sighed and her shoulders sagged. "I don't know what to do."

"And you want me to tell you what to do?" Alice chuckled a deep, heavy clown chuckle. "C'mon, Millie, we're too old to be telling each other what to do. What do you feel deep down that you want to do?"

Mildred smiled. "I'd like to meet him." She shrugged playfully. "It sounds exciting to meet someone new like this."

"Then go for it, Millie. Excitement in life gets rarer and rarer. Just take precautions." Alice chuckled. "And I'm not talking about birth control."

"What do you mean?"

"There are a lot of sharks in them there waters. And they're looking out for women to prey on. So be careful."

"Well, that's the little voice that keeps whispering in my ear. As a woman, I have always had the fear of becoming a victim. Now, as an *old* woman, I seem to be more afraid."

"Well, don't tell him too much about yourself just yet."

"What do you mean?" Mildred frowned.

"Does he know how much money you've got? Does he know where you live? Things like that."

"No." She tried to remember. "I'm sure none of that was mentioned." She frowned again, searching her memory. "No, I'm absolutely sure we never talked about those things. I mean, he does know I'm in Sarasota. He lives in Sarasota, too.

That's why he wants to meet with me. We live close by." She searched her memory once more. "No, no addresses were mentioned."

"Good. Keep it that way for awhile." Alice shrugged. "You never know. And if you go to meet him, take somebody along. That way, at least, there'll be a third party in the picture, in case there's some funny stuff behind this meeting. And if you want to get serious about this, do a background check on the guy. You know, hire a private detective to check the guy out, see that he's on the up-and-up. Can't hurt. And it can give you some peace of mind."

"Seems a bit much, don't you think?" Mildred said.

Alice just shrugged, setting her bells to tinkling.

"Suppose he finds out I did that?" Mildred said. "He might feel angry with me."

"Girl's gotta do what a girl's gotta do," Alice said. "There are risks attached to everything we do. Take the risk. If he's a nice guy, like you said, he should understand. If he doesn't, well, maybe he isn't the kind of guy you think. And it would be best to find that out, too."

Alice spotted a scruffy-looking man come through the front door, step to the counter, and say something to Grace. Grace pointed toward Alice, and the man looked over. He made a strange face.

"Looks like my taxi is here, Millie. Gotta go."

"Thanks, Alice."

The clown stood up. "Hang on, Millie. I'll talk to you when I get back later."

"All right," Mildred said. "I told Timothy I'd give him an answer tonight."

"Good. Should be back about noon. We'll do lunch and talk some more about this Timothy guy. See ya later." The clown gave her a small wave with a white-gloved hand, then walked clumsily in the flappy shoes over to the guy at the counter.

When Benny, The Colonel and Charlie came around the far corner of the building, they saw a cart filled with oyster plants sitting next to the thick clump of hibiscus plants that bordered the property. There were also oyster plants in pots laid out beneath some of the hibiscus, placed where they were to be planted. As they approached the area with the potted plants they could see that some plants had already been put in the ground.

"It looks as if Mr. Yamaguchi has been working," the Colonel said. "There are plants already in the ground."

"Some tools on the cart, too," Charlie said.

It was only when they reached the area where plants had already been put in the ground, that Benny saw the shoe lying beneath the bushes. He didn't say anything to the others. He just pointed to the shoe. The Colonel stepped forward, crouched down, pulled aside the branches, and found the man wearing the shoe.

"Jesus," Benny whispered.

"Damn," Charlie said.

CHAPTER 2

The two kids walked through the front door and stepped over to the desk. Both were in that gawky preadolescent stage. One, a redheaded kid, was a foot taller than the other. He carried a black plastic box containing computer disks. The kids looked out of place among the old people who moved about the lobby.

"We're supposed to meet Dr. Innes, Grace," Georgie Allan said. He was twelve years old and the shorter of the two.

"Yes," Grace smiled. "He told me you were coming. Who's your friend?" Grace was in her fifties. She was a tough-looking woman with a solid, stocky body, dyed brown hair, cold blue eyes, and a warm disposition exactly the opposite of the way she looked.

"This is Artie Dunsworth. He's going to help us with Dr. Innes's computer."

"Nice to meet you, Artie," Grace said, as she stood. "If you two boys will take a seat over there"—she pointed to one of the sofas—"I'll see if I can find him." She came around the desk as the kids went to the sofa and sat down. She walked across the lobby toward the dining room.

Peter spotted Grace entering the dining room. "Looks like your computer support has arrived," he said, and with a nod of his head indicated Grace coming toward their table.

Walter turned and saw Grace motion in the direction of the lobby. Walter nodded in thanks and pushed himself away from the table. "Well, all, I must leave." He struggled to stand, using the cane for support. "It is time for me to enter the twenty-first century. *Star Trek* here I come."

"Good luck, Walter." Peter grinned.

"Yes," Eleanor said, "and just remember, a child can master the thing. So, don't be intimidated by it."

"Children can do a great many things I have never been able to master. This may be another. But thank you for the vote of confidence." He turned and limped out of the dining room following Grace.

As Grace and Walter walked across the lobby toward the two boys, Benny came rushing in from the front entrance. He saw Georgie Allan and his friend on the sofa, then he saw Grace and Walter and headed them off.

"Grace," Benny said, in a low voice. He did not want the boys to hear him. "You gotta call the police. Now. We found Yamaguchi dead in the bushes." He pointed toward the far wall of the lobby. "Looks like he's been stabbed."

It took a moment for the full impact of the words to find their way into Grace's frame of reference. "God!" she said under her breath, and rushed over to the desk.

"Killed!" Walter said, also in a low voice.

"Yeah, Doc. Looks like it," Benny said. "Maybe you ought to come take a look."

"Yes." Then, in a normal voice to the two boys sitting on the sofa, "Georgie, I think you and your friend will have to wait a little longer. There's been an accident, and I must go see if I can help."

"We can come back later," Georgie said, and looked to Artie.

"Yeah, Dr. Innes." Artie shrugged. "Sometime after lunch?"

"That will be just fine, thank you," Walter said. Then to Benny, "Take me to the scene."

Grace hurried straight into Jessie Cummings's office.

Jessie took one look at Grace's face and knew something bad had happened. *Be calm,* she told herself. *Whatever it is, be calm.* "What's the matter, Grace?"

"Benny just told me that the gardener is dead."

"God, that's awful," Jessie said, but she was puzzled by the terribly emotional look on Grace's face. People died suddenly, but did Grace know the man that well? "How did it happen?" Even as she said it, she was thinking that she'd have to get another landscaping firm. Her responsibilities had a way of staying in the forefront of her mind.

"Benny said he was stabbed outside." Grace pointed at the far wall.

"Stabbed!" Now Jessie completely understood the look on Grace's face. "Somebody stabbed Mr. Yamaguchi?" It was a rhetorical question, but she had to say something while her mind raced around trying to get a grasp on what she'd just heard.

Grace nodded. "That's what Benny said."

"Did you call the police?"

"Not yet."

"I'll call them." Picking up the phone she punched in the numbers as she spoke, "You get some of the help—waiters, kitchen personnel, whatever—and have them make sure no one tramples over the scene until the police arrive. And tell Benny I'd like to talk to him." She put the phone to her ear, "One more thing, Grace, don't tell anyone about this just yet. I don't want to get everyone's heart racing until we know more about what happened." Then into the phone, "I'd like to report a killing . . ."

Detective Ardley and two policemen in uniform arrived a half hour later. By that time, word of Yamaguchi's death had spread throughout the Home like a fire out of control. Peter, Eleanor, and Betty had joined the crowd around the body. Some of the staff stood around to keep people at a distance from the crime scene.

When the police showed up, Jessie Cummings met them outside the front of the building. Detective Ardley, a big man with a head of thick white hair, a bulging waist and a sweat-stained sport shirt, got out of the car and, followed by the two uniformed policemen, stepped up to her.

"Well, Ms. Cummings," Ardley said, his voice like fine gravel, "we meet again. Or . . . how does it go? We have to stop meeting like this." He grinned.

"It isn't funny, Detective," Jessie said. "We're talking about a dead man." There was a snap in her voice. She did not like this man, and had assumed she would not see him again after the traumatic incident two months before.

"You must forgive me," Ardley said, with no sincerity. "But with my job I am always talking about dead people." Then, "One of your 'inmates' murdered by the family for their money?"

Jessie took a deep breath to hold down her anger. "The gardener has been killed." She turned away from the policemen. "If you follow me, I'll take you to the body."

"One moment, please," Ardley said and nodded to one of the uniformed policemen who went to the patrol car and returned with a thick roll of yellow crime-scene tape. "Okay, Ms. Cummings, lead the way."

They followed Jessie around to the side of the building. There were more than twenty people, clustered in small groups, standing by the hibiscus bushes. Three of the people were staff members, kitchen help that had been directed by Grace to keep the area clear. The groups of people were talking nervously among themselves, their attention and comments directed at the area beneath the hibiscus bushes.

"The gardener been working for you long?" Ardley asked.

"Three months," Jessie Cummings said. "The landscapers we had before were getting sloppy. Mr. Yamaguchi's group came highly recommended."

"Do a good job?"

"Great job."

"Think the former landscaper might be desperate for his old job back?"

"With landscapers coming out of the woodwork in Florida, why would he think I'd hire him back?"

"Good point," Ardley said. "Who found the body?"

"Three of our residents were out walking and came upon Mr. Yamaguchi."

As they approached the site, the attention of the small groups shifted from the bushes to their approach. Ardley spotted Benny and Peter's group and walked toward them.

"Anyone I might happen to know?" Ardley asked, looking at them as he moved closer.

Jessie, frowning, looked back and forth between the group and Ardley. "Mr. Ashe was one of those who found the body."

Ardley frowned as he dug into his memory. ''Benny, isn't it?'' Ardley said. ''And his friend . . . Benington. Yes. Mr. Benington not with him this time?''

''No. Colonel Winston and Charlie Aspen.''

Peter with his back to Ardley, was talking to Benny. ''Does this sort of thing happen often around here?''

''Not normal, if that's what you mean. But crime has a way of bunching up on you.'' Benny saw Jessie coming toward them with Ardley at her side. Benny frowned and said out of the side of his mouth, ''Houston, we have a problem.''

Peter turned to see Ardley. *Damn,* he thought. He said, ''Bloody hell, here we go again. Doesn't the police department have anyone else besides this Detective Ardley?''

Ardley stopped in front of them. ''Good morning, Mr. Benington, Mr. Ashe. We meet again over a dead body. Sort of makes me wonder about you both.'' He smiled with no humor. ''I will be talking with you, Mr. Ashe, in a few moments, if you don't mind?''

''I was with Benny when we found Yamaguchi,'' Charlie said.

''And I, too,'' Colonel Winston said.

''Ah yes. Ms. Cummings informed me of that,'' Ardley said. ''I would appreciate it if you would all hang around while I finish here. We can talk then. I'm very interested in what you all have to say.'' He looked to Jessie. ''Possibly Ms. Cummings could find us a private place to talk?'' Jessie nodded. Ardley looked back at the group and smiled coolly. ''I'll see you all shortly.''

Ardley turned away, and Jessie and the two uniformed policemen followed him. Ardley then moved through the people toward the hibiscus. On the ground he saw the legs of the gardener sticking out from beneath the bushes. He also saw that the earth around the body was freshly turned topsoil, and there were a number of footprints in the soft dirt. He sighed. He knew that a clean crime scene was too much to hope for, but cleaner would have been nice. Now he'd have to find out who disturbed the scene and how.

''I had directed some of the staff to keep people away until you got here.'' Jessie Cummings had stepped to Ardley's side.

''Not soon enough,'' he said, making it sound as if she were at fault.

Jessie swallowed her anger and said nothing.

''I would appreciate it if you could take the witnesses inside. I'll be there as soon I finish going over this.'' He nodded in the direction of the body.

''Yes, Detective, I'll do that.'' *The quicker this gets over with the better,* she thought.

''Thank you,'' Ardley said and turned his attention to the crime scene.

Jessie went back to the group. ''The detective wanted me to take you three—Benny, Colonel, and Charlie—inside now to wait for him.''

Benny said, ''The Doc also checked out the body.''

Jessie shrugged. ''Then you, too, Doctor.'' Walter nodded.

Benny turned to Peter. ''Slick, you gotta come with us, too. You got a way with words, and I don't want that cop pulling a fast one on me.''

''I don't think you need me, Benny.'' Better to keep a broad distance from the police was Peter's thought. Especially Ardley. Ardley had done him a favor, but that didn't mean he couldn't change his mind. Ardley had suspected correctly that Peter had tiptoed through the criminal world in the past as a jewel thief. Peter didn't want him to pursue an investigation in that direction.

''Well, if you won't come, then I'll have to get my lawyer.'' Benny said this loud enough for Jessie to hear.

God, Jessie thought, in the words of Yogi Berra, it was déjà vu all over again. ''Please, Peter. I don't want this to drag out. We've had enough of the police around here recently.''

Peter didn't want this to drag out, either. The faster Ardley got out of there the better. He sighed in resignation. ''All right, Benny. But, please, hold your tongue while we are with the detective.''

''Sure, Peter.'' Benny shrugged and grinned. ''You know me.''

God, did he, he groaned inwardly. He smiled. ''Yes. That is why I asked you.''

The two uniformed officers immediately began laying a yellow ribbon of crime-scene tape on the ground in a wide circle, pushing through the bushes to the other side, with the body at the center of the circle. One of the officers went to the patrol car, returned with a camera, and began taking pictures of the scene, while the other stood around protecting the scene from further disturbance. The technicians would take pictures when they came, but Ardley liked to have a set of the scene as he found it.

Ardley took out his notepad and pen, then stepped forward slowly, examining the ground where he walked, careful not to obliterate any of the existing footprints. He knew he had to be thorough, because this was the only time he would see the scene in this way. The medical examiner would be there soon, the body would be removed, the scene would be disturbed. He took his time, trying to pinpoint anything that might appear insignificant, but could be important later in the investigation. He made notes as he walked. When he reached the body, he looked at the branches of the bushes above, made notes on his pad, then he crouched down and moved the branches back to get a better view of the dead man.

He wrote in his notebook: *One puncture wound mid back, right side. No signs of struggle. Earth disturbed as if body was dragged, or crawled a few feet. No broken branches on bushes. Victim facedown. Left arm extended over head, hand open, palm up. Not much blood. Death quick? Victim Asian, old. Small trowel near extended right hand. Potted plants all around. Seven empty pots nearby. One hole dug for next plant. Probably putting in plants when killed. Dressed in work clothes of sorts. Scene disturbed, many footprints, and some punctures in ground from crutch or cane?*

He took one more look around the body, then rose slowly to his feet, with a soft grunt. It was getting tougher to get up from a crouch, the bones were getting old. He walked over to the uniformed policeman who had been taking pictures.

"Call the station and get somebody out here to make casts of those footprints. It's topsoil, so it should be firm enough. When the medics get here you can leave. Have the film developed, and drop a set of eight by tens on my desk. I'll see you back at the station." Ardley turned and walked toward the building.

"Yes, sir," the man said to Ardley's back.

Ardley stepped inside the lobby of Coral Sands, and Grace called to him from behind the desk.

"They're in the card room," she said. She pointed to the corridor at the rear of the lobby. "Second door on your right. Ms. Cummings said if you need her she'll be in her office."

Ardley nodded and walked across the lobby.

"What do you mean 'killed!' " Jacobson's voice shouted at the other end of the phone. Jacobson was the owner of Coral Sands.

"Killed, as in stabbed to death," Jessie Cummings said. She was seated at the desk in her office. She had called Jacobson to let him know what happened, before some reporter contacted him. She knew the press would soon be all over Coral Sands.

"I don't like this," Jacobson said. "So soon after the other killings. Coral Sands could get a reputation as being unsafe."

"I don't know what to tell you."

"Tell me to calm down. Tell me not to get an ulcer. Tell me to take a vacation. It's what my wife tells me. Why not you?"

Jessie smiled. "I'll keep you informed."

Ardley entered the second room on the right. The five men were seated around two card tables that had been pulled together. Ardley walked over and sat in the one empty chair at the table. He took out his notebook, opened it, and laid it on the table in front of him. Then he took out his pen, clicked out the point, and poised the pen over the notebook.

"Okay," Ardley said. "Who wants to start?" He looked at The Colonel. "How about you?"

"Not much to say," The Colonel said. "Benny came up to us . . ."

"Us?" Ardley said.

"Charlie"—nodding in Charlie's direction—"and myself. We were out walking. I go out every morning . . ."

"You are?" Ardley interrupted.

"Alexander Winston, Colonel U.S. Marine Corps, Retired."

Ardley wrote in the notebook, then looked up. "You and"—he looked over at Charlie—"Mr. . . . ?"

"Charles Aspen," Charlie said.

To The Colonel, "You and Mr. Aspen go out walking every morning and . . ."

The Colonel interrupted, "No, we do not. *I* go out every morning. This morning I met Charlie outside, and we walked together for awhile."

Ardley nodded and made notes.

The Colonel continued. "Benny came up to us while we were walking and asked if we had seen the gardener, Mr. Yamaguchi. Neither of us had. Earlier I had seen the potted plants on the other side of the building and the three of us walked over there to see if Mr. Yamaguchi was around." He shrugged slightly. "We found him dead."

"You went over to the body?" Ardley said.

"Yes."

"Did you touch or move the body in anyway?"

"No," The Colonel said. "I did touch it, but did not move it. I put my fingers on his neck to see if there was a pulse. There wasn't."

"Anyone else here walk over to the body?"

Walter nodded. "I did. I'm a doctor, and went to see if I could help in some way. I, too checked for signs of life."

Ardley noticed the cane leaning against Walter's chair, and looked back at his notes. He crossed out *crutch* and underlined cane.

Benny said, "I took a closer look, too."

Charlie said, "I kept my distance."

"And you, Mr. Benington?" Ardley said.

"I have no part to play in this," Peter said.

"Then, Mr. Benington, what are you doing here?" Ardley said.

"Benny asked me to come along." Peter shrugged, trying to tread lightly over that.

"I wanted to make sure you didn't try snowing us. Slick, here, is as sharp as a shyster lawyer," Benny said. And Peter groaned, now he knew he shouldn't have come along.

Ardley gave Peter a look that would dissolve metal. "I am not fond of lawyers."

Peter groaned, again. This was not good.

"Why?" Benny said. "They don't let you put anything over on them?"

Damn, Peter thought. Benny and his runaway mouth. Why did he let Benny get him into this?

Ardley looked at both men as if he were examining a couple of ugly bugs. The look lasted long enough to make Peter very uncomfortable. Then Ardley looked at the others and said in an emotionless tone, "I will have someone here later to take prints of your shoes, to compare with those around the body. You needn't be in them. You can leave them with Ms. Cummings."

Then to Benny, "Mr. Ashe. Why were you looking for Mr. Yamaguchi?"

Benny shrugged. "We were going to have breakfast together. I waited in the dining room, but he never showed. So I went out looking for him. I met The Colonel and Charlie, and asked if they had seen him. They offered to come along with me and look for him."

"You all knew Mr. Yamaguchi?"

Everyone nodded except Peter and The Colonel.

Peter was relieved to be able to say, "I had not made his acquaintance." That would help him keep far away from this incident and the police. As long as he didn't allow Benny to drag him into it further.

"I was not interested in knowing the man," The Colonel said. He pulled himself up as if knowing the man would demean him.

Ardley caught the meaning. His senses were trained to pick up nuances and dig out what was behind them. "Why is that, Colonel?" Ardley said.

"I don't think it is necessary for you to know that for your investigation."

"You let me judge what I need for my investigation." Ardley had expected simply to spend a few minutes and go through the routine of taking all their statements. If he had anticipated this attitude from one of them, he would have interviewed each man separately. One-on-one interviews were easier for getting at the truth. Most people did not want to unburden themselves in front of a large audience.

"I'd rather not say."

"Colonel Winston, I insist." Ardley said it all in a quiet tone, but there was the power of authority in that tone. When The Colonel did not respond, Ardley continued, "Did you dislike the man for any reason? Hate him?"

The Colonel sat still, looking around at the others.

"Are you a bigot, Colonel?" Ardley stressed the word 'bigot', and made it sound foul and disgusting. "A dumb-ass white supremacist, maybe?"

The Colonel sat upright with as much dignity as his old body could evoke. "Calling me names does not change the fact that my feelings have nothing to do with your investigation of Mr. Yamaguchi's murder."

Ardley took a deep breath and let it out slowly, demonstrating control over his emotions. "It has every bearing on the killing. People are murdered for a reason. Usually by people close to them—in relationship or in proximity. Sounds like you fit one of those categories, Colonel." Ardley let that hang in the silence that followed.

The Colonel looked around at the eyes of the others looking back at him. He didn't quite know how this had all turned on him. Finally, he summoned up a sigh of surrender, and said, "How old are you, Detective?"

"Fifty," Ardley said.

"Well, then, son, this may be difficult for you to understand, but I'll tell you anyway.

"Before you were an idea in you father's pants, I was fighting for this country. Walked on half the damn islands in the Pacific killing Japanese and watching my friends getting killed by them . . ."

"Well, I . . ." Ardley said.

"Don't interrupt me, son. What I have to say normally isn't said. It's kept in the dark places of people's minds. So, let me tell it once and get it out of the way here. Then maybe you'll understand a little, and can get on with your investigation."

"Yes, sir," Ardley said.

"I'm not going to bore you with the screams and gore that still haunt me at night, even after all these years. No matter how I tell it, telling it can not come close to the horror of actually seeing it, of living it.

"And, I'm not alone in this. You go over to Shoney's restaurant. They have pictures on their wall of people married fifty years or more. Half those pictures are old wedding pictures, and just about every man is in uniform. The war was in every family, it sat at the table in every home.

"And we weren't out protecting some shitass piece of real estate, or propping up some asshole dictator. We were fighting for the very existence of this country—for home and mom and apple pie.

"In Europe it was the Nazis, a bunch of thugs who took over their country and tried taking over the world. In the Pacific it was the Japanese. Not a bunch of thugs, but an entire alien people bent on committing suicide for their emperor in order to kill as many of us as they could. It was an ugly, inhumane culture that considered the individual nothing but a piece of shit. I fought them and killed them. And I spent almost two months in one of their camps. I was lucky. They killed many soldiers who tried to surrender. They felt to surrender was a dishonorable act for a soldier. I saw what they could and did do to people.

"People"—The Colonel shook his head sadly—"such an unemotional word. I saw friends, human beings like you here, slaughtered. Cut wide open, screaming as their blood ran into the earth . . ." He stopped speaking, and took a deep breath, fighting the horrors back into the dark part of his mind. "I said I wasn't going to get into that.

"What I'm trying to get at is, there was a real hate for the Japanese. A real hate. A hate that is rooted in your bones. A hate that doesn't go away . . . ever. The kind of hate a man harbors for the murderer of his little child. That kind of hate.

"I'm not apologizing for it. It's there, it's real, and it's a part of me. And I am not alone. There are many of us, even in this house, who carry that hate quietly. You won't find any sympathy among us for a dead Japanese. Some of us think the Japanese didn't lose the war, only a battle. They are fighting the war still—and are winning. Doesn't help alleviate the hate to see their power growing." He thought a moment, then nodded. "You may even find your killer among us."

Colonel Winston then struggled to his feet. Stood straight as he could and looked at them. "I think I've said all I'm going to say about this." He turned and walked away.

They all watched him go.

Walter Innes, his eyes following the man, said quietly to no one, "The War doesn't end until the last soldier dies."

The silence that followed was like a heavy weight over the room. They looked at each other, trying to gather the present around them and push away the vision of the past they had just seen.

Ardley had been taken aback by the old man's speech. For a few moments there he saw a young soldier and the horror and the hate. Finally, he broke the silence, "Did you serve in the War, Mr. Ashe?"

"Yeah," Benny said. His mind slipped back in time for a moment, then quickly ran from what it saw. "In Europe. Walked all over France shooting Germans."

"And you, Doctor?" Ardley said.

Walter Innes nodded. "Europe. I was a medic, trying to put together the bodies ripped apart by the Nazi bullets."

"Mr. Aspen?"

"Saw the hills in Korea for awhile," Charlie said. "Wasn't old enough for W.W. Two."

"Mr. Benington?" Ardley said.

"Too young, I'm afraid. I was between wars. Drafted at the end of the Korean mess, and sat around in the horrible heat of Panama for two years. Then came home before they could find another war for me to fight in." Then he frowned at Ardley. "You think perhaps The Colonel is right, and the killer may be among us?"

Ardley said evenly, "Hate is a real good motive for murder."

CHAPTER 3

Alice, wearing her clown outfit, came through the front door and gave Grace a weak wave as she headed across the lobby.

Grace smiled and nodded in recognition. ''How'd it go, Alice?''

''Those kids were a rough audience,'' Alice said over her shoulder. Her voice was tired. She continued to walk toward the far end of the lobby.

Grace smiled. *Yeah, but you loved it, or you wouldn't do it*, she thought. Like they said, the circus was in your blood, even after all those years.

Ted Walden passed Alice without a glance in her direction. He was headed toward Grace.

Ted Walden, tall and frail, had the sad look he'd worn on his face for the past three years. He first put it on the day the doctors diagnosed his wife with Alzheimer's. And he'd worn it ever since. Grace watched him approach the desk. His wife had died only two months ago, so it was unreasonable to expect him to change so soon, but Grace felt the look would never go away. The sadness was carved too deep for him to ever remove it.

Grace glanced at the clock—11:30. ''Good morning, Mr. Walden.''

''Good morning, Grace,'' he said. Sadness coated every word he spoke. He stopped at the desk and looked at her, sadder than she'd remembered him ever looking. ''I don't know what you can do about it, but something was stolen from my room.''

''Oh, my, that's awful,'' Grace said with genuine concern. The rooms were not locked so that people inside could be reached quickly in an emergency. With the money the residents needed to have to get into Coral Sands there was no reason for them to steal from one another. ''What was it, Mr. Walden?''

''My wife's necklace,'' he said. ''I had it lying on the table in front of her picture. I'm sure it was there last night. When I got up this morning, it was gone.'' He stopped to swallow down the emotion that threatened to surface. ''Kept it there since she died. It meant a lot to me, Grace.''

''We will try to get it back for you, Mr. Walden.'' But she truly wasn't convinced it was stolen. She'd handled many complaints of stolen things that turned up later to have been misplaced. The elderly sometimes had trouble remembering where they put things. Though, Grace thought with an inward shrug, I've had that problem much of my life. ''I will report it to Ms. Cummings immediately. And we'll do everything possible to get it back for you.''

Mr. Walden handed her a Polaroid photo. ''This is what it looks like. It took me a while to find the picture.'' The photo showed an array of jewelry laid out on a white surface. A circle was drawn in pen around the necklace.

''Won't you need this picture?'' Grace said, holding the photograph out to him.

''No,'' he said. ''The picture was taken for insurance coverage. But, I've given the rest of the jewelry to our daughter. So, I won't need it unless I get the necklace back.'' Then he choked back the swelling emotions. ''It was my gift to Elizabeth on our first anniversary.'' He sighed. ''It has more value to me than to any thief.''

''I'll see that Ms. Cummings gets this,'' Grace said. ''And, again, I'm sorry, Mr. Walden.''

He shrugged at the hopelessness of it all. ''Thank you.'' Then he turned and walked back the way he had come.

She watched him go, and his suffering tugged at her heart.

• • •

"Sorry you had to see this," Ardley said. They were standing outside by the crime scene. Yamaguchi's body was tucked into a heavy-gauge vinyl bag, and was being hoisted onto a gurney by two uniformed policemen. Standing next to Ardley was a tall Japanese man in his fifties, his skin the color of old leather. His face betrayed no emotion.

"Did your father have any enemies?" Ardley asked. "Someone who might do this?"

"My father was a kind and gentle man." The man spoke in an even, controlled tone. "He loved gardening, loved plants, loved life, and loved his family. Only a person possessed by demons would hate my father."

"Did he always work so early in the morning?"

"Yes," the son said. "It was much cooler in the morning. Can get pretty hot as the day goes on." Ardley nodded to that. "But I think it was the light. The early sunlight is softer and more gentle. It fit his personality."

"Who gets the business, now that your father is dead?" Ardley spoke in even, matter-of-fact tones.

The son looked at him a long moment. Ardley was patient.

"You think I would kill my father for the business?" he said at last.

"I don't think anything," Ardley said. "I rule out possibilities. What I am left with is a motive, and maybe the killer."

The son nodded. "It was not his business. My brother and I started the landscaping operation years ago. When my father retired—he worked for IBM—we offered him a job. Something to keep him interested."

It was Ardley's turn to nod. "How is business?"

The son sighed in resignation. "We don't need his money, either. We do quite well on our own."

"Did he fight in World War Two?" Ardley said. He thought that someone in the Home might have recognized him as an old enemy, and set things right after all that time. Stranger things had happened.

"Yes, he did," the son said. "He was with the Neisi regiment in Europe, the four hundred and forty second. They fought the Germans. They were trying to show America that, as Japanese-Americans, they and their families were loyal Americans. They fought hard and bravely because they had something to prove. They suffered eighty percent casualties. He never said if things were better for their families because of their sacrifice. He never talked about the War. Keeps the medals in a drawer." The son shook his head. "It is so hard to believe that this gentle man was a soldier."

"That's all the questions I have for you," Ardley said. He could believe this gentle man was a killer of men. He'd met a number of kind, gentle men who'd slaughtered people. "Again, I'm sorry for your loss. We will do what is necessary to bring the killer to justice."

The son shook his head. "That, Detective, is no consolation." He turned and walked away.

Jessie looked at the picture. There was an array of jewelry laid out on a white cloth. Some of the jewelry was quite impressive, but the necklace circled in pen was not. A thin silver chain with a tiny open heart in diamond chips. Not something of value to a thief, she thought. "He said it was taken from his room?"

Grace was standing by Jessie Cummings's desk. "Last night. He said it was there when he went to bed, but was gone this morning."

"He thinks someone came into his room in the middle of the night?"

"Well," Grace said, "we do require the doors to be unlocked. So, it's possible."

"But why?" Jessie said. "It's not what you would call an expensive piece of jewelry."

"It's always possible he misplaced it. Except, he had it in front of a picture of Elizabeth. Some sort of shrine, I guess. So, it is more likely he wouldn't have moved it."

"Yes," Jessie said. "I see." But she didn't see. The necklace was not something worth stealing. But, she thought, neither was the gravy boat. Peculiar. Could they be linked? She wondered. Then she shook her head. "Too strange," she said, more to herself. Then to Grace, "All right. Let me think about what to do about this. I'll keep the picture."

Grace left the office. Jessie sat there for a long time trying to figure out how to handle this issue of the missing necklace, and the odd theft of the silver gravy boat. Finally, she said aloud to herself, "The hell with it. Give it to somebody else." If she had done that with the silverware episode two months ago, it would have been resolved sooner and with fewer headaches. She flipped through the Rolodex, found the number she was looking for, picked up the telephone, and dialed.

"Coswell Investigations," the man said at the other end of the line.

"Michael, this is Jessie Cummings at Coral Sands. You've done work for me before."

"Yes. I remember. Couple of times. One of the help was stealing from the residents. What can I do for you Ms. Cummings?"

"We've got some peculiar thefts going on here. I was hoping you could find out what's happening."

"I'd be happy to help. When do you want me to start?"

"Tomorrow all right?"

"As a matter of fact, I'm between jobs right now. I could be there in the morning," Michael Coswell said. "The usual fee—three hundred dollars a day."

"And the usual role."

"The hired handyman. Okay, I'll bring my tools. As often as I play that role, I'm getting pretty good at it. Maybe I'll start doing handyman stuff on the side."

"Well, then, we'll deduct the training expense from your fee," she smiled.

"Now, now. No more talk like that," he said, a grin in his voice. "I'll see you in the morning."

After she hung up the phone, she debated calling Jacobson, the owner, and telling him about hiring the detective. She decided to let it alone for the time being. He always got upset when she spent money, and she didn't want to deal with his temper right then.

Mildred entered the dining room at noon, and saw Alice sitting with Benny and some other people at a table near the broad windows at the back of the room. She was disappointed. She thought Alice would have sat alone at a table so they could talk. She headed toward them. Mr. Petersen was standing by the table entertaining the group. From the way Benny was laughing, and from what she could hear, Mr. Petersen was Henny Youngman today.

"Marriage is compromise. For instance, my wife wanted to buy a mink coat, and I wanted a new car. We compromised. We hang her mink coat in the garage.

"A guy goes to court for a divorce. The judge asks, 'Why do you want a divorce?' The man answers, 'Every night I come home from work, and instead of my wife being alone, I find a different guy hiding in our closet.' The judge says, 'And this causes you a lot of unhappiness?' 'It certainly does, your Honor, I never have any room to hang my clothes!'

"Two guys dressing in a locker room. The one guy sees the other struggling into a girdle. 'When did you start wearing a girdle?' The other guy says, 'When my wife found it in the glove compartment of my car.' "

"Mildred!" Alice said. "Over here!" Then to Mr. Petersen, "Sorry Henny, but we have to cut the show short."

"I understand, sweet lady," Petersen said. "And I leave you with this one thought: Some men are born great, others have greatness thrust upon them . . . like Dolly Parton's husband." He wiggled his fingers in a friendly wave and walked off.

Benny was laughing so hard tears were running down his face, and he was having trouble catching his breath.

"Doctor," Peter indicated Benny, and smiled at Walter Innes. "That must be a terrible affliction. Isn't there something you can do for him?"

"What affliction are you referring to?" Walter Innes asked with a straight face. "His not being able to catch his breath, or the fact that he laughs at those jokes?"

Mildred sat in the only empty chair at the table. "Hello, everyone."

Alice introduced her to Peter, Walter, Eleanor, and Betty. "I'll have to wait until he stops laughing before I introduce Benny," Alice said. Benny was still choking on suppressed laughter.

Mildred smiled. "Benny and I have been friends for a very long time."

Benny gave Mildred a little wave of recognition, while he

tried to hold back the laughter. Mildred smiled and waved back at him.

Alice said to the others, "This is the woman I was telling you about. The one who wants to meet this guy she met on the computer."

Mildred blushed with embarrassment and anger. To Alice, with an edge to her voice, she said, "I spoke to you in confidence, Alice. I expected this to be kept between us."

"Sorry, Mildred, but I felt it was too important to not look for help. Me and these people"—she indicated everyone at the table—"were involved as a group in solving Marjorie Boyd's murder two months ago. They are good people. You can trust them."

"So, do you intend to meet this man?" Walter asked.

"Well . . ." Mildred hesitated. She felt uncomfortable, but she was cornered, and could not avoid talking about it. "I've been giving it some serious thought."

"Go for it," Eleanor said. "Life is full of risks. If you don't take the risks, it's just boring."

"I think it's exciting," Betty said in her twittering voice, "and so romantic."

Peter said, "But you really know nothing about this man?"

"How much do you know about someone you go out with the first time?" Eleanor said. "It's always a chance you take."

The waiter showed at the table with a large round tray crammed with dishes of food. Everyone stopped talking until the waiter had finished putting the plates of food on the table. He turned to Mildred. "Madam, can I get you something?"

"Just coffee and toast," she said. The waiter nodded and left. Then to the others, she said, "I've no appetite with all this excitement in my life today."

"Like any risks one takes," Walter said, "it has its elements of danger. I've had a number of women patients who became victims in such situations."

"I don't think I'm likely to be raped." Mildred smiled at the absurdity of it.

"Well," Benny said, finally composed, "you read a lot about women getting raped at all ages. And there are other things that could happen, too. Lots of nutcases out there roaming around off the leash."

"So," Mildred said, annoyed now, "I should spend my life locked in a room looking out at the world?"

"There are prudent measures that one could take," Walter said. "Any gambler knows he must minimize his risks."

"Yeah," Benny said. "You . . ." He stopped talking as the waiter came to the table and placed Mildred's toast and coffee in front of her. "Anything else I can get anyone?" he inquired.

They all indicated things were fine as they were, and the waiter left.

"As I was saying," Benny said, "You gotta tip the odds in your favor."

"And how do I go about doing that?" Mildred said, not convinced it was possible.

"Well," Walter said. "The Spanish use a chaperone system."

Mildred made a noise of derision. "Me, with a chaperone! Get serious now, everyone."

"Walter has made an interesting point," Peter said. "Possibly someone should go with you to this first meeting."

"Oh, yeah. And I introduce him to Timothy as my chaperone. Timothy will think I'm bonkers."

"You know, Mildred," Eleanor said, "it isn't such a bad idea. At least then one of us will have seen the man. His knowing that he can be identified by someone other than you may be enough to discourage him if he has trouble on his mind."

"And if he doesn't?" Mildred said. "If Timothy is a genuinely nice guy, it may be enough for him to think my elevator doesn't go to the top, and I'd never see him again."

"You could tell him your car wasn't working, and you were offered a ride," Betty said. "That's believable, I think."

"Yeah," Benny said. "You let me know when you're going to see this guy, and I'll drive you. I'll get Caroline to come with me. It'll look even better that way with the two of us taking you. Like we really were giving you a lift."

"If you want," Alice said. "I'll drive you."

"Oh, I don't know," Mildred said. "It all sounds so silly."

"If," Benny said, "he decides to cut you up and stuff you in a trunk, it won't sound so silly then."

"Well," Alice said, "you think it over. It's your decision.

But you know we're here to help if you need us.''

That was true, Mildred thought. And annoyed as she was, it was a comfort knowing that.

''Served in World War Two? In the Pacific?'' Jessie was puzzled, and annoyed. Detective Ardley had a way of getting under her skin.

''Yes,'' Ardley said. He was seated opposite her desk.

''I don't understand the request? You want me to go through the residents' files searching for people who fought in the War in the Pacific. Why should I do that? If you don't mind my asking.''

''If you do it, it can be done discreetly,'' Ardley said with patience. ''If I must get a court order and have my people go through the files . . . Well, there are no guarantees about discretion.'' He then frowned. ''Mr. Ashe led me to believe you do have such information? Every resident fills out a form with a request for his past history?''

Benny had a big mouth, Jessie thought. ''Yes. So we can direct them to events that might interest them, and people who share a common experience. Remember, the files contain only what they were willing to tell me. But *why* do you need this?''

''Please keep this search of the files to yourself for now. No sense in getting everyone excited.''

''No sense in getting everyone excited! I'm excited! Will you answer my question—why do you need this?''

''I'd like to stop by tomorrow and see what you've discovered.'' Ardley said, his tone still even, his delivery matter-of-fact.

God, she hated this man! She wanted to scream at him. Instead, she forced herself to get very calm, and in a voice as even as Ardley's, she said, ''Detective, unless you give me a good reason for getting this information, you had better get to work on your court order. And, I will contact our attorney to see that the privacy of our residents is protected.''

There was a long moment of silence as they looked at one another. Jessie was not going to give Ardley an inch right then. She had had enough of this man playing with her. It was time he took her seriously. Suddenly Ardley let out a deep sigh.

''All right, *Ms*. Cummings,'' stressing the 'Ms.' ''But I

would appreciate it if you did not tell anyone about this. My job is to first gather facts. Then I sift through it looking for a good reason why someone was murdered.'' He shifted in his chair, trying for a comfortable position. Then he told her about Colonel Winston's little speech. ''And there might be something in what The Colonel said. At this point in the investigation, I'm just gathering facts. I promise you I will not do anything to invade the lives of the residents unnecessarily.''

It was Jessie's turn to say nothing for a long time. She'd won her point, but there was no award to go with it. ''I'll try to have the information for you tomorrow. Say around eleven or so.''

''I will be here personally to look it over.'' He rose and headed for the door. He stopped, turned, and said, ''Thank you for your cooperation, *Ms.* Cummings''—once again stressing the 'Ms.'

She won a small battle, but not the war, she thought, holding her temper in line.

No sooner had Detective Ardley left than Grace came through the door.

''What is it, Grace?'' Jessie said, clearly not in a friendly tone.

Grace, surprised, took a step back.

Jessie saw the look on Grace's face. ''Sorry,'' she said. ''Just a little edgy.'' Edgy, hell. Pissed was more appropriate. But no reason to take it out on Grace.

''Well,'' Grace said. ''What I've got to tell you may make you more edgy.''

God, what now? Jessie thought. ''Let's have it out and get it over with.''

''Okay. A number of the residents are . . .'' she searched for the right word ''. . . upset about having a killer and a thief on the loose in the Home.'' Jessie's deep frown caused Grace to hesitate. ''The hell with pussyfooting around, they are scared and want you to do something to protect them.''

''Like what!'' Jessie snapped, then backed off. ''Sorry, again.''

''It's okay,'' Grace said. ''This sort of stuff gets everybody a little edgy.''

Jessie smiled wearily. ''Yes, I guess so.'' She sighed. ''You can tell them, whoever they are, that I'm making arrangements for their protection.''

Grace grinned wryly. ''And what do I say when they ask me what that is?''

''Tell them we're checking on hiring a security firm to patrol the grounds.''

''Are we really considering that?''

''Yes,'' Jessie said. ''But I'm sure Jacobson won't approve the expense. And I'm not sure how effective they'd be against in-house thefts. But it may quiet them down a bit. Don't give this any fanfare, and no public announcements. The word will spread quietly on its own.'' Jessie gave Grace a weary look. ''Okay?''

''All right,'' Grace said, then grinned. ''I'll do my best to keep the animals quiet.''

''Thank you,'' Jessie said.

''You think Mr. Yamaguchi's death and the thefts are related?'' Grace said.

''No. I'm sure Mr. Yamaguchi's death has nothing to do with the residents. And the police can handle that situation. My concern is the thefts. People should feel they're possessions are safe in their apartments.''

''Talk is the police think it's someone in the Home,'' Grace said.

''God,'' Jessie said, throwing up her hands. ''The rumor mill really works overtime in this place.''

''Still,'' Grace said, ''it's possible.'' She hesitated, knowing what she had to say was going to annoy Jessie. ''The press is outside.''

''Shit!'' Jessie put her head in her hands. ''I don't want to talk to them. I don't want them interviewing any of the residents, getting people more upset than they are. Do what you can to send them on their way, okay?''

Grace nodded. ''Okay.''

It was four-thirty in the afternoon when Yamaguchi's son entered Jessie Cummings's office.

''Mr. Yamaguchi,'' Jessie said. Her sincerity and emotions were genuine. She had lost a parent and knew the deep wrenching pain firsthand. "I don't have any words to express how sorry I am about your father."

"I know," the man said. "Words are insufficient expressions of emotion."

He swallowed visibly. "I have spoken with my brother, and we feel we must relinquish our obligation to you. To come here every week and tend the grounds where our father died would be a constant reminder of our loss." He hesitated. "I hope you understand."

"Yes, of course," she said.

"We have enjoyed the working relationship, and hope we have satisfied your requirements with the ground work."

"Completely satisfied. I am sorry you must leave us."

After Yamaguchi's son left her office, Jessie, in frustration, leaned over and pounded her forehead on her desk. Please God, let this day end, she thought.

It was seven-thirty when Mildred powered up her computer and signed on to the Microsoft Network. It took a few moments for the connection to be made. Some nights the system was slow. Tonight it seemed even slower, because she was anxious to speak with Timothy. Her heart was pounding. She was as excited as a girl going on a blind date. Once on the Network, she clicked the list of Favorites, then chose Beach Blanket 2F chat room, and clicked on it. It was a private room limited to two people. Timothy reserved the room for seven thirty every evening for them. The screen changed to the chat window, and across the white talk area appeared:

FineLace has entered the conversation

Mildred could see Timothy was already there, his online name—Shy-Guy—was listed in the upper right of the screen.

Shy-Guy: Hello, Mildred. I've been waiting for you.
<Shy-Guy smiles warmly at Mildred>

Mildred typed "Good evening, Timothy. <smiles>" and hit the ENTER key. On the screen printed:

FineLace: Good evening, Timothy. <smiles>
Shy-Guy: How was your day, dear one?

How was my day? she thought. *How* was *my day?* Not much sleep last night, not much food today, not much on her mind except what she was going to say to Timothy. But she wasn't going to tell him that.

FineLace: Not much happening to me personally, but . . .
FineLace: there's been some unpleasant excitement around the Home.
Shy-Guy: ?
FineLace: The gardener was killed this morning. Terrible.
Shy-Guy: Killed? Explain, please.
FineLace: They found his body this morning on the grounds. He was stabbed to death.
Shy-Guy: Stabbed! How awful! What sort of place do you live in where such things can happen?

Timothy knew she lived in Sarasota, but he didn't know where in Sarasota. And, although it was a roundabout question, she remembered what Alice had said, and she felt alarm bells go off.

FineLace: Ugliness has a way of finding you where ever you are.
Shy-Guy: Did you know the man?
FineLace: No, not really. But it is still a tragedy.
Shy-Guy: All death is a tragedy. The ceasing of life. Tragic.

He was right about that, she thought. Well, maybe not completely right. She could think of some deaths that were a godsend. But it was a nice poetic thought. She typed:

FineLace: Not a subject I want to get into.
Shy-Guy: Understand. The weather is too nice, life too pleasant to discuss morbidity.
FineLace: How was your day, Timothy?

She figured she'd change the subject. She knew they both

were stalling, waiting for the right moment to face the question of their meeting.

Shy-Guy: Not much to speak of. Spent most of day wondering if I did the right thing, pushing you for a meeting.
Shy-Guy: Don't want to jeopardize what we have together.
Shy-Guy: Yet, feel there should be more than this for us.

Well, she thought, guess the time has come. And she still wasn't sure what she was going to say.

FineLace: I've done a lot of thinking today, too.

And all last night, she thought.

FineLace: It's not easy to risk something as nice as our friendship.
Shy-Guy: I want to see you, want to meet you. But I'm afraid you won't like what you see.

She smiled.

FineLace: I worried the same thing, Timothy.
Shy-Guy: You should not have worried. You could not be anything but beautiful.
FineLace: At my age the beauty is gone. For good, I'm afraid.
Shy-Guy: Age is what makes a woman beautiful. She grows to a wonderful whole person, without the pretense . . .
Shy-Guy: There are no facades to hide who she is. And from what I know of you, you are beautiful.
FineLace: <blushes>
FineLace: My silver-tongued Timothy <smiles sweetly>
FineLace: You sure know how to touch a woman's heart.
Shy-Guy: You've been thinking all day, and I've been thinking all day. What conclusions did you reach?

After that, she knew what she was going to say.

FineLace: I think we'll take the risk and meet. All life is risk. If we don't meet we may always regret it.

Having said that, she felt better, as if life's electricity was back in her system. There was a long delay with no response from Timothy. She checked the MSN icon in the right corner of the screen to be sure she was still connected. Wouldn't be the first time she'd been moofed in the middle of a conversation. Maybe there was a problem at his end. She was just about to ask if he was still there when—

Shy-Guy: I can't find fault with the logic. You're right. We don't meet, we'll never know what could have happened. So, let's do it.
<smiles with warm anticipation>

Suddenly she felt as excited as a schoolgirl cutting classes for a date.

FineLace: Well, now that that's settled. Where do we meet? And When?
Shy-Guy: Your call, dear one. I think we should meet on territory you feel safe.
FineLace: I hadn't really thought about it, Timothy.
Shy-Guy: Then let me suggest the Beach House in Bradenton. For dinner? You know the place?
FineLace: Yes, it is a nice place.
Shy-Guy: Good. How about seven tomorrow night?
FineLace: We may have trouble getting a table. They don't take reservations.
Shy-Guy: We'll give it a try. They have a nice combo playing on the deck overlooking the Gulf. We can dine outside and watch the sunset.
FineLace: Sounds nice.
Shy-Guy: Seven, then? In the bar. I know you're not a drinker but it's comfortable there.
Shy-Guy: How will I know you?
FineLace: And I you?

There was a pause before he answered:

Shy-Guy: Got it! Carry an umbrella. Only a new tourist carries an umbrella. And I'll do the same.

She laughed.

FineLace: LOL. Great idea.
Shy-Guy: I'll be the only old guy with an umbrella sitting at the bar. Tomorrow at seven, then.
FineLace: I'll be there. <smiles>
Shy-Guy: If for some reason I am late, I'll telephone the bar, and ask for Mildred.
FineLace: You expect to be late?
Shy-Guy: I have complete faith in Murphy. I want to meet you badly enough to have something go wrong. <g>
FineLace: Understand <smiles>
Shy-Guy: Then goodnight dear one, till tomorrow at seven.
FineLace: Goodnight Timothy.
Shy-Guy has left the conversation

She sat there smiling at the computer screen for a few moments, savoring the warm excitement she felt. She didn't know how to describe the feeling. It was as if she felt . . . young again. Yes! That was it—young, and alive! It was a wonderful feeling. She hadn't experienced that in so long, so very long a time. She took a deep sigh and moved the mouse pointer to File, pulled down the menu, and clicked on Save Chat History. The computer whirred for a couple of seconds. Then she clicked on Exit and shut the machine down. With the excitement she was feeling, she didn't know if she'd get any sleep that night, either. But if she laid awake, she would do it with a smile on her face and a warm happy feeling in her heart. No better insomnia than that.

CHAPTER 4

Benny was wearing a light blue blazer, blue silk shirt, and dark gray trousers. Peter found it fascinating that a woman could exercise so much influence over Benny that he would abandon his scruffy clothes. Caroline was the woman responsible for Benny's transformation. Caroline, a bent fragile old lady, was the genteel Southern belle who Benny had met outside a supermarket. When he saw her he was smitten, and, as they say, the rest was history.

Caroline was sitting next to Benny, and they both were sitting across from Peter and Eleanor. Though Caroline was frail and bent with osteoporosis, she glowed as if there was a light inside her. Peter marveled that love at any age could bring such a glow. It gave him hope. He was sixty and there was the promise of a lot of years ahead. It was comforting to see that those years could still hold such joy.

The Golden Apple Dinner Theater was putting on a production of *A Funny Thing Happened on the Way to the Forum.* The dinner theater was in the heart of downtown Sarasota a few steps from the Clown College—formerly the Opera House—and in sight of Patrick's restaurant. Benny had asked Peter and Eleanor to join them at the Golden Apple Dinner Theater as his guests. They both gladly accepted.

They were enjoying the food and passing around small talk about the theater and the delicious food, when suddenly Caroline said, "I certainly would not like to turn this conversation to such sordid things, but Benny told me about the awful thing that happened at Coral Sands today.''

Peter said, ''Yes. It was a shock.''

''I can hardly believe the Lord would permit such things to happen in this beautiful place,'' Caroline said.

''With all the killing going on in the world,'' Eleanor said, ''shamefully, Mr. Yamaguchi's death seems insignificant.''

''That is the problem with today's communications,'' Peter said, ''we learn too much about what is happening. Not beneficial for upholding one's faith in civilizing mankind.''

''Yeah,'' Benny said. ''I read somewhere where they found the missing link between the apes and civilized humans, and it was us.'' Then, more seriously, to Peter, ''What do you think about that detective's idea of it being someone in the Home?''

''Someone living in that wonderful place killed the man?'' Caroline said. ''My Lord!''

Peter shrugged. ''Nowhere is it written that killers must be young and poor.''

''Well,'' Benny said, ''I don't like the idea of that detective snooping around, digging into people's pasts. Could hurt a lot of innocent people just trying to live out the rest of their lives in peace.''

Eleanor nodded, feeling a twinge of concern. She understood exactly what Benny was talking about. ''That's true. Not everyone has led a smooth, boring life. Some have carried terrible things with them to get to here.'' Terrible things, she thought. It would be awful if some of those things were resurrected from where she had buried them years ago.

''Yes,'' Peter said. He knew what Benny was referring to, because Benny and he had exchanged personal confidences one evening. Benny had fled from the wrath of a mobster named Bobby Dee, who went to prison as a result of Benny's testifying against him. Benny had also robbed the man of a considerable amount of money. Bobby Dee had vowed to have Benny killed, and almost succeeded once when Benny was in the Witness Protection Program. Benny had been at the Home for sixteen years, under an assumed identity, hiding from the law and Bobby Dee. Benny was sure that Bobby Dee was still out looking for him. And Ardley digging into the past would find that Benny did not exist, that his identity was false. Could be a lot of trouble for Benny.

Could be a lot of trouble for Peter, too. Peter's background was in insurance and specialized in retrieving stolen jewelry at a cost to the insurance companies . . . Some of the jewelry he had stolen himself.

"Well," Peter said, "you can thank the good Colonel for planting the idea in Ardley's head."

"The Colonel?" Caroline said.

"Colonel Winston," Benny said. "A retired Marine who fought in the Pacific during the War."

"World War Two?"

"Yeah."

"What did he say?" Eleanor said.

"The Colonel," Benny said, "went off half-cocked about the War and that there were still people, even in the Home, who would like to see all Japanese dead. He included himself as one of those people."

"There's not much any of us can do to stop Ardley's investigation." Peter shrugged. "And maybe The Colonel is right."

"And maybe The Colonel is the one," Benny said.

Later, after the show, the foursome left the restaurant and walked through the lighted streets toward the parking lot a block away. They had all come in Benny's car. Peter and Eleanor lagged behind Benny and Caroline. Eleanor walked with her arms holding on to Peter's left arm.

"Did I tell you," Peter said, "that you look stunning tonight?"

She smiled. "You're flirting with me. But I will be honest. I worked especially hard at looking good tonight."

He smiled. "I'm glad."

"I was even going to wear my diamond brooch, but"—she frowned—"couldn't find the darn thing anywhere."

"You don't need diamonds to make you look beautiful."

"Tell me something," she said in a low voice.

"Anything, dear lady," Peter said, also in a low voice. It felt good to have this woman near him, holding on to his arm. It felt good to whisper to her secretly.

"I take you to be a man of the world," she said. "A man who has courted and seduced women."

Peter grinned. "Now, a gentleman would not talk about such things. They are private encounters between two people. It is best they remain private."

"I'm glad to hear you say that," she said with a smile. "But, tell me. How do you go about seducing a woman? Is there a special technique?"

Peter smiled at her and his heart skipped a joyful beat. "Well, I might invite her to my apartment for a late night drink and some quiet conversation."

"Hmm," Eleanor said seductively. "That sounds like it would work very well."

"It depends on the woman, you see, and how willing she is."

"Yes, I can see that," Eleanor said.

It was late at night. The corridor was quiet, gently illuminated by a few soft lights on the walls. The bare feet that stepped over the thick carpet of the hall did not feel the carpet's surface, the senses sending signals to the mind did not record the corridor, did not record any of the surroundings, for the mind was in another time, another place, another reality. The mind, until recently, had not visited that other world in a very long time, the memories locked behind a formidable door in a dark dusty corridor. But now the feet walked on hard dry earth, among makeshift housing, illuminated by a bright tropical sun. The housing was of wood barely held together, poor protection from the vagaries of the weather. The foul smells that rose with the heat, raked the senses and tore at the throat with every breath.

It was a hellish world where demons ruled and others suffered, where men were beaten and brutally slaughtered. Where women were abused, demeaned, raped, tormented, and killed. Where children suffered and starved and died—their deaths at times the relief of a burden. Where people betrayed people, sold their souls for a few more breaths of life. Where love and compassion did not exist, and ugliness and cruelty were cherished. All this under the incongruity of blue skies and the peaceful swaying of palm trees.

The mind, filled with hot hate, walked through this world cursing the God that looked down upon it and let it be, and cursing the demons to suffer in agonies beyond those ever dreamed for damnation.

The mind made these trips to the demon world at odd times. The feet would be walking on Florida soil, then without warning, the next step would land in another time on the dry parched earth of this hell, where the mind once again was struggling for survival, enduring horrors and suffering only men could inflict on men.

It was the hate that gave the mind and body strength. The hate burned like a roaring fire out of control, and it fed the soul the heat of life. In that world, when a person stopped hating they gave up and died. This mind, this body, would not give up the hate. It cherished it, nurtured it, burned into the mind the scenes that fired up the hatred. This mind, this body would survive.

The woman's hand reached up and gently knocked on the door.

Peter looked up and smiled with hope. He poured sherry into the two stemmed wineglasses he'd set out on the cocktail table. Then he got out of the chair and walked to the door on trembling legs. He was as nervous as a schoolboy on his first date. The knock came again. He took a deep breath to quell his nervousness, and reached for the doorknob. He turned it slowly, and pulled the door open. Eleanor was standing in the hall, dressed in white silk lounging pajamas, her feet bare.

"Well," she said in a soft voice. "Are you going to invite me in?" She smiled. "Or do you work better in hallways?"

God, he wanted to shout his joy at seeing her there. He stepped back to make room for her to enter. "It is not work, to show such a lovely woman affection."

Still smiling, she stepped past him into the apartment. "You certainly have a smooth line."

He closed the door and reached out a hand to her shoulder to stop her. She turned to him. He stepped up to her, took her face gently in his hands, and looked deep into her eyes. The smile left her face, and her gaze probed his. His voice a soft whisper, he said, "There are no lines here, no pretense. I speak the truth of what my heart feels.'' His face moved close to hers. ''Eleanor, I think you are the woman I have been searching for all my life.'' He put his lips gently on hers. Her lips hesitated, then surrendered willingly to the softness of his lips.

CHAPTER 5

It was nearing nine in the morning when the man came through the front door of Coral Sands. He was dressed in dark blue pants and shirt, a workman's uniform, and he wore a leather tool belt and carried a large metal toolbox. He looked awfully young, Grace thought, as he came up to her desk.

"Can I help you?"

"Yes," the man said. "I'm here to see . . ."

"I remember you," Grace said suddenly. "You're that private detective we had working here a while back. Mr. Coswell, isn't it?"

He grinned. "Old people are supposed to have bad memories."

Grace smiled. "I forgot. I assume Ms. Cummings called you?"

"Yes. Yesterday," Michael Coswell said. "Didn't she tell you?"

Grace grinned wider. "I guess she forgot. I'll tell her you are here." She stepped over to Jessie's office and poked her head inside the doorway. "Mr. Coswell? Says, you are expecting him." Grace then stood back as Jessie came out of her office, walked around the front desk to Michael Coswell, and shook his hand.

"Good morning," Jessie said.

"Morning, Ms. Cummings."

"That handyman outfit suits you."

"It's become the uniform of the job," he smiled.

"Let's go into my office where I can give you the details of what's been happening." Then she turned to Grace, "Not a word to anyone." Grace nodded. Her innocent look did not fool Jessie. She knew Grace was the major leak in her office. She just didn't know how to stop her. Grace had been there a long time, and was too good at her job to fire her. Besides, she liked Grace. They had a very good working relationship. Just no way to plug her mouth. "If everyone knows he's here, he won't be able to find out who's been doing the stealing."

"I understand," Grace said. What good is a secret if you can't share it with anyone? she thought.

Michael Coswell followed Jessie into her office.

A few minutes later Eleanor came down to the lobby and walked over to Grace. She thought Eleanor looked different somehow. Younger, maybe?

"Good morning, Grace." Eleanor's tone was light and cheerful.

"Good morning, Eleanor. What can I do for you?"

"Well," Eleanor said, "I'm not sure if this is anything. I heard about the thefts yesterday, and last night when I was getting ready to go out I couldn't find my brooch. At the time I thought I mislaid it somewhere. But, this morning I searched everywhere. I can't find it."

"Oh my," Grace said with a sigh. "Well, give me a description of the brooch." She looked quickly around to make sure no one was within earshot, then she leaned forward and spoke in a low confidential tone to Eleanor, "Jessie is inside with a private detective she's hired to find out about these thefts. I'll give him this information right away."

"A private detective?" Eleanor said.

"Don't tell anyone I told you about him," Grace said. "This is just between you and me, okay?"

"Not a soul," Eleanor said. "But it's good to know something's being done about this."

Grace was confused by Eleanor's reaction. She didn't seem particularly interested. As if her mind were somewhere else.

"A silver gravy boat and this schmaltzy necklace?" Michael Coswell said. He was seated in the chair opposite Jessie's desk. Jessie was seated behind the desk. He was holding the photograph of jewelry Ted Walden had given to Grace. "Sounds to me more like somebody misplaced a few things than a thief on the loose. You really want me to check this out?"

"More for the residents' peace of mind," Jessie said. "They get nervous very easily."

"But they don't even know I'm here?"

"Trust me. They'll know all about you within the hour. We have a very active grapevine here." No way will Grace keep this to herself, she thought.

Michael Coswell smiled. "Well, I can bone up on my handyman skills."

"And get in a little gardening." Jessie smiled. "Our gardener was putting in some plants on the far side of the building. Maybe you could finish that up for me?"

"How long you want me here?"

"Hopefully things will calm down in a couple of days."

"Then you don't think these things were stolen, either?"

"Truthfully, no. But things here are very tense right now. Knowing you are here will help." Then she smiled. "And there are some plumbing problems that need to be corrected. Grace knows what has to be done."

Michael Coswell shrugged. "It's your money." He stood up, and grinned, "And plumbing is my strong point."

It was then that Grace came into Jessie's office. "There's been another theft." She handed Michael Coswell the description of Eleanor's brooch, and looked at Jessie. "Eleanor Carter just reported her brooch was missing. Worth thirty thousand, she said. She didn't seem too upset about it."

"Well," Michael Coswell said, "now that's more like it."

Jessie just shook her head. It's going to be another bad day, she thought.

Detective Ardley came through the front door and was moving toward Grace's desk when Michael Coswell came out of Jessie's office. The two men spotted each other immediately.

"Ralph!" Michael Coswell said. "Haven't seen you in a dog's age."

"How you doing, Mike?" Ardley shook Coswell's hand. Then he looked over the man's work clothes, "Maybe I should say, what are you doing? Business been bad? Got a new line of work?''

Michael Coswell laughed. ''Nope. I'm in disguise. Though I'm getting pretty good at this handyman stuff. And speaking of work, what are you doing here?''

''Guess you didn't hear about the killing yesterday?''

''Killing! No. No wonder Ms. Cummings said the residents were edgy.''

''The gardener was stabbed. His body was found under the bushes yesterday morning.''

''Damn,'' Michael Coswell said.

''Don't have any more than that right now,'' Ardley said. ''And while we're on the subject, what are you doing here?''

''Seems there's a thief on the loose. Ms. Cummings wants me to see what I can find out.''

''Thief?'' Ardley frowned. ''Strange she didn't mention that to me.'' He wondered what else she hadn't told him.

''Think there might be a connection?''

''I don't know. Just watch your back, Mike,'' Ardley said. ''Maybe someone has a grudge against this place and is taking it out on the help.''

''Well, well, well,'' Alice said with a knowing grin. ''Don't we look different today.''

Eleanor tried to sound innocent, ''I've had this outfit a long time, Alice.'' They were standing in the lobby. Eleanor was on her way to the dining room when Alice came off the elevator and saw her.

''Did you wear it when the fireworks started?'' Alice laughed loudly.

Eleanor blushed, but tried to hold to her innocent stance. ''What are you talking about?'' She was afraid to ask the question, but didn't know what else to say.

''So, Mr. Suave finally scored'' Alice laughed again—''and from the look on your face it was a good match.''

''Now, Alice, cut that out.'' Eleanor couldn't give her words the force that said she was serious.

''And, I'll tell you one thing, it looks good on you. I've never seen you look happier. I hope he doesn't become a disappointment.''

Eleanor smiled, and said secretly, ''It *was* a good night. And truthfully, I really like him.'' Then more seriously, ''But please don't spread this around?''

Alice grinned. ''Me? All anyone has to do is look at you, and they'll know.''

''Please, Alice?''

Alice shook her head. ''No one will hear it from these lips.''

Grace, sitting at the front desk on the far side of the lobby, was smiling. With the acoustics of the lobby, she could hear every word they had spoken. So, she thought, that's why Eleanor looked different, and why her mind seemed someplace else.

''I know I'm a bit early, Ms. Cummings,'' Ardley said, as he lowered himself into the chair opposite her desk. He said it matter-of-factly. There was no apology in his voice.

''Well,'' Jessie said, ''I was expecting you at eleven. I haven't had time to go through all the files yet.'' It was a lie. She had gone through them last night, but she didn't want to give him the satisfaction.

Ardley shrugged, ''I really came early for a different reason. I can't put a man on the inside of this place without his standing out in the crowd. Is there anyone on the premises you trust, that would cooperate with the police?''

''You mean, spy on his friends, don't you?'' Jessie said.

Ardley gave another shrug. ''I would be more inclined to say he would be protecting his friends. Until we know what we're dealing with, everyone is in danger.''

It annoyed Jessie that she had to agree with him. ''There's one person who knows just about everyone in the place—Benny Ashe. He's like the mayor of Coral Sands. I can't guarantee his cooperation. I don't think he's very fond of you.''

Ardley sighed. ''I believe that's true.'' Then he frowned at Jessie. ''What's this I hear about a thief on the premises?''

''I don't truly think it has anything to do with Mr. Yamaguchi's death.''

Ardley didn't say anything. He just sat quietly, looked at her, and waited.

Finally Jessie said, ''I don't think there *is* a thief on the premises. The objects, except for Eleanor's brooch, have no real value.'' She gave a little shrug. ''I suspect these things have simply been misplaced. Old people have a tendency to misplace things.''

''Well, suppose you tell me about these thefts anyway. I like to have a clear picture of what's going on around a murder scene.''

Peter descended to the lobby in the glass elevator about ten minutes after Eleanor had gone into the dining room. He had lain in bed, thinking, a long time after Eleanor had left his room this morning. Life had taken a new and pleasant turn for him, and he needed, no, wanted to soak it all up, drink in the new feelings that invaded his body and his mind. Finally, he got up and dressed and headed down for breakfast.

The lobby looked different, warm, more exciting. Peter's mind was filled with a whirling fog of feelings that were all good, happy, drunken feelings. And all the feelings whirled around Eleanor. Last night was a pact made and sealed in ecstasy. He was a man in love. The sights, the scents, the feelings of last night with Eleanor filled his mind. She was a part of him still, commanding his thoughts, touching every part of his body with her essence.

It amazed him that he could have such feelings for a woman. He had been with many women. All sorts of women, from all walks of life, and there were times when he had thought he was in love. He couldn't believe how wrong he had been. Never in his wildest imagination did he think he could feel this way. And he was thankful that he had lived long enough to meet this fantastic woman.

Eleanor was not simply another woman, another person. There was a magical mist around her. She was the Sphinx, harboring the answers to all of life's secrets. She was a goddess who blessed him with her magic. She was the promise that life could be absolutely wonderful. She was the soul that poets strained futilely to describe. He desired to be in her presence always, to look at her, to smile with her, to become an inseparable part of her.

As Peter got off the elevator, he chuckled to himself. What would his son, David, think of him if he could see him now? Probably chalk it up to a sure sign of senility. Peter knew that he, himself, would have thought that of his own father. An old man acting like an infatuated teenager would have seemed ridiculous to him. Funny how things look different on the other side of the fence.

Ardley came out of the dining room and confronted Peter.

"'Morning, Mr. Benington," Ardley said without a smile.

The way Peter was feeling at that moment, he feared nothing Ardley said or did. He felt invincible, surrounded by the haze of warm love.

"Good morning, Detective," Peter smiled.

Ardley gave Peter a strange look. "You feeling all right today?"

"Just fine," Peter said. "What can I do for you, Detective?"

"I was looking for Mr. Ashe . . . Benny. Have you seen him today?" Ardley couldn't help looking at Peter, trying to figure out what was different about the man.

Peter nodded toward the dining room, "He's not in there?"

Ardley shook his head.

"Then, I can't help you. Normally we all get together for breakfast. You might try outside. Sometimes he goes walking after he's eaten." Sometimes, Peter thought, he spends the night with Caroline, but he wasn't going to let Ardley know about that. Peter had once thought it funny for a man Benny's age to be spending the night with a woman. That was before last night and Eleanor.

"Thanks," Ardley said. He hesitated, gave Peter one more examining look, then nodded. "Thanks," he said, and turned toward the door leading out to the swimming pool.

Ardley stepped through the door and out to the deck around the swimming pool. He saw the two old men sitting in the gazebo near the edge of the lake, and headed toward them. He was still puzzled by the way Peter looked. I'd swear, he thought, the man was deliriously happy.

As he approached the two men, he saw one of them was wearing a T-shirt with NECESSITY IS THE MOTHER OF DECEPTION written on the back.

"Excuse me, gentlemen," Ardley said. Neither man turned around. "Either of you see Mr. Ashe this morning?"

Sailor Hat looked at Gray Hair. "Mr. Ashe?"

"I think he means Benny," Gray Hair said.

"That's his name?"

"Yep."

"Haven't seen him today, officer."

"Me, neither," Gray Hair said.

Ardley was about to turn away, then said, "Were either of you in World War Two?"

Sailor Hat nodded. "Navy."

"Army Intelligence," Gray Hair said.

"Army Intelligence!" Sailor Hat said. "No wonder it took us so long to beat the Germans. And me sitting out in the Pacific on that destroyer all the while, bobbing up and down, throwing my guts up into the ocean."

Ardley thought for a moment about pursuing his questioning, then, looking at the two men, decided it was futile, gave it up, and walked back to the building. Inside he headed across the lobby toward the front desk. It was then that Benny came through the front door. They saw each other at the same time.

"Mr. Ashe!" Ardley said, and then walked toward Benny. Ardley saw the expression on Benny's face harden and become wary. Ardley stepped up to Benny. "I would like to speak privately with you, if you have a moment?"

"I have a choice?" Benny said. "Will I need a lawyer?"

Ardley did not react to Benny's remarks. "Is there a place we can sit down without being interrupted?"

Benny frowned, took a deep breath in surrender, and said, "The card room is usually not busy so early in the morning."

"Fine," Ardley said. "Please lead the way."

"So, how is our computer expert this morning?" Peter asked, as he pulled out a chair and sat down at the table.

Walter Innes grunted. "Bits, bytes, gigs, ROM, RAM," Walter said, "I don't know what in blazes the kids are talking about. I'm not learning about the computer, I'm learning a second language."

Betty giggled.

Alice laughed aloud. "I know just what you mean, Walter. I see kids all the time, but I don't understand what they are saying anymore."

Eleanor smiled. "You mean you are not out there scanning

the web and visiting chat rooms and doing magical things with your computer?''

''I didn't get past plugging the darn thing in,'' Walter said.

''Well''—Peter smiled—''you must have learned something yesterday afternoon.''

''I learned that there's a lot more to learn than I thought.''

''C'mon,'' Eleanor said. ''It can't be as bad as that.''

''Well, I did learn that when the computer says to press any key, that there is no ANY key. And when I don't put in the right information, it admonishes me for entering a Bad Command. But it never congratulates me on entering a good command. What I thought was a cup holder, was really the load drawer for CDs.'' Walter shook his head slowly. ''The only thing I mastered yesterday afternoon, was how to turn on the computer. Which, by the way, is easier than turning it off.''

They all laughed at that.

''It was intimidating to see those kids in action.'' Walter said. ''Georgie and his friend, Artie, were carrying on a conversation while Artie was flipping his fingers all over the keyboard, and the computer was dancing to his every whim. Made me feel damn old. I didn't even know enough about what they were telling me to form an intelligent question.''

''The only consolation I can offer,'' Peter said, ''is that, in my experience, the first lesson in anything is usually the hardest.''

''God,'' Walter said, his eyes wide, ''I sure hope they don't get any harder!''

''I think,'' Alice said, ''that things are moving too fast for us to catch up with them. New stuff everyday with the computer.''

The waiter came over to the table, interrupting the conversation. He put a plate of toast and scrambled eggs and a cup of coffee in front of Eleanor. Then he turned to Peter. ''May I take your order, sir?''

''The scrambled eggs look good,'' Peter said. ''I'd like a double order, with home fried potatoes and bacon. Rye toast and coffee. Oh, yes, and a glass of orange juice.''

''Yes, sir,'' the waiter said, and walked away.

''My God, Peter,'' Walter said. ''You're eating like a man

in love." With a small smile on his face and a knowing look in his eyes, he looked at Peter, then Eleanor.

Peter didn't acknowledge Walter's look, and Eleanor avoided his gaze. God, Peter thought, is it that noticeable? There was a moment of embarrassed silence that, thankfully, Peter thought, was broken by Benny's arrival.

"There's Benny," Betty said, and smiled. "I think he and Caroline make such a nice couple."

"From the look on his face," Alice said, "he didn't have a good night with her."

Benny's expression was fierce anger. He came up to the table, pulled out a chair and sat down.

"You guys ain't gonna believe what just happened to me," Benny said.

"It is obvious from your expression," Peter said, "that whatever it was, it was not good nor pleasant."

"You got that right, Slick," Benny said. "That Detective Ardley asked me to help him out. Do you believe it! Me, he asked."

"I find that difficult to believe, Benny," Peter said.

"Yeah," Alice said. "Sounds nuts to me. Why don't you tell us what you've been drinking?"

"C'mon, Alice. The guy wants me to help him with the Yamaguchi killing."

"A new low for law enforcement," Walter said.

"I think that's exciting," Betty twittered. "A real adventure."

Eleanor asked, "What did he want you to do?"

"Well, he wants me to keep my eyes out for anyone in the Home acting weird."

Alice laughed. "Now I know you're kidding. Everybody in this place acts weird. Even me. I dress up like a clown. There's Mr. Petersen who thinks he's Henny Youngman; Elaine Singleton, a drunken born-again Christian; Jimmy Ernest, who never comes out of his room except at night—I think he's got a vampire complex; Gregory, who goes out with his golf clubs every day and never plays golf; Wilson who walks around all day talking to himself; Himmler who is still secretly a Nazi; Kitty who wears more makeup than Tammy Faye Bakker and acts like a harlot; Hillary who goes out every day and searches through people's garbage cans; Aaron who—''

''Yeah, yeah,'' Benny interrupted. ''That's what I told him. If he's looking for weird, he came to the right place. He's looking for a nutcase screwy enough to kill Yamaguchi. At least that's what I thought he was saying.''

Peter didn't know some of the people Alice mentioned, but the idea that there were a lot of nutty people walking around made him question once again if his moving there was a smart idea. ''Ardley really thinks someone in the Home killed Yamaguchi?''

''Naw, I don't think so,'' Benny said. ''I asked him that. He said he was covering all the bases. He still hadn't done a thorough check of Yamaguchi. Yamaguchi's son described the man as a saint. Ardley said every saint he ever heard about had enemies that killed them. So, he suspects there was more to Yamaguchi's life than the sons knew. Maybe someone he knew hated him enough to kill him. And, he told me there also might be someone out to get at Jacobson, and was trying to give the place a bad reputation.''

''Ardley told you all that!'' Eleanor said. She didn't believe the man would confide such information to Benny.

''Yeah, well, I found that hard to believe, too. But, he was trying to get me to help him. Make me feel part of the team. That's what he told me, anyway.''

''And you believe him?'' Eleanor said.

''Believe him—yeah. Trust him—no,'' Benny said. ''That's why I'm telling you guys. He asked me not to say anything to anyone. Anyway, I don't know what he's not telling me.''

''Well,'' Walter said with a shrug, ''there is a possibility that someone in the Home did kill Yamaguchi. The mind is a terribly complex organ that we do not begin to understand. Things happen when a person gets older. Torments emerge from the dark to haunt us. I have witnessed people who have regressed in their rage—dredging up old hates and reacting with the same violence felt years before.'' He stopped, aware that the others at the table were looking at him. ''All I'm saying is that it is possible,'' he said defensively. Then with a subtle smirk, he added, ''Perhaps Eugene could help us here?'' To Betty, ''You think you could ask Eugene what's going on here?''

Eleanor gave Walter a look warning him not to treat Betty lightly.

''I will do that,'' Betty said with complete innocence, as if she didn't notice the smirk on Walter's face, ''when I talk to him tonight.''

Eleanor looked at Betty with concern. ''Has Eugene helped you anymore with your problem?''

Betty shook her head in annoyance. ''But he did say I should tell you all what's going on.'' She hesitated. ''I just don't know how to do that. It's so''—she lowered her eyes, ''embarrassing.''

''I think we have all seen too much of life to be embarrassed,'' Walter said in a quiet tone.

''But a person is judged by how their children turn out,'' Betty said. She was clearly upset by all this. ''It isn't fair. If your child becomes a criminal, everyone blames the parents. How can they do that? Eugene and I did our best to raise him right.''

''You got a kid that's a crook?'' Benny said.

''No, no, no,'' Betty said, waving away Benny's question. Then she looked down, avoiding everyone's eyes. In a weak voice she said, ''This is not easy for me.''

''Betty, we are your friends,'' Eleanor said, ''and we want to help you.''

''Yes,'' Walter said, ''and Eugene said you should tell us for that reason. We can help.''

''Oh,'' Betty said, shaking her head. She was near to tears. ''I don't see how you can.''

''Then trust in Eugene's judgment,'' Peter said, not sure why he was pushing this.

Betty took a deep breath, then blurted out, ''My eldest son, Andrew, is trying to have me declared incompetent and get control of my money.'' She wasn't relieved to have it out in the open. No matter how one looked at it, it was still dirty laundry.

''Shit,'' Benny said.

''Damn,'' Alice said.

"I assume," Walter said, "that Andrew has resorted to a determined attorney?"

Betty nodded, lowering her eyes in despair. She felt betrayed and alone.

"Lawyers and their legal papers can be very intimidating," Walter said.

"I just don't know what to do." It came out as a plea for help.

"And what does Eugene say you should do?" Eleanor said.

"Oh," she waved the notion away, "he just says to trust him, that everything will be all right."

"Do you have a lawyer to help you with this?" Walter said.

"No," Betty said. "A man came to see me. Said he was a lawyer the court sent over. I told him to go away. I didn't like him. Eugene didn't like him." She was too confused and overwhelmed by her son's betrayal. Shaking her head, her hands twittering helplessly in the air. Her voice breaking with emotional strain.

"I'll get you a lawyer," Benny said, hot anger in his voice. What sort of son-of-a-bitch son would try to take advantage of Betty? "I know a good one. He'll help you. We ain't gonna let this son of yours do this to you."

"How far along is this process?" Walter said. "Has his attorney contacted you? Has a court date been set?"

Betty made a deep sigh. She couldn't believe this was happening to her. "I got some sort of legal paper saying I have to go to court in four days."

"Four days!" Eleanor said.

"The bastard isn't wasting any time," Alice said, her anger clearly in her face.

"I'll get that lawyer right now," Benny said to Betty. "Don't you go anywhere. I'll be right back." He pushed back his chair, stood, and walked out of the dining room.

"He was such a good boy," Betty said. "Why would he turn on me like this? I'm his mother. And I'm not incompetent."

Everyone exchanged concerned glances. They were all thinking the same thing. She was going to have a tough time of proving her competence with Eugene hanging around in the background.

"I'm not," Betty insisted in her fragile high voice. "I can manage my own affairs."

"Don't worry," Eleanor said. "As Benny said, we aren't going to let this happen to you. I'm sure each of us is willing to testify to your competence. That alone should be enough to discourage him."

Everyone at the table nodded that they were willing to come to her aid. It made her feel better. Maybe this was what Eugene knew would happen if she told them.

Peter had nodded, too. He wanted to help this fragile little woman, but he wondered what sort of testimony he could give in her behalf if the issue of Eugene came up. Eugene was going to be her real problem in this.

CHAPTER 6

"Eight people who mentioned they were in the Pacific theater during War Two," Jessie Cummings said. "Six men and two women. The other four in the stack of folders just mentioned they were in the War but did not say which theater of operations."

"Somehow I thought there would be more than that," Ardley said. "Of course it narrows the field of prospects."

"There could be more. Remember, this information was voluntary. At lot of people don't want to be involved with the retired military groups."

"I understand."

"If your killer is a veteran gone over the edge," Jessie said, "there's a lot of retired military outside Coral Sands."

Ardley looked up from the folder he was reading. "Trying to remind me how difficult my job is?" He sighed. "Well, I guess it's time to interview these people," indicating the folders in his lap. "Could you set up a private place for me to talk to them? I really don't want to drag them down to the station."

Jessie looked up at the calendar on the wall. "The craft room isn't going to be used today. You can do it there. But, please be discreet when you talk to them. I don't need any heart attacks to deal with."

"Discretion is my strong point."

"I find that hard to believe!" She grinned.

Ardley smiled. "That's the first time I've seen you smile, Ms. Cummings. You should do it more often."

Jesus, she thought, is this rude sexist flirting with her?

''Grace!'' Jessie called out.

''Yes!'' Grace hollered back and then showed up at the office door.

''Detective Ardley wants to speak with some of the residents in private. I told him he could use the craft room today,'' Jessie said, and Ardley handed the folders to Grace. ''Would you please contact these people and schedule them to meet with the detective?''

Ardley said. ''You can schedule them a half hour apart. I'll be here all day.''

''Providing they're all here,'' Grace said.

Ardley nodded. ''Providing they're all here.''

''And, Grace, contact some landscapers. We need to find a replacement for the Yamaguchis.''

Grace nodded. ''Okay.''

''Also, please spread the word for everyone to protect their valuables. Just in case there really is a thief on the loose. I'm sure everyone knows about the thefts, but I want them to know we're on the job.''

There were mountains of clouds in the distance, the huge tops a bright white in the sun, when Benny parked the car in front of a two-story, brick building in downtown Sarasota. Betty, Peter, and Benny got out of the air-conditioned car into the bright heat of Florida. Betty was hugging a large manila envelope. They walked toward the building.

''We're in for some rain later.'' Benny nodded toward the clouds.

''It'll help to cool the air,'' Betty said. ''The night will be very pleasant.''

''Eugene tell you that?'' Benny said.

Betty made a face at him.

''Now, Betty, I just want you to tell this guy everything,'' Benny said.

She let out a deep sigh. ''I will. But I know he is not going to like Eugene.''

''If the guy doesn't know everything, there's no way he's gonna be able to help you.''

''Eugene,'' Peter said, ''is going to be a problem for you.

He will be difficult for the judge to accept. It is best if your lawyer is not surprised at the hearing by your son mentioning Eugene.'' He's going to have to be a terrific lawyer to rationalize Eugene, Peter thought.

''Yes, yes,'' Betty, annoyed, waved them away. ''I know that.''

Benny stepped up to the glass door, pulled it open—the cool air from inside spilling out onto him—and stepped aside to let Betty go in first.

Bill Fresno's office was a study in clutter. Besides the numerous stacks of paper, there were five briefcases jammed with paper. The office was a reflection of the man. Bill Fresno, a man in his thirties, acted as if he had someplace important to be and was already late. His dark hair was disheveled, his white shirt was opened at the collar, and his tie hung loose.

While Betty brought him up to date, Bill Fresno went through the documents in the envelope Betty had given him, fidgeted, moved around in his chair, checked his watch repeatedly, and even got up a few times to pace. It was during one of his pacings that Betty mentioned Eugene. He stopped cold, and frowned at Betty.

''Who is this Eugene?'' he said.

''My husband.''

''You have a husband and he's not here with you?''

Betty put on her peaceful innocent face. ''Oh, he's here.''

Bill Fresno's eyes widened under his frown, as he glanced perplexed about the office. Oh, oh, he thought, a real bedbug.

Here we go, Peter thought.

Bill Fresno phrased his next question carefully. ''Do you see your husband here?''

''Of course not.'' She said it as if the question were absurd.

''Mrs. Jablonski, would you mind explaining what you mean when you say your husband is here?''

''Well,'' she said very seriously, ''he's always at my side.'' She left it at that, as if it were explanation enough.

''I'm sorry, Mrs. Jablonski, but I still don't understand.''

Betty took a deep breath and sighed at his denseness. She then spoke slowly and carefully as if to a child. ''Eugene passed away eight years ago . . .''

''Ooh, he's dead.''

''Yes, but he's always with me.''

Bill Fresno relaxed. It wasn't that bad, keeping the memory of her husband alive. That was okay, a sign of real affection, true love, even. That would be a good argument in court. Betty's next statement quickly changed his opinion.

''He protects me,'' Betty said, ''and advises me on everything.''

If this weren't so serious an issue, Peter would have laughed at the expression on Bill Fresno's face.

''Oh oh,'' Bill Fresno said, putting a hand up to rub over his face, trying to rub some clarity into his mind. ''You lost me again, Mrs. Jablonski.''

''I talk to him every night, and he tells me what to do.'' Simple as that.

''Please, let me try to understand. You talk with your husband every night?''

''Yes.''

''Does he talk back to you?''

''Well, of course he doesn't speak aloud.'' What a dummy this lawyer was. ''He's dead. He spells out the words on the Ouija board.''

Bill Fresno didn't sit, so much as collapse in his chair behind the desk. ''Oh, boy,'' he muttered. He was right the first time—a real bedbug. Then in a normal tone, ''I'm sorry, but I don't think I can help you, Mrs. Jablonski.''

''You gotta help her,'' Benny said. ''They're going to take her apart if you don't.''

Bill Fresno looked at Benny. ''Even with me helping her they are going to take her apart.'' He slapped the folder of papers Betty had given him. ''She's been examined by a committee of a couple of doctors appointed by the court. They say she has a problem.'' He leaned forward over the desk and looked hard at Benny. ''This stuff about Eugene doesn't bother you?''

Benny turned to Betty. ''Would you mind stepping outside for a few moments while Mr. Fresno and I talk?''

''No.'' It was a firm 'no.' ''I'm staying right here. Anything you want to say about me can be done to my face.''

It was Peter who jumped in next. ''As I understand this, the issue of incompetence is much different than that of being an eccentric. Betty is totally capable of making her own decisions and seeing to her own welfare. Both of which she does very well.''

Benny looked at Peter with wide-eyed admiration. The man was good!

Bill Fresno frowned. He had to admit to himself that was a pretty good argument. Might be an interesting challenge—defending this woman against her hungry relatives.

''I am not eccentric,'' Betty said.

Bill Fresno looked at her while he drummed his fingers on the desk, and ran the whole scenario through his mind.

''Being different don't mean you can't take care of yourself,'' Benny said.

''I'm not different,'' Betty said. ''You speak of me as if I were crazy.''

''No,'' Bill Fresno said. ''He speaks of you as if you were not crazy. He's concerned that the judge will think you're crazy. My problem is to convince the judge that you are perfectly, or maybe imperfectly, normal.''

''Then you'll help her?'' Benny said.

Bill Fresno shrugged. What the hell, he thought, I think I'm a terrific lawyer. Maybe it's time I tried to prove it. ''Can't promise you anything except I'll do the best I can. I just hope it's good enough.'' Then he looked at Betty, ''Mrs. Jablonski, you'll have to tell me everything about Eugene.''

CHAPTER 7

Jimmy Ernest came into the craft room and sat at the table opposite Ardley. Jimmy Ernest was wearing a cotton robe over his pajamas. He saw the question on Ardley's face. "I usually sleep during the day, and am up at night."

Ardley nodded.

"It's from the War. Since I got out of the Marines, I couldn't sleep when it was dark. Got a job as a night watchman. Fit my schedule to a tee."

"The War? You mean World War Two?"

Jimmy Ernest nodded. "The Japs'd sneak into the foxholes at night. One morning I found two of my buddies with their throats slit in the next foxhole. I wasn't gonna let that happen to me." He chuckled coldly. "I didn't get much sleep during the War." He shrugged. "So, I sleep during the day. Nothing bad about that. I don't have to worry about a sunburn. You meet more interesting people at night, anyway."

"How do you feel, now, about the Japanese?"

"I don't want to talk about that," Jimmy Ernest said in a quiet tone.

"Why don't you want to talk about it?"

Jimmy Ernest sat there and said nothing.

"I would like to hear what you have to say."

Jimmy Ernest shifted uncomfortably in the chair. "I don't want to talk about it."

"Is there something you're trying to hide?"

"Look"—Jimmy's face went cold and his voice was hard—

"I got all that stuff locked up in the back of my head. Took a lot of years to get it there. I ain't gonna let it out again. And I ain't gonna let you let it out again."

Hillary Mason was a tall, thin man with every muscle and vein showing through his skin. The gray hair on his head stuck up in all directions, and his blue eyes were hazed over and washed out. He had a tremor in his right hand. The clothes he wore were one up from ragged.

"I was in a prison camp for a year. Three hundred seventy-two days. You ever been hungry?" His eyes wandered, and he never looked directly at Ardley. It was as if he were talking aloud to himself.

Ardley didn't answer.

"Try eating something that looks and smells like vomit, with live bugs in it. We were so hungry we fought over the stuff. That's hungry. The Japanese bastards used to laugh at us fighting over the slop. When they got tired of that, they'd take one of us out and beat the living shit out of him. After a while, they did more than beat us.

"I got married before I was shipped to the Pacific. God bless her, that woman stayed with me after the War, even when she knew I couldn't . . . couldn't do it anymore. Couldn't love her the way a man was supposed to. Couldn't father any children."

Gladys McGovern was a tiny, round, grandmotherly woman with huge breasts and a gentle smile. But when she spoke about the War, her voice became distant, her eyes looked at another time.

"I was a nurse during the War. I was home in the states visiting my family when my husband, Greg, was taken by the Japanese in the Philippines. I never saw him again. After the War a man came to see me. I don't remember his name. Said he was in the prison camp with my husband, and when my husband was dying, this man promised him he would come see me and tell me that my husband loved me, and I should go on with my life." She stopped for a moment, and Ardley saw she was someplace else. "Greg *was* my life."

• • •

When the interviews were finished, Ardley had more suspects than he could handle. And more weirdoes than he expected. Ardley found out, for one, that Hillary Mason spent his time going through other people's garbage cans. Christ, the guy's got enough money to live in Coral Sands, and he goes out digging in other people's garbage. Unbelievable.

"Mr. Fresno is a very intense person," Betty said. She was sitting in the backseat in Benny's car. They were driving back to Coral Sands. "That can't be good for his health."

"Well," Benny said, "it's not his health we're worrying about. We want somebody who's gonna do the best job protecting *your* health."

"But, I'm very healthy."

"If the judge says you're incompetent," Benny said, "they'll put you away somewhere."

"Away somewhere!"

"The judge will assign someone," Peter said, "to oversee your needs and care for you. That will be your son. I am sure he will not take on the responsibility of seeing to your every need. No doubt he will place you in a nursing care facility where they will feed you and take care of you."

"Oh, my," Betty said. This was a shock to her. "And I thought I would only have to give up control of my money." Betty sat back. Her situation had become more desperate. There was a lot she would have to discuss with Eugene that night.

To change the subject, and let Betty contemplate the seriousness of her situation, Peter said to Benny, "Are you going to see Caroline this evening?"

"Yeah. We're going to the Beach House for dinner. We're taking Mildred to meet her computer admirer there. Once they get together, Caroline and I are gonna have dinner. You and Eleanor can come along if you want."

"I believe Eleanor may have other plans for the evening," Peter said.

"Oh. I thought you and her were getting rather close."

Peter smiled. It was tough keeping secrets in a closed community. "I believe we are," he said.

• • •

It was a little past six when Jessie Cummings came out the front door on her way home. Mike Coswell was coming toward her.

"You still here?" Jessie said.

"Vigilant to the last," he smiled, and stopped by her.

"We're not paying you by the hour."

He laughed. "It's not the money. I'm going to stick around and see if I can't get most of those plants in the ground. They can't take much more time in the pots."

"They'll hold," Jessie said. "They get plenty of water when the automatic sprinklers go off at two in the morning."

He shrugged, still smiling. "Then let's say I'm working on a little theory about the thefts."

"What sort of theory?"

"Maybe I should call it a hunch more than a theory. I think they happened at night, and I'd like to stick around. See what I can come up with."

"Suit yourself."

"Any chance I can get a meal for my effort?"

Now Jessie smiled. "I knew there was a price in there somewhere." Then she nodded toward the front door. "Tell Grace I said it was okay."

"Thanks." He stepped past her. "I'll see you in the morning."

"Good night," she said, and left for home.

"I'm so excited for you, dear!" Caroline said. She was seated in the front passenger seat of Benny's car. Benny and Caroline were driving Mildred to Mildred's rendezvous with her computer admirer. "Such a romantic adventure!"

"Well," Mildred said, "I'm numb with the excitement." She really didn't like the idea of everyone being involved in her life like this. It made her feel foolish, and she vowed it would never happen again. It was a mistake taking Alice into her confidence. "I haven't slept right in two days since this started. I hope I don't fall asleep on him."

Benny laughed. "You should hope you do!"

"Oh, Benny," Caroline said. "She didn't mean it that way, silly man."

"Do I look all right?" Mildred said.

"You look just superb," Caroline said.

"Except for the umbrella," Benny laughed. "You look like a tourist."

"That's the idea, so he can recognize me." Mildred smiled, "We thought it would be more discreet than my holding a rose in my teeth."

"You better hope he doesn't meet some lady tourist he thinks is you," Benny said.

"I'm not sure how we're going to do this," Mildred said. "He's expecting me to be alone."

"Hey," Benny said, "we'll go in the bar area with you, and take a seat someplace nearby. When he shows we'll come up and say hello. You introduce us, and then we'll leave you guys alone. That way he'll know he's been seen. If he's up to something funny, it may change his mind that people could identify him later, if you know what I mean."

"I guess that's all right."

"Don't worry, dear. We will be dining in the restaurant, if you need us."

"Thank you both for helping me."

Benny had no trouble finding a parking space near the entrance to the Beach House. During the season, when all the snowbirds were in town, both parking lots would have been filled and it would have been impossible to find a parking space. The Beach House sat on the beach in Manatee County just north of Sarasota and overlooked the Gulf of Mexico. There was a huge wooden deck across the back of the restaurant, where customers were treated to fresh sea breezes and live music while they dined and drank and enjoyed the spectacular sunsets. Inside, the restaurant was air-conditioned, and the side facing the Gulf was a wall of windows, so the diners inside could also enjoy the sunsets. The music from the deck drifted inside the restaurant.

Benny, Caroline, and Mildred went inside past the maître d's station and turned left into the bar area. It, too, had windows overlooking the Gulf. The bar area was not especially crowded. Mildred looked expectantly at the people in the bar. There were a number of older men scattered about, most with women, none with an umbrella.

Benny and Caroline took a table two over from the table

where Mildred had sat down, and ordered drinks—white wine for Caroline, beer for Benny. He, too, had scanned the room, checking out all the men. They seemed not at all interested in Mildred.

"I think this is so romantic, meeting a strange man," Caroline said.

"Not a smart thing to do," Benny said.

"Well, darling man, it was how I met you."

Benny smiled. "Yeah, but I ain't strange."

Caroline laughed a small genteel laugh.

Benny checked his watch—6:58. Well, they were a couple minutes early. There was still time for him to show. It pissed Benny off that a guy would leave a woman like Mildred waiting. If it had been him, he would have been there early. Well, it takes all kinds.

He looked over at Mildred. Damn, she seemed so frail, so fragile, sitting there with such expectations, so vulnerable. To Benny all women were vulnerable, and men either respected them or preyed upon them. Benny again looked over the men in the bar, and wondered if the son-of-a-bitch was there toying with Mildred.

"With all the scattered clouds out there, it will be a beautiful sunset."

"Yeah," Benny said. "But I've been in Florida so long, I don't get the thrill I used to at watching them."

"I was like that until I met you, dear man. You reawakened my spirit, and let me see that life can be exciting at any age. Maybe I can reawaken your spirit, and you will enjoy them again."

"Since I met you, all I want to look at is you. The heck with the sunsets."

Caroline smiled lovingly. Benny's speech and manner were crude, but he was a romantic and had such a warm and loving heart. Her life had little romance before Benny arrived on the scene. She felt privileged that such a man would take notice of her at all.

Benny noticed one man in particular, a white-haired guy with a shoestring tie and fancy western belt buckle, who kept looking over at Mildred. The man caught Benny's eye a couple of times, when he looked in their direction, and quickly looked away.

The next time Benny looked at his watch it was ten after seven. Mr. Belt Buckle had left, and two other older men had come into the bar. But no one moved to talk to Mildred, who by this time, was looking concerned.

It was seven-thirty when Benny went over to Mildred. "Looks like he changed his mind, Mildred."

"I hope nothing has happened to him." She was worried. "Timothy said he would call if he was going to be late."

"Sitting here like this is not going to help him if something happened. And, honestly, if the man let you wait this long, he isn't worth getting involved with."

"Could we wait a little longer?" Mildred said.

"We'll wait as long as you want. Why don't you have something to eat? Maybe it'll make you feel better."

She gave Benny a weak smile. "My stomach's so tight with expectation, I don't think there's room for food."

Benny smiled and nodded. "Hang in there. Just let us know when you want to leave."

"Okay."

It was eight o'clock when Mildred decided it was time to leave. No one said anything. The situation had become embarrassing to each of them. Benny paid the check, and they all left the restaurant. They drove back in silence. Mildred felt the fool, and Benny and Caroline felt sorry for her, sorry she had been so misled, and sorry because they knew how embarrassed she was.

When they entered the lobby of Coral Sands, Peter and Eleanor were coming out of the dining room, and Benny signaled them not to say anything to Mildred. Mildred didn't want to see anybody right then, she was too ashamed. She went straight to the elevator and up to her apartment. Peter and Eleanor came over to Benny.

"What happened?"

"Nothing, that's what happened." Benny was angry. "The s.o.b. didn't show. Damn dirty trick."

"God," Eleanor said, "she must feel awful."

"It was terrible to see her hopes dashed like that," Caroline said. "It can not be easy for a woman at any age."

"Well, the bastard better not show his face around me." Benny said. "I'll break his nose."

Peter smiled. "Something you're good at."

Eleanor smiled, and Benny couldn't help but grin.

"After this I gotta have a drink," Benny said. "You guys interested?"

Peter and Eleanor exchanged questioning glances. "Sure," Eleanor said. "Why not?"

Mildred entered her apartment, went over to the computer, turned it on, and sat down. She was hot with a mixed bag of emotions: worry about what might have happened to Timothy; embarrassment at being stood up in front of her friends; anger that he did not call her; and, worst of all—foolishness at having dared to dream romantic dreams at her age.

She waited for the desktop to appear, then clicked on the Microsoft Network, and clicked on connect. After a moment the connection was complete, she clicked on Favorite Places, then on Beach Blanket 2F chat room. The room was empty. Timothy was not there. Not that she really expected him to be there, but there was always that chance.

She clicked back to MSN Central, then E-mail. When the E-mail screen came up she clicked on Compose a Message and entered Timothy's address in the To box, then she started typing . . .

> I'm hurt and disappointed, Timothy. I waited for an hour, and you didn't show up. After all that talk about wanting to get together, about taking the relationship a step further, you back out at the last minute. How rude and insensitive. I thought you were not capable of such rudeness. How wrong I was. I'm so angry I don't know what to say . . .

As she was typing, an E-mail message came in for her. It was from Timothy! She stopped typing and opened his message.

> Sweet Lady, forgive me. I have no rational excuse for not meeting you as we planned. I could make one up, but

honesty is the one thing we've had in our relationship. I got "cold feet." My handle isn't Shy-Guy for nothing. When the time came to meet you, I paced and fretted and worried that you wouldn't like me in the flesh. I can't describe the agony I went through, trying to get my feet moving in your direction. But I never made it out the door. I stayed in my room, upset by my weak spirit, wanting to crawl into a hole somewhere and hide.

I'm so confused and disappointed in myself. I know I must have hurt you terribly. All I can do is apologize with all my heart, and ask you to forgive me.

I'll be on the Beach Blanket tomorrow night if you still want to speak to me.

She read the message twice, her anger turning to warm compassion. The poor man, to be so afraid of living. She forgot her hurt and her disappointment, and her heart reached out to him, her eyes blurred by tears. After she deleted the message she had been writing to him, she shut off the computer.

It was dark outside, the sun had set a short while before. She looked out at the dark world and wondered how many Timothys there were—afraid to go out of their homes, their only contact with people through this skinny phone line and a computer. How sad some people's lives were.

The next morning, just after sunrise, Colonel Winston was out for his usual morning stroll around the grounds of Coral Sands. It was another beautiful morning: sunny, the sky a soft blue with a confusion of clouds, and the air moved in soft, cool breezes. He liked the mornings best of all. The world was still asleep, so all he heard and smelled were the stirrings of nature. The palm trees swayed gently, and birds called playfully.

It had been his habit all the years in the Marines to take early morning walks. It was a peaceful time, even in wartime.

Finding the gardener's body the other morning had jolted him back in time to the War. The doors to the dark corridors in his mind had been yanked open, and the horrors hidden there had come running out. It would take time to push them all back into the dungeons of his mind where they belonged.

But the walk and fresh air were improving his spirits. He walked taller and with renewed confidence along the carpet of thick grass. Until he reached the spot where Yamaguchi's body had been found.

The crime-scene tape had been removed yesterday, but the spot was clearly marked in his mind. He wanted to shy away, but something made him peer into the shadows under the brush where Yamaguchi's body had been found. His eyes widened and he stopped cold. God! There were two shoes sticking out from under the brush!

CHAPTER 8

When Ardley and the rest of the police arrived, Jessie Cummings was waiting for them outside the front entrance to Coral Sands, having arrived only five minutes before. She had been rousted from her bed by the telephone call from Shirley Danzig, the night clerk just going off duty. Jessie told Shirley to contact the police and not let anyone near the body, then Jessie grabbed some clothes, did the best she could do with hair and makeup, and drove over to Coral Sands. She hadn't even had time to get a cup of coffee to put a spark under her thoughts. Jessie had asked Shirley to get her a cup while she waited for the police.

While she was waiting Jessie thought more seriously about getting a security firm to patrol the grounds at night. It would help to ease the minds of the residents. Providing Jacobson would spring for the expense. Not something he was likely to do.

When Ardley got out of the police car, Jessie could see he wasn't doing much better than she. He looked weary. For some reason, that made her feel good.

"Good morning, Detective," Jessie said with little enthusiasm.

Ardley didn't respond with a greeting. All he said, in the grumbling tone of one not yet fully awake, was, "Why can't people kill one another at a decent hour of the day?" He heaved a hard sigh. "Who is it this time?"

"I just got here myself. All I know is Colonel Winston found the body. He's waiting at the scene."

"You sure he's dead?" Ardley couldn't suppress a large yawn.

"Shirley, the night clerk, told me The Colonel had said the man was dead. I assume The Colonel knows dead when he sees it."

Ardley nodded. His eyes were still heavy with sleep, and his thoughts struggled to come together. He let out a wide yawn that watered his eyes.

"You look like you could use a cup of coffee," Jessie said.

"Nectar of the gods." Ardley groaned. "Please, if you can get me some?"

At that moment Shirley came out of the building with a cup of coffee in her hand for Jessie. "Cream and sugar," Shirley said. Shirley was a skinny woman whose wrinkles and hard lines made her look older than she was. Her short hair, in need of a combing, was a mix of blond and gray, and she wore no makeup.

Jessie gave Ardley a questioning look.

"Just fine with me," Ardley said.

Jessie handed him the cup. "Shirley, would you please get another?"

Shirley nodded and went back inside.

Ardley sipped at the hot coffee. "I am in your debt, Ms. Cummings." This time he did not overly stress the Ms. "Where's the body?"

"Shirley said it was around the side. The Colonel is waiting there for us."

Ardley sighed. "Well, let's go see." He signaled to the two policemen in uniform to follow, then Ardley and Jessie headed around the side of the building. One policeman was carrying another large roll of yellow crime-scene tape.

As they walked, Ardley kept taking large gulps of the coffee, trying to get himself wide awake.

Mildred, dressed for the day, came down to the lobby. She had a breakfast appointment at the hospital. She did volunteer duty there, and this day she was to have breakfast with her friend Connie Shaw, another volunteer. Connie was a very sweet person, and Mildred had decided to confide in her about Timothy. Mildred did not want to talk any further about Timothy to her friends at Coral Sands. She was afraid of generating more embarrassing episodes like last night. Mildred had all she could do to face everyone when she had returned to the Home last night after being stood up by Timothy. She didn't want to go through that again.

She crossed the lobby, waved a good morning to Grace who had just showed up for work, then went out the front door. Mildred saw the police cars but paid them little attention. There had been police cars around for the past few days, since Yamaguchi had been stabbed. She got in her red Honda, started the car and drove out of the parking lot. She didn't notice the dark blue car that was parked across from Coral Sands. Nor did she notice it start up and follow her as she drove away.

Colonel Winston was standing guard over the murder scene. There was no one else around. The Colonel and Shirley had kept the incident to themselves.

"Good morning, Colonel," Ardley said as he stepped up to the man.

"Wasn't a good one, I'm afraid." He nodded in the direction of the brush. "Like the last one—stabbed in the back."

"Know who it is?" Ardley gulped the last of the coffee and handed the cup to Jessie.

"I believe it is the private detective that Ms. Cummings hired."

"God, I never told him about Yamaguchi being killed," Jessie said with sudden guilt.

"I did," Ardley said. "And I told him to watch his back."

"The footprints around the area are mine," Colonel Winston said. "I did not see any other prints in the dirt."

"That was like before. All the footprints were accounted for. Nothing of the killer's. Unless . . ." Ardley let that hang, though he completed the thought in his mind . . . *The killer is the one who found the body.*

The Colonel gave Ardley a puzzled look.

"When did you find him?" Ardley knew he was sounding gruff, but he still wasn't awake. The coffee had yet to do its stuff.

"I was up and walking early. Just after sunrise. The body is cold. He must have been killed last night."

Ardley looked at Jessie. "What would he be doing planting in the dark?"

"Maybe just before dark," Jessie said. "I saw him working out here around six last night when I was going home. It looks like he put most of the plants in the ground."

Ardley saw only two pots with plants in them. The rest of the pots were empty and stacked to one side. He peered around and spotted the sprinkler heads flush with the ground. "When do the sprinklers go on?"

"Every other day at two in the morning."

"That accounts for no footprints . . ."

"The Lord punishes the sinners!"

Ardley nearly jumped out of his skin. "Damn," he said, turning around to face Elaine Singleton, his heart pounding, the adrenaline surging into his system. She was standing just behind them. Her hair disheveled, her eyes glassy from drink. She was barefoot, and wearing a nightgown that had seen better days.

"Stay to the path of righteousness and ye shall see the Lord!"

"Lady, do you have to shout?" Ardley said. "The Lord didn't make me deaf." Then he nodded to one of the policemen to take her away.

The policeman took Elaine by the arm and guided her away. Elaine shouted over her shoulder, "Repent your sins, before it is too late!"

"She's an alcoholic," Jessie said. "Harmless, but at times a nuisance."

"Why don't you put her somewhere?" Ardley snapped. He was trying to get his adrenaline flow back to normal, and to clear the panic his mind had been thrown into. But, now he was wide awake.

"You mean in a hospital?"

"Wherever people like that can get care."

"I suppose we could do that," Jessie said, "but you see she's terminally ill. Doesn't have more than a year. She won't get any better care than here. We protect her from herself, and we let her live the way she wishes. What more can a person ask for their last days?''

She suddenly realized The Colonel was standing there listening, and turned to him. ''Not a word of this to anyone. Her son took me into his confidence. No one, not even Grace, knows about this.''

The Colonel nodded. ''You have my word.''

Ardley turned away, his anger at being frightened had subsided. This wasn't a conversation he wanted to engage in. He nodded to the remaining policeman, who stepped toward the crime scene with the roll of crime-scene tape and began marking out the area. Ardley stood there watching him roll out the tape. Mike Coswell's death didn't fit the crazed veteran theory. That line of investigation could be dropped. The idea that someone was trying to discredit Coral Sands now looked better.

Ardley turned to Jessie. ''Ms. Cummings, I'd like to have the name of that landscaping firm you fired. Also, any disgruntled employees you may have dismissed over the past say . . . six months.''

Jessie nodded. She didn't ask why, because she knew what he was thinking.

Ardley looked back at the murder scene. His investigation of Yamaguchi's past would continue. Wouldn't be the first time someone killed a couple of people to hide the real victim. Ardley had found that Yamaguchi liked to gamble, but wasn't very good at it. Could be something there.

He also learned that Yamaguchi had a very hefty life insurance policy with his boys as the beneficiaries. A check on the solvency of the boys' business was next on the list. Then a check on their individual debts. Money, in this case $250,000, was always a good motive for murder.

There was no need to investigate Mike Coswell's past. The killer of Yamaguchi would have had no idea that Mike would be brought on to investigate the thefts. So, Mike wasn't the target.

He wondered how many more killings would be done before the murderer felt his real victim would be well-hidden?

Ardley turned again to Jessie Cummings. ''I'd like to have

a couple of my people work around here undercover for awhile.''

''I understand,'' she said. She pointed. ''Mr. Yamaguchi was going to continue the bed of oyster plants beneath the hibiscus all along the border. Maybe they could finish that?''

Ardley followed where she pointed. ''I'll have some people here later today.''

''Have them see Grace. She'll be able to direct them on the plantings. I'll have her order another truckload of oyster plants for delivery this afternoon.'' Then she frowned at Ardley. ''But what about at night? Michael was killed sometime last night.'' A couple of policemen patrolling grounds at night would be better than hiring a security firm. And she wouldn't have to clear it with Jacobson.

Ardley thought about it a moment, then nodded. ''I'll have a couple of uniforms stay on the grounds for the next few nights.''

''Another killing?'' Peter couldn't believe his ears. What sort of place *was* this!

''Yeah,'' Benny said, ''Grace just told me.''

''How awful,'' Eleanor said.

''Oh my, oh my,'' Betty said, distressed. ''Eugene never said anything about this.''

They were sitting around a table in the dining room waiting for the waiter to bring them breakfast. Walter and Charlie were also at the table.

''Who, may I ask, was killed this time?'' Walter asked, resting his chin on the handle of his cane.

''The private detective Jessie hired yesterday,'' Benny said. ''Found him under the bushes, stabbed like Yamaguchi. He was finishing up the planting Yamaguchi had started.''

Charlie shook his head sadly. ''Gardening must be a tough profession nowadays.''

People getting killed seemed to be a favorite pastime around here, Peter thought. He almost left after the first killings, which had occurred shortly after he arrived two months ago. Now there were two more! This wasn't what he had pictured retirement to be. He looked at Eleanor. If it weren't for how he felt about that woman, he'd pack up and leave now. He realized, suddenly, that he was no longer a free spirit. He was tied to Eleanor in a way he had never thought possible.

"That about shoots down The Colonel's theory," Benny said.

Betty shook her head. "It could still be a deranged person in the Home."

"Someone who hates gardeners," Walter said, with a straight face.

Benny looked at Betty. "Did you ask Eugene about this like you said you were going to?"

"No," Betty said. "I had so much to ask him about last night, I forgot."

"Did you ask him about the lawyer?"

"Yes. And he said that Mr. Fresno was the right man for the job. Those are Eugene's words." She hesitated. "But I still think Mr. Fresno is too tense. He makes me nervous."

"What else did Eugene have to say?" Eleanor said.

"Well, I told him that I thought this whole thing with my son was just about the money. Then I asked him about—if I lose in court—would I be put away in some nursing home? He said, I was right and it was all about money. Money was the key, was what he said. He also told me that I shouldn't worry because I'm not going to lose."

If you believe in miracles, Peter thought.

"That should have made you feel better," Eleanor said.

"But it didn't." Betty was clearly worried. "I don't know, I'm still scared about all of this legal stuff, and courts and lawyers and all that. They have so much power, they can do anything they want to you."

"He sounds sweet," Connie Shaw said. She and Mildred were at breakfast in the hospital cafeteria. Connie was a thin, pleasant woman with close cropped gray hair and a face filled with smile wrinkles.

Mildred smiled. "I thought so, too."

"Imagine being so shy. The poor man."

"I was surprised at that. He wasn't shy on the computer. And he is an intelligent man."

"I guess the two—intelligence and confidence—don't necessarily go together." Connie forked a tiny portion of food into her mouth. "So, do you think you will ever meet with him?"

"Truthfully, I've been wondering the same thing myself."

"I mean, do you want to meet with him, after his standing you up like that?"

"I spent much of the night thinking about that. And I think I would still like to meet him. He sounded like a person who would be fun to know."

"I suppose because he's shy about women doesn't mean he's shy about everything."

"Yes, you're right. When I spoke to him online, he was extremely pleasant." Mildred frowned and shook her head. "That's not the right word." Then she brightened. "*Fun*, he was fun to be with. A good sense of humor, a quick mind. I liked talking to him. Once we get past this timidity, I think I would enjoy his company."

"Well, girl," Connie said, "I think you should go for it. We're all lonely and looking for someone to make us happy. There aren't enough single men out there for all us old bags. I envy you your Timothy. And if you decide not to see him, give me his E-mail address. I'll go buy a computer and learn to use it, so I can contact him myself."

Mildred smiled. Even though Connie made it sound like a joke, Mildred knew Connie was serious. And she was right about her being lonely. Mildred was so tired of being alone. Friends were okay, but she missed sharing the small intimate moments with someone. Johnny had been dead almost ten years now. When he died she had suffered so from losing him that she swore she'd never get involved with another man. She didn't want to experience that pain again. But now she felt very differently about it, and longed for someone to hold her hand, and smile warmly at her.

"Time to get to work," Connie said, with a sigh standing and picking up her tray.

Mildred also got up, picked up her own tray from the table, and followed Connie to the area where they were to leave the dirty trays. As they walked, Mildred was thinking warmly about the coming evening and speaking again to Timothy.

It was eleven in the morning when Mildred left the hospital. She volunteered for only a few hours each morning. Her next stop was a couple hours with Meals-On-Wheels, where she delivered lunches to people who couldn't get out of their homes. As she walked across the hospital parking lot she saw the dark blue car, and noticed the man standing by the car. She thought for a moment that he looked familiar, and was almost going to wave at him. But she remembered Benny's remark about all old people looking alike, so she didn't wave. She got in her car and drove away.

"Another killing! What the hell is going on!" Jacobson shouted.

He was so loud that Jessie had to hold the phone away from her ear.

"You'll probably get the details on the six-o'clock news."

"I already saw they had the name of Coral Sands in the paper yesterday when that gardener was killed. I don't need more publicity like that! It'll ruin me!"

"The police are keeping an eye on the place. Right now they're posing as landscapers and mowing the lawn."

"We paying them?"

"No."

"Has anybody moved out?"

"No."

"Well, that's something. We got to come up with a way to negate this negative publicity. Think on it, will you?"

"Yes."

"Maybe some way to improve security?"

"How are things at Camelot Woods?" Jessie tried to change the subject.

"Well, so far it has not become a major crime scene." His tone was sarcastic.

"I'll check with some security firms. Get some estimates, and get back to you."

"Fine."

Fine? Jacobson must really be worried, she thought.

"Have you ever thought of leaving this place?" Peter asked. He and Eleanor had come out of the lobby, crossed the swimming pool deck, and were walking down toward the lake.

Eleanor gave him a puzzled look. "No. Why do you ask?"

He shrugged. "Just wondered if this whole scene became tiresome after a bit." It was a half-truth. He just couldn't say outright that the eccentric people living here and these killings had him unnerved.

"Well, it hasn't become 'tiresome' in three and a half years. In fact"—Eleanor smiled—"it's been rather exciting at times."

Peter chuckled. "Well, it has certainly been that since I've been here. It is much like living in a Shakespearean tragedy—bodies scattered all around. People dropping like the proverbial flies."

"Yes, it has been upsetting the past few months."

"Tell me this is not the normal run of things here in Coral Sands."

She laughed. "So that's what's bothering you. No. We don't have a lot of people being killed here. But, lately we've had our share."

They walked in silence for a few moments. Then Peter said, "Would you consider moving away from here?" He wanted to say—would you move away with me? But he wasn't ready to make such a commitment to their relationship. Their relationship was still too new to build any future on.

"I can't say that circumstances won't arise to make me change my mind. But as of now, I don't see myself leaving here."

Well, he thought, maybe the circumstances will change. Maybe their relationship would grow stronger. Then he stopped himself. He couldn't believe he was thinking those thoughts! He, Peter Benington, committed to a woman? Absurd. He'd never had such feelings of commitment to a woman since he married Janice so many years ago. And that had ended a dismal failure.

"I got a call from Betty's attorney," Eleanor said.

Peter nodded. "We gave him your name and the names of the others who said they'd testify on Betty's behalf."

"Do you think she has a chance of fighting off her son?"

Peter shook his head. "I don't see how she can shake Eugene's influence. Mr. Fresno is going to have to be one fantastic attorney to win this case. Fresno is having Betty see a psychiatrist today. That should be an interesting interview."

"Poor Betty," Eleanor said. "To have her own son turn on her like that."

"Money can make people do many strange things." He thought about how his own life had been influenced by money. He'd done many strange things to possess money.

"Another one dead," Gray Hair said.

Peter and Eleanor had wandered close to the gazebo where the two men were sitting. Sailor Hat wore a T-shirt that read ATHEISM—A NON-PROPHET ORGANIZATION.

"Two in a row," Sailor Hat said.

"Gardening is getting very dangerous these days."

"Gardening is real close to farming, handling those fertilizers and stuff. And farming has always been dangerous."

"Farming dangerous?"

Sailor Hat nodded. "Sure is. I know, you think it's a healthy occupation. If it's so healthy then you tell me, how many farmers we got retired here?"

"None that I know of."

"My point. Short lives. It's the air pollution. Worse than any city."

"Air pollution! On a farm? Out in the open, under the sky, with the air crisp and clean? Hard to believe you're serious."

"It's the kind of pollution you can't see, so you're not prepared for it."

"What did you mix in that orange juice you drank at breakfast?"

"Ever been on a farm?"

"Visited some."

"Then you've smelled all that cow shit and animal odor. Anything smells that bad can't be good for you. Makes your nose curl up. What do you think it's doing to your lungs? And it's in the air all around the farm. Pollution you can't see, but sure can smell. Yes sir, farming's a dangerous occupation."

Peter and Eleanor held their laughter as they walked away.

It was after dropping off the lunch at the third stop on her route that Mildred noticed the dark blue car and the man she had seen in the hospital parking lot. Coincidence? she thought. Possible, but she couldn't bring herself to believe it. The question then was what was going on? If he was following her, then why? She would take notice at the next stops to see if the man was still with her.

Mildred arrived back at Coral Sands a little past three. She had skipped her exercise class that was scheduled after the Meals-On-Wheels tour was finished. The blue car had stayed with her all the while she delivered the lunches. It had frightened her enough that she wanted to get back home. The dark blue car had followed her home. Now she was more frightened.

She came through the front door of Coral Sands and Grace called to her.

"Hey, Mildred! Got something for you."

"Hi, Grace." Mildred walked over to the front desk.

Grace was standing behind the desk, and next to her on the counter was a large vase of flowers, a mix of pinks and yellows and whites.

"These came for you." Grace smiled, and pointed to the vase.

Mildred's eyes widened. "They're beautiful! Are you sure they're for me?"

"Says so on the card." Grace pointed to the card hidden in the flowers. "And who's this Timothy?" Grace smiled. "Holding out on me, eh? Keeping this guy for yourself."

Mildred smiled. "I didn't want the competition." Timothy sent the flowers! How absolutely wonderful! she thought. Mildred opened the card. It read: *To Dearest Mildred, the prettiest Arial Font I've ever known. With sincere apologies, Timothy.* How very sweet, she thought.

"What's an Arial Font?" Grace asked.

Mildred, admiring the flowers, grinned. "Just a computer term, Grace."

"You met this guy on the computer?"

Mildred nodded, her fingers gently caressing the blooms.

"Well, now. I didn't know the computer could get you a date. I'll have to get one of those machines right away."

Mildred picked up the vase. "Thanks, Grace," she said, and headed for the elevator.

"Well, well, well." It was Alice coming in from the swimming pool area. She intercepted Mildred. "If that's from a funeral, from the look on your face, it was somebody you were happy to see go.''

''Oh, Alice,'' Mildred said, still smiling. ''It's from Timothy.''

''Computer loverboy,'' Alice said. ''I thought that was finished last night?''

''No. He sent me a very nice apology. Something came up at the last minute and he couldn't make it,'' she lied. ''And he sent me these flowers.'' She looked at Alice. ''Pretty, huh?''

''Beautiful. I don't want to bust your bubble, but now he knows where you live.''

''Oh Alice, stop being so suspicious. He's a sweet, gentle man.''

''They said the same thing about Ted Bundy. Nicest man you'd ever want to meet.''

''C'mon, Alice. Ted Bundy didn't meet people on the computer. He snatched women from the street.'' And she suddenly remembered the man who had been following her all day, and she stopped smiling.

Alice saw the quick change in Mildred's expression. ''What's the matter? Somebody walk over your grave?''

''You know . . . some man's been following me all day.''

Alice grinned. ''I wish I could say that. Heck, half the women in here wish they could say that.''

''No. I'm serious, Alice. I saw him in the parking lot at the hospital this morning. Then he followed me as I delivered the lunches for Meals-On-Wheels.''

''You don't have any idea who it is?''

''When I first saw him I thought for a moment that I recognized him, that I had seen him someplace before. But I wasn't sure where.''

''Why don't you put away those flowers, and come back down. I'll see if I can find Peter. He seems pretty experienced, maybe he can advise you on what to do. We can even talk to the police. Right now this place is surrounded by them.''

Mildred gave Alice a puzzled look.

''If you look outside you'll see the grounds being mowed and all that. Cops. They came this afternoon. Grace told me they want to keep an eye on the place after the two murders.''

"There's been another killing!"

"Yeah. A private detective that Jessie had hired. Found his body this morning under the hibiscus about where they found Yamaguchi's body."

"My Lord," Mildred said. "What's going on around this place?"

"I don't know. But nobody'd believe it if they saw it on a soap opera. The real world's uglier than fiction."

"Too much of a coincidence," Benny said. "I mean, she goes to meet this guy from the computer, and he doesn't show. Then today there's someone following her. Sounds fishy."

"Is he still outside?" Peter said.

"Nope. No sign of the blue car or the guy."

Mildred nodded in confirmation. "When Benny and I went outside, the blue car was gone. But the man did follow me home."

"The two incidents do not necessarily have to be related," Peter said. Peter took a drag on his cigarette. He limited his smoking to ten cigarettes a day. "Life is filled with coincidences that border the impossible. I'm sure you have experienced your share of them."

They were seated at one of the white resin tables out by the swimming pool. The sun had slipped behind Coral Sands and the entire area by the pool was bathed in a comforting shade. Without the heat of the sun's rays, it was a pleasant and pretty day. With them at the table was Alice and Mildred.

"Yeah," Alice said. "The Denise Darcel factor."

Everyone looked at her with a question on their face.

"Denise Darcel was a French woman, a movie star. She played in *Battleground*, a war movie in the late forties, I think. Anyway, during World War Two, in France, she met and fell in love with an American soldier. The War forced him to leave her and move on with the fighting. Now, that was in France in the forties. Forty-odd years later, and she has moved into a retirement community in Arizona. One day she's at the local bar having a drink. She starts talking with the guy on the stool next to her. Yep, same guy. And love blossomed anew." Alice shook her head. "What kind of odds are there in that? Thousands of miles away, and all those years later, to end up sitting on the bar stool next to each other. You just never know.''

''Yeah.'' Benny had to agree. That was why, even after all those years, he was still on the lookout for somebody from the old neighborhood who could tell Bobby Dee where he was living.

''I feel that Benny has a valid point,'' Eleanor said.

''I am not saying that this possible coincidence is not something to be concerned about,'' Peter said. ''But, I do not think we should jump too hastily to certain conclusions.''

''What do you think I should do?'' Mildred asked. She was trying not to show her fear. For a few moments upstairs, when she was arranging the flowers, she had almost convinced herself that there was nothing to worry about. Maybe the guy even worked for Meals-On-Wheels and was checking up on the deliveries. But the little voice down deep inside her wouldn't shut up. It kept telling her there was something here to worry about, and the fear remained. So she had gone downstairs and found Alice with Peter and Benny.

''You say that you don't know the man?'' Peter said.

''No. I did think, at first that he looked familiar. But I couldn't remember where I had seen him before. And then I remembered what Benny had once said about all old people looking alike.'' Mildred shrugged. ''I figured that's what it was. He looked like somebody I once knew.''

''Too bad,'' Benny said. '' 'Cause then we could go break his leg or something.'' Though the others smiled, Benny was serious. He didn't like the idea of men taking advantage of women. He felt deeply that women should be protected from those animals. Given the opportunity, he would have intervened, and probably punched the guy out to teach him a lesson.

Eleanor put her hand on Peter's arm. ''Aren't there laws against stalking someone?''

Peter nodded. ''I believe there are.''

Peter took a long drag on his cigarette, giving his mind a chance to consider the problem. ''Well,'' Peter said, ''I assume the first thing to be done, is to seek legal advice.''

''You want lawyers involved in this!'' Benny couldn't believe what he was hearing.

Peter shook his head. "I doubt very much if a lawyer would be of any good in this situation. No, I was referring to the police."

"Oh, my. The police?" Mildred said. "I don't know if this is serious enough to get the police involved."

Benny made a face. "I never heard of the cops being good at anything like this."

"Yeah," Alice said. "My only experience with cops has been after a crime has happened. I don't think it's a crime to drive around the streets following someone."

"If the man is stalking her, then it is a crime," Eleanor said.

"I don't know if he's stalking me," Mildred said. "I mean, it just happened today. I may not see him again tomorrow."

"Possibly the police could advise us on ways to approach this *before* a serious crime has been committed." Peter stubbed out the cigarette in the ashtray he had brought outside with him.

"You're not thinking of talking to Ardley?" Benny asked.

Peter nodded. "The man has a lot of experience. It could not hurt to talk to him." Peter looked at his watch. "It's going on four o'clock. Let me give him a call and see if I can arrange for us to meet with him today."

"I feel very nervous about talking to the police about this," Mildred said. She was afraid of being classified as an old lady who imagined things.

"If they can't help us, we're no worse off," Eleanor said.

"Better we talk to the police now," Alice said, "than after they find your dead body."

Mildred had no reply to that. The little voice inside her whispered that such things were very possible. The world was filled with strange people who did strange and terrible things.

CHAPTER 9

The policeman who walked through the front door looked like someone from Hollywood's Central Casting. Tall, dark hair, a build like Sylvester Stallone, and the brightest blue eyes Grace had ever seen. If there was a merciful God in heaven, she implored him to immediately make her twenty years younger.

"May I help you, officer?" Grace smiled. She knew that twenty years earlier such a line would have gotten her the right response. Not now.

"I'm Officer Jerry Otis. I've been assigned to watch your place tonight." He smiled.

God, Grace thought, his smile was beautiful. She could feel her heart melt. He could watch her place every night. Where were such men when she was young?

"Yes. Of course." She couldn't take her eyes off him, and she had trouble thinking clearly. "Yes, yes. Jessie—Ms. Cummings—told me there would be a policeman around all night."

His grin grew wider, and Grace's blood pressure rose.

"Not all night, I'm afraid." He smiled still. "I'll be relieved at midnight."

"Of course." Grace grinned. It was a nervous grin. Did he know what a wonderfully disturbing effect he had on women? Whatever he had should be bottled so all men could have it. What a wonderful world it would be. "So, how else can I help you?"

"Well, I'd appreciate it if you alert your staff to my being here because I'll be wandering around tonight. I don't want to get shot as an intruder. Detective Ardley told me there were a lot of nervous people here."

"Yes. Yes, of course." Grace couldn't keep her mind on the conversation. She just wanted to look at this beautiful creature. "Ah, let's see. Yes, you'll have to know where things are. Like the bathroom and . . ."

"The kitchen might be a nice place to know, too. I could use a cup of coffee every now and then." Now he gave her a broad innocent smile.

With that smile, Grace thought, she'd do anything he wanted. If only he wanted anything from her. Then she chuckled to herself at the foolishness of her emotions.

"Come. Follow me." To my bedroom, she added mentally. "I'll give you a quick tour and introduce you to some of the people. Of course, most of these people will be gone after six. But I'll stay around and introduce you to the night staff, too."

"Thank you, ma'am."

Grace groaned inwardly. Talk about a word that destroyed one's dreams—"ma'am."

Detective Ardley looked worn out. He was slumped in the chair behind the desk when they came into his office. The office looked worn out to match the man. It wasn't much to look at as offices went. But it was typical of those shown for the police on television. It was small and cluttered. There was one chair other than the one Ardley occupied. Ardley signaled Mildred to take the chair, and Mildred sat down.

Ardley bypassed the civilities. "Okay, you called this meeting. So, what's up?"

Mildred looked up to Peter to explain.

"Mildred"—Peter nodding in Mildred's direction—"noticed someone following her today. An old man in a blue sedan. It has disturbed her, and us."

Ardley looked at Mildred. "You want to tell me about it?"

"Well," Mildred said, "first, I saw him in the hospital parking lot. I do some volunteer work there. Then when I was delivering lunches for Meals-On-Wheels, I saw him again. And he followed me to each of the places where I delivered the lunches. Then he followed me back to Coral Sands."

"You know him? Ever saw him before?" Ardley asked.

Mildred shook her head.

"This the first time something like this has happened to you?" He asked this to rule out the paranoid old lady complex—always seeing threatening men following her.

"Yes."

"Did this guy make any advances to you? Threaten you in anyway?"

"No."

"Ain't there laws against stalking?" Benny threw the words at him like a challenge.

Ardley sighed. He was holding on to his patience. It had been a long and rotten day for him, and he wanted to go home. "Stalking is a persistent following and harassing. One day does not constitute stalking."

Benny frowned in anger. "You saying there's nothing you can do to protect her?"

Ardley nodded. "I'm saying there's nothing the police can do to protect her. I'm not even sure she's being threatened."

Benny stood there with his jaw clenched in anger.

"I understand your position, Detective," Peter said. He jumped in before Benny could blow off more steam with his mouth. "Perhaps you could suggest what we can do to stop this man from following Mildred?"

Ardley leaned forward with his arms on the desk. "Personally, I don't think there is much here for everyone to get excited about. But, if this guy persists, and you can get me his name and where he lives, I'll go have a little talk with him. If he has anything criminal on his mind, knowing the police are involved could be enough to scare him off. That's the best I can offer at this time."

"Thank you, Detective," Peter said, and quickly grabbed Benny to guide him out of the office before Benny opened his smart mouth again. "I think we have taken enough of Detective Ardley's time."

The three of them left Ardley's office and went outside to Benny's car.

"Good thing you pulled me away, Slick," Benny said. "I was ready to tell that guy off. Damn police. Never help when you need them."

"The police are responsible for solving crimes," Peter said. "There is nothing in their mandate that specifies preventing crimes. But he did offer to help, providing we can identify the man following Mildred. We came here for advice, and he gave it to us. Now, let's get in the car and go home."

Mildred sat before the computer screen waiting for the connection to be made to the chat room and Beach Blanket 2F. It was seven o'clock on the button when she signed on to the network. But again, the network was slow, and it seemed to take forever to get from screen to screen. Finally, the Beach Blanket 2F screen came on, and there was Shy-Guy already in the room.

Shy-Guy: Hello, dear lady. I've been waiting for you. I was afraid you might not come.
FineLace: Hello, Timothy. Thank you for the flowers. They are beautiful.
Shy-Guy: I know they can not make up for the disappointment of last night.
FineLace: How did you know where to send them?
Shy-Guy: You had told me about the killing of that poor Oriental man. Then I read about it in the newspaper. The paper mentioned Coral Sands. Doesn't take a rocket scientist to put that all together.
FineLace: Well, thank you again. I have them on a side table near the window. There I can see them wherever I am in the apartment.
Shy-Guy: I hope we can put yesterday behind us.
FineLace: Well, the flowers are a good start. <g>
Shy-Guy: It may take a while before I get up the courage to see you. Please understand.
FineLace: I understand, dear man. <smiles affectionately> We will meet when the time is right for both of us.
Shy-Guy: You are such a warm understanding lady. I do not feel worthy of your interest.
FineLace: Please don't make more of me than I am. <g> For one thing I'm no lady.
Shy-Guy: lol.

Shy-Guy: Well, I think you are a lady. And I worry about you living in a place where a man has been killed.
FineLace: Crime has a way of finding you wherever you are.
Shy-Guy: Have the police found who did it?
FineLace: No. And I'm sure you'll read about this in tomorrow's paper, but there was another stabbing last night.
Shy-Guy: Another stabbing! Was the person killed?
FineLace: Yes.
Shy-Guy: How awful.
Shy-Guy: Was this person related to the Oriental man?
FineLace: No connection. This was a private investigator that the manager of Coral Sands had hired to investigate the thefts that have taken place recently.
Shy-Guy: There's a thief in Coral Sands, too! Doesn't sound like a nice place to live.
FineLace: Yes, I guess it sounds bad. But it isn't. It is a very nice place to live. Sometimes bad things happen even in nice places.
Shy-Guy: What are the police doing about all this?
FineLace: The best they can, I hope. There's a policeman patrolling the grounds tonight. That should help.
Shy-Guy: I am worried about you.
FineLace: Please don't worry. Worrying is nonproductive. I can take care of myself. And I have plenty of friends here who I can depend on. I couldn't be safer anywhere else.
Shy-Guy: I will still worry. Part of caring for someone is worrying about them.
FineLace: Yes. You are right. I worry about you.
Shy-Guy: About me? What are you worried about?
FineLace: I worry that you won't overcome your shyness. There is so much life you are missing because of it.
Shy-Guy: Funny, I don't like the idea of you worrying about me. Yet, it says you care about me. I like that.
FineLace: I do care about you.
Shy-Guy: And I, sweet lady, care very much about you. With that, I must say goodnight. Tomorrow night, again?
FineLace: Tomorrow night, again. <smiles>
Shy-Guy: Goodnight, dear one.
FineLace: Goodnight, Timothy.
Shy-Guy has left the conversation

Mildred sat looking at the screen. Her heart felt warm and happy, and sad at the same time. Timothy was such a sweet man. It was nice to have the affection of such a man.

She pulled down the File menu and clicked on Exit Room. A message popped up in the middle of the screen: DO YOU WANT TO SAVE CHAT HISTORY? She clicked on Yes. The screen blinked, and there was a momentary whirring of the disk drive. Then she signed out, and the computer screen returned to the desktop.

Mildred looked over at the flowers and sighed. *Am I ever going to get to meet this man?* she wondered.

Peter hadn't wanted to go to the poker game. He preferred to be with Eleanor. In fact that was all he wanted to do—to be with Eleanor. He still could not believe he felt that way about a woman. But Eleanor had insisted he go. Too much togetherness was not good, she had said. Reluctantly he had agreed.

He was ten minutes late getting to Benny's apartment. Everyone was already there.

"Hi, handsome," Alice said. "We've already played a round of hands. I missed your money."

"Hello, Peter," Walter said. "Alice is, once again, taking us to the cleaners."

"Yeah." Charlie grinned. "At this rate I'll have to sign over my car to her."

"I saw your car," Alice said. "As wrecks go, it's a good example."

To Peter, Benny's apartment, decorated in early Salvation Army, fit the atmosphere of a poker game. All it needed was a lot of cigarette smoke and a dealer with a green eyeshade.

"Want a beer?" Benny asked, as Peter sat down at the table.

"Yes. That will be just fine." Peter took out his money and stacked the coins. He had counted it all before he came, so he'd know at the end of the night whether he had won or lost.

"Anybody else?" Benny said.

There were no takers, so Benny got up, went into the kitchen area, and pulled a can of beer from the refrigerator. He came back to the table, placed the can on the cardboard coaster on the table near Peter, then sat down.

"Thanks," Peter said, and pulled the tab on the top of the can. It popped with a *fizz*. He took a long gulp of beer. It was icy cold and clawed satisfyingly at his throat. "Good." He sighed. "I needed that."

"You ready there, Handsome?" Alice started dealing out the cards. "Five card draw."

"So, how is lovely Eleanor managing without you?" Walter said.

"Now, Doctor, please don't start on me."

"Yeah." Alice grinned. "I thought lovebirds were inseparable."

"All right"—Peter put his hands up defensively—"all right. Let's have all of this out of everyone's system. Then we can play cards. Are there any more remarks that must come out? Come on. Let me have them."

"I got one," Benny smiled. "Are you practicing safe sex?"

Everyone, including Peter laughed.

"If you need any new positions." Alice grinned. "I've got a deck of cards with all of them on it."

Benny laughed. "So, that's where those cards went."

"Well, I didn't want them to go to waste with you," Alice said.

"Ho ho ho," Charlie said. "We going to see a fistfight here?"

Walter picked up the cards in front of him and looked at them. "I open." He threw a dime into the pot.

"How is dear Mildred doing?" Walter asked.

"You mean about being stood up or about being followed?" Benny asked.

"She's being followed?" Charlie tossed a dime into the pot. "I call."

"Yeah," Benny said. "Some guy was tailing her all day. We talked to the police, a lot good that did. They can't help her. They said they gotta know who the guy is first, before they can do anything."

"Seems poor Mildred is getting more than her share of problems," Walter said.

"I call." Peter tossed in his dime, though he didn't have much faith in his pair of tens. "Mildred agreed to permit Benny and Caroline to follow her tomorrow. If the man shows himself again, Benny will get the license number of the car. The police should be able to take it from there.''

''So, you're into detective work, eh Benny?'' Alice threw in twenty cents. ''I raise a dime.''

Benny threw in his hand. ''Damn, Alice how did you get so lucky?''

Walter added a dime to the pot. ''I call.''

Charlie threw in his hand.

Peter looked forlornly at his pair of tens, then tossed in his dime, and threw down three cards.

Alice dealt out the cards. She took two for herself.

Peter picked up his three new cards. There was another ten. Three tens. Not bad, he thought.

There was another round of betting, then Walter showed his two pair. Peter laid down his three tens. Alice grinned, and showed her three jacks.

Alice scooped in the money. ''Sorry guys,'' she smiled.

''If you were sorry you'd let us win a few,'' Walter said. ''I'm going to change decks. I don't like this trend of Alice winning every hand.'' He reached over to the counter nearby and took another box of cards. Then to Peter, ''You think there's any connection between this man following her and her being stood up by computer man?''

Peter shrugged. ''I honestly don't know.''

''Well,'' Benny said, ''I think there is. Just too much of a coincidence to me.''

Walter was struggling with the box of cards. ''I can't seem to get this box open, Benny. Where do you buy your cards?''

''Here let me have it,'' Benny said, and took the box from Walter. ''Old people don't keep up their upper body strength. You gotta do more exercising, Doc.'' Benny tried to flip open the top, but it wouldn't come out. Benny frowned at the box. ''Ah, here it is. There's a piece of Scotch tape over the end.'' Benny lifted the edge of the tape with his fingernail and started peeling it back. ''Funny,'' he said, ''I don't remember putting ta—'' The flap of the box flew open sending a dozen large black cockroaches bouncing onto the table!

The reaction was instantaneous. Everyone, except Walter, jumped to their feet with fright, toppling a few chairs, and shouting things like ''God Damn!'' and ''Son-of-a-bitch!''

and "Jesus Christ!" Only Walter Innes remained stoic and seated and said calmly, "My Lord." The rest of them stood around the table breathing heavily, and looking at the fright in each other, and looking at the cockroaches on the table. Peter's heart was doing a drunken tap dance, testing his beta-blocker medication.

"What are you trying to do, Benny, give us a heart attack!" Alice shouted. "One of us could have dropped dead right here!"

Charlie said, "My blood pressure must be up to 240!"

Benny stepped to the table and leaned over it, peering at the cockroaches. They weren't moving. He prodded one with his finger, then picked it up. "Plastic," he said.

"Plastic!" Alice said. Then she chuckled through her anger, "That son-of-a-bitch Mad Joker. If I ever get my hands on him, I'll pull his heart out through his mouth. Scaring the shit out of me like this."

"What I find amusing it everyone's reaction to an insect a million times smaller than us," Walter said.

"Oh, blow it out your ass, Walter," Alice said.

Charlie and Benny chuckled.

What Peter found interesting, but not amusing, was the Mad Joker's ability to move freely and unnoticed within other people's apartments.

The poker game broke up a little after eleven. Alice walked away a gloating winner. Peter and the other men left the game licking the wounds in their pride. Tired, ready for bed, Peter went back to his apartment.

When he returned to his apartment, Peter was disappointed to find that Eleanor wasn't there waiting for him. They hadn't made any arrangements to meet, but he had hoped she would be there. He didn't want to admit it to himself, but it hurt to think that she did not need him as much as he needed her. He had hoped her head and heart were as filled with him as his were suddenly filled with her.

"Oh well," he sighed. He changed into a pair of shorts, poured himself a snifter of Amaretto, lit a cigarette, and sat in the chair by the window overlooking the lake.

• • •

The barefeet once again stepped from the rug in the corridor to the dry earth of another time, to a scene from that other world. The mind viewed the scene as if it were present and yet apart. There was a coldness to it's viewing. No outrage, no anger, no hate. All that was covered over, reserved for private moments when it was not dangerous to feel and express it all. The entire scene was surreal, made more so by the bright sun, and the soft rustle of the palm fronds in the breeze. From somewhere a bird called playfully.

The woman on the roadside, frail with hunger, scabbed with sores, weary with disease and abuse, stood defiant before the three Japanese soldiers. The mind knew this woman, had known her before. A diplomat's wife—young, well-bred, who never had soiled her hands. A genteel bigoted woman with a steel core to rule over the servants and those lower in class. In her imprisonment that steel core held her together, and had enabled her to stand up to the prison guards. For two years she had endured, as all prisoners endure, with the hope of an end just around the corner.

The Japanese soldiers gestured and shouted commands at her, commands she understood only too well. Commands she pretended not to understand. Then one of the soldiers hit her square in the chest with the butt of his rifle. The mind imagined the pain the woman must have felt. The woman's face went wide with the pain, but no sound came out as she crumpled to the ground.

There were other eyes watching the scene. Two other prisoners stood helpless before the guns of the soldiers. The mind could see that the other prisoners were trying not to see. The mind looked again at the woman, now on the ground, weeping with the pain, and with the hopelessness of her situation. The mind wanted to help, wanted to come to her rescue, to carry her away from all this horror. But the mind, too, understood its helplessness. It did the only thing it could do—watch. Watch every detail of what was happening. Watch to someday report, to someday seek justice for this woman. Though the mind knew justice in that world was a myth of the weak, the mind also knew that someday there would come a time when justice would return.

The soldiers tore off the woman's clothing, rags that were

once clothing, while she lay helpless on the ground clutching at the pain in her chest. Then one of the soldiers took her by the hair and her sudden screams tore at the air, tore at the mind. The soldier dragged her screaming into the shrubbery, while the other soldiers kept their guns on the remaining prisoners. People physically too weak to aid, even if they were so inclined. The mind listened to the screams and the grunts and the shouts, the blunt smacks of fist to flesh from the shrubbery. And then the screams stopped. The time dragged treacherously slow as the mind watched, looking for some glimmer of hope in the soft stirrings and human sounds that came from the shrubbery. It was a long time before the soldier came out of the shrubbery, hitching up his pants. He picked up his rifle and grunted something to the other two men. One of the soldiers put his gun down and went into the shrubbery. No screams this time, nothing but soft guttural sounds. The mind watched. Time appeared to stand still. Then the second soldier came out from the shrubbery and picked up his rifle. The third soldier put his gun down and disappeared into the bush. Another long time passed before he reappeared and nodded to the first soldier.

The first soldier then directed the prisoners to get the woman and bring her out. The mind moved toward the bushes along with another prisoner. The prisoner picked up the woman's clothing. Together they pushed into the shrubbery, one of the soldiers just behind them, and found the woman. She lay lifeless on the ground. There was no blood, except the smears from some of the opened scabs. She looked physically unharmed, the bruises would develop later. One look at her eyes showed the harm had been much worse than physical. The eyes were dulled, no life, no defiance left in them. Together they dressed her as best they could in the torn rags, and helped her walk back to the road. She uttered not one sound. The mind knew she would utter no more sounds to the day they killed her.

Peter had been sitting by the window looking out at the lake for a long time, remembering how Eleanor showed up at his door in silk pajamas and barefeet, and how excited and overjoyed he was to see her. He had gone through four cigarettes, finished the glass of Amaretto, and poured himself another. Though he was tired, he didn't want to go to sleep. Actually, he didn't want to go to sleep alone. After the other night with Eleanor, sleeping alone had no appeal. It had been a wonderfully comforting feeling having her in bed beside him through the night. Now, without her, the bed seemed cold and forbidding.

Peter sipped at the Amaretto, then took a long drag on another cigarette. Suddenly he wondered if what he was feeling was really the ecstasy of love, or the first stages of senility, of his mind going into decay.

Oh, boy. Time to go to bed, he thought. With such thoughts running loose, it was better to try sleeping than dealing with them. He stubbed out the cigarette and drained the glass of Amaretto. Then, as he was about to rise from the chair, his heart skipped a few beats, and his mind filled with hope and joy, as he heard a soft knock on the door.

CHAPTER 10

After Eleanor left his apartment to get primped for the day, Peter stayed in bed and languished in the wonderful way he felt. He knew that married people lived longer than single people, but, jokingly, he always thought they did it for spite. However, if they had this kind of feeling for each other, no wonder they lived longer. God, this was fantastic. He wondered if his son, David, felt this way about his wife, Marlene? Peter sure hoped so.

He would have liked to stay in that cocoon of warm ecstasy forever. But, with Eleanor no longer beside him, the ecstasy was slipping away. So, he finally got out of bed to get ready for the day. He didn't get far, though. As he passed into the living room his eyes caught the view of the lake through the sliding glass doors. Pretty view, with the sun and the swaying palm trees and the bright blue sky. He lit a cigarette and sat admiring the view. Everything looked so alive and wonderful since Eleanor had entered his world. It was pure pleasure to be alive.

When Peter finally showered, shaved, dressed, and went down to the lobby, everyone was already in the dining room having breakfast. He saw Alice, in her clown outfit, leaving through the front door of the lobby. Peter entered the dining room. Most of the gang were at a table near the windows. He walked through the tables toward where they were seated. When he saw Eleanor, she gave him a smile that melted his heart. At the table he sat in the chair Eleanor had reserved next to her.

"Good morning, everyone," Peter smiled. "It is nice to see you here, Caroline."

Caroline gave him a warm smile and nodded.

"Morning, Peter," Betty twittered.

"Well, well, well," Walter said. "We were getting worried about you, Peter." He grinned slyly. "We were beginning to think your heart may not have been able to handle the strain of last night."

Eleanor playfully slapped Walter's arm. "Oh, Walter, stop that."

Peter looked to Benny. Time to change the subject. "I thought you were going to follow Mildred today?"

"Yeah. She gave me a list of the different places she's gonna be and when. I tell you, that woman is busier than a prostitute working two beds."

"Oh, Benny." Caroline clucked her tongue. "Such talk."

Benny turned to Caroline. "Sorry. Kinda slipped out." Then to Peter, "I didn't want this to turn into a parade—this guy following Mildred, and me and Caroline following him. So this way we can just go to where she's gonna be next. See if the guy shows there." He looked at his watch. "First place is the hospital. We're gonna pick up on her there in about an hour."

"You will be careful," Peter said, "not to confront this man. It could be dangerous."

"Don't worry. I ain't gonna do nothing that stupid."

Peter wasn't convinced. He had seen Benny in action. "If you need to, you may call me here. Eleanor and I will be here throughout the day."

"We will?" Eleanor gave Peter an innocent look.

"Charlie offered to spell us if we wanted," Benny said.

"Where is Charlie?" Peter asked.

"He skipped breakfast this morning," Betty said. "He's out walking. He's trying to lose some weight."

"Oh, Betty," Peter said, "how did it go yesterday with the psychiatrist?"

"Yes," Walter said. "What did the good doctor say?"

"Oh, he didn't say anything." She waved her hands in disgust. "Just gave me all these tests. I thought I was back in school. It is all so silly."

"What," Eleanor asked, "did the doctor say, after you took all those tests?"

"He said 'goodbye.' That was all." Betty frowned, annoyed. "And Eugene was no help. When I told him about it last night, all he did was laugh."

"Laugh?" Walter said incredulously.

"Yes." Betty moved her hands on the table imitating their movement over the Ouija board. "H-A. H-A."

"I guess it is a positive sign that they didn't cart you off in a straitjacket." Walter's expression hinted at a grin.

Eleanor gave Walter her warning look about making fun of Betty.

Benny frowned. "I don't think them shrinks know anything. Look at all the nuts they let out. There's always something in the newspapers about some nutcase the shrinks said was cured, and then the guy goes out and kills somebody."

Walter sighed. "Yes, medicine, but especially psychiatry, is more an art than a concrete science. It's the skill of the artist that is the difference between success and failure."

Peter said, "That's why Mr. Fresno sent Betty to a psychiatrist he can depend on to testify on her behalf."

"I've done my share of testifying as an expert witness," Walter said. "What happens is, each side produces their own expert, and the experts contradict each other. Effectively canceling out the expert testimony." Walter shrugged. "Such is our system of justice."

"You are such a pessimist," Eleanor said.

"Well, yes, I am. I will not deny it." Walter smiled. "We are each entitled to our own religious beliefs." Then to Benny, "If, perchance, you should need my assistance, I, too, will be in all day. I have another computer class with my young teachers."

"Have you tried to do anything on your own on the computer?" Eleanor asked.

Walter snorted. "Yes. Last night I played with it. At one point I touched a key and the computer said I had performed an illegal operation. In my career I've done a few. But, I wondered how the computer knew?"

• • •

Benny and Caroline drove into the parking lot of Blake Hospital about ten minutes to eleven. The parking lot was huge, and jammed, and the parking slots and aisles were narrow. Benny's yellow 1978 Mercury Marquis was like an ocean liner in a stream. Benny maneuvered the car with great care through the lot looking for a place to park where they could see the front entrance in order to see Mildred leave. He finally gave up trying to find a slot, and settled on parking in the aisle that gave him a good view of the entrance.

"She should be out soon," Caroline said. She was holding the written itinerary in her hand. Caroline was small, and with her osteoporosis bend her head barely poked up over the dashboard.

Caroline had no sooner spoken the words when Mildred walked out of the building. They saw Mildred stop and look around.

"Probably looking for her stalker," Benny said.

Benny and Caroline watched as Mildred then walked to her car, climbed in and backed the car out of the parking slot. Over the tops of the other cars it was difficult to see Mildred's gray Toyota. They had barely a view of the top of the car.

Benny started the engine. "She should pass close 'cause the exit is right over there. You keep an eye on her car. I'm going to watch to see if any other cars pull out after her."

The parking lot suddenly became busy, with a number of cars leaving and a handful coming into the lot. Mildred's Toyota passed on the way to the exit.

"She has passed and is leaving," Caroline said.

"Okay. We'll wait here and see if a blue car comes by."

Two other cars passed them before the blue sedan came into view.

"That might be the car," Caroline said. "There's an older gentleman at the wheel."

Benny laughed. "In Florida that is not unusual. Most of the cars have old guys like me driving them."

Benny guided the car toward the exit and kept the blue car in sight. "We'll follow him for awhile. See if he's keeping an eye on Mildred. If he ain't, we know where she's gonna be next, and we'll pick her up there."

Caroline nodded, and looked at the itinerary in her hands.

''Meals-On-Wheels. She is involved in many giving activities.''

They drove for ten minutes following the blue sedan. The sedan stayed close behind Mildred's Toyota. When Mildred turned into the small parking lot in front of Meals-On-Wheels, the blue car pulled into the parking lot of a lawyer's office across the street from the Meals-On-Wheels building. Benny drove on past.

''You're passing Mildred by, darling,'' Caroline said. ''Why aren't you stopping?''

''I don't want to attract attention to us. That guy'll get suspicious. We'll turn around at the end of the street and park where we can see him.''

''But, he wasn't following Mildred, dear man. He went into that lawyer's parking lot.''

''Don't mean nothing yet.'' Benny turned the car around and parked by the curb, the blue sedan visible across the street and down a bit. ''We'll see if he follows her from here.'' Benny reached behind him and grabbed a pair of binoculars from the backseat. ''Meanwhile, we'll get that guy's license number, just in case I'm right.'' He took off his sunglasses, put the binoculars to his eyes, and peered at the sedan. ''You got your pen ready?'' It took a little adjusting of the binoculars to bring the car in focus. He could just make out the license plate.

''Yes. I'm ready,'' Caroline said. She held a pen poised over a small notebook.

''S-F-4-H-4-2. It's a Florida plate. I can't make out the county.'' He lowered the binoculars and looked to Caroline. ''You got that?''

''Yes,'' she said, and looked up from the notebook. Suddenly she started giggling uncontrollably. ''Oh, Benny.''

''What? What's so funny?''

''Where on this dear earth did you get those binoculars?'' She managed to say this through the hand she held over her mouth to mask the giggling.

''I saw them on a sofa in the lobby in Coral Sands on our way out.'' He shrugged. ''Thought I'd borrow them. Seemed like a good idea. Why?''

''That was naughty of you, taking what doesn't belong to

you.'' She was still giggling, and she pointed to his face.

Benny turned the rearview mirror so he could look at his face. ''Damn,'' he said. There were two black circles around his eyes. ''The Mad Joker strikes again.'' Benny tossed the binoculars onto the backseat. He was clearly annoyed, and felt foolish.

Still giggling, Caroline produced a couple of tissues from her handbag, and tried to wipe the black rings away, wetting the tissue daintily with her tongue, and daubing carefully around Benny's eyes. ''I'm sorry, my dear man, but it's not coming off easily. That will teach you not to take things that are not yours.'' She fussed the tissues back into the handbag. ''You'd better wear your sunglasses until we can get that silly stuff off your face.'' Then she giggled again.

Benny put his sunglasses back on. The lenses were large enough to hide most of the black circles, except from a side view.

Benny saw Mildred come out of the building with meal containers, and load them in the back of her car. She returned to the building and came back with a six-pack of juice, put that in the car with the meals, and closed the trunk. She looked once around, then got in the car and drove out of the parking lot. Almost immediately the blue sedan drove out of the parking lot across the street and took off after Mildred.

''He's our guy.'' Benny started the car and took his place third in line in the tailing parade.

It took Mildred an hour to deliver the meals. At each stop she got out of the car, brought a meal into the house, then stayed for a short while before coming back out and driving to the next house. Benny kept a good distance back from the blue car, which stayed with Mildred all the way. After the last meal was delivered, she drove over to Goodwill and dropped off some clothing. Finally she went to University Plaza, parked the car, and, carrying a small purple sport bag, went into Shapes. The blue sedan parked two aisles over, facing in the direction of Shapes.

''According to this itinerary, she's going to be working out in there for about two hours,'' Caroline said.

''Well, we'll go back to Coral Sands and tell Peter what

we've got. He can talk to Detective Ardley while we come back here and pick up following Mildred."

"Yes. We should not leave her alone with that man following her. Also, while we are there I'll see if Grace has something to remove that ink from your eyes."

Benny guided the car slowly around to the parking aisle where the blue sedan sat. "I want to get a close look at that guy."

"Okay, dear. But don't do anything foolish, you hear?"

"Yeah, I hear."

He moved the car slowly down the aisle until he approached the blue sedan. There was an empty parking space right next to the sedan. Benny guided the car into it.

Caroline's heart jumped to her throat. "Benny," she pleaded, "don't do anything."

The man in the car looked over, and Benny peered at him a moment. Then Benny backed the car out of the slot and drove away.

Caroline let out a long sigh of relief, her hand over her breast. "For a minute there I thought you were going to get out of the car."

"I know that guy," Benny said.

Just before noon Eleanor and Peter were seated in lounge chairs out by the swimming pool. There was no one else around. Peter had mixed up a batch of piña coladas in a thermos, and had brought out two glasses. Eleanor and he were enjoying the warm weather and sipping the cool drinks.

"You sure make a good piña colada." Eleanor sighed. It was pleasant to lie there in the chair and just look at the sky. Large mountains of clouds were floating in from the east, and the sun danced all over them, showing whites and grays in exciting forms against the bright blue sky.

"It is nice here like this," Peter said, also with a sigh. But he wasn't looking at the sky. His eyes were on Eleanor.

"It's too bad about Betty," Eleanor said, her eyes on the sky. "I was sitting here thinking that I have not a care in the world. And there's Betty, fighting for her very life."

"Well, I wouldn't get too comfortable if I were you. Good

old Mr. Murphy says: If you're feeling good, don't worry. You'll get over it."

She chuckled. "I guess that's true. Things never stay the same. It must have been terrible for Betty to visit that psychiatrist. Having some stranger judge your capabilities."

"And she has a good reason to be concerned," Peter said. Then he noticed beyond Eleanor toward the lake that Tweedledee and Tweedledum had left the gazebo and were walking toward them. "It must be time for lunch. Those two old men never seem to leave the gazebo except for food."

Eleanor glanced over toward the lake and the two men, then returned to looking at the sky.

Only when the men got closer could Peter read Sailor Hat's T-shirt. NEVER PUT OFF TO TOMORROW WHAT YOU CAN DO TODAY . . . UNLESS IT CAN WAIT.

"Where does he get all the T-shirts?" Peter wondered aloud. "I don't think I've seen him with the same one twice."

"Haven't a clue," Eleanor said. "You know, in all the time I've been here I know nothing about those men."

"Well," Peter said, "I haven't known you very long, but I'd like to know about you." Everything about you, he thought.

"What you see isn't enough?"

"I want to know what you think and feel," he said. "I want to know your history. The things you experienced that gave you joy. I want to know all about you."

"The past is not me. We are never what we once were. There are experiences in everyone's past they would like to change. Incidents that were embarrassing or just plain stupid. Things they did that were unkind or selfish. Those incidents are not me, and they are not you. And I am not the same person I was then. To know me, is to experience me now, for that is who I am."

He gave Eleanor a lecherous grin. "Then let's add to our experience, shall we?"

"You must think I'm easy," she smiled.

"No. But I was hoping."

She laughed. "You'll have to wait for dessert."

• • •

When Benny and Caroline returned to Coral Sands it was just before three in the afternoon. Benny did not remove his sunglasses when they entered the lobby. Immediately he and Caroline went looking for Peter. Through the windows they saw him with Eleanor, Alice, and Charlie in the lounge chairs by the swimming pool. Petersen, as Henny Youngman, was standing in front of the group and throwing jokes at them. Alice was laughing aloud, and the others trying on various versions of chuckles.

"Damn," Benny said. "Henny Youngman is here and I'm missing the show."

"That, dear man, is not Henny Youngman," Caroline said.

"I know that. The guy's name is Petersen, but there are times when he thinks he's Henny Youngman." Benny shrugged. "Sometimes he thinks he's Fred Astaire, sometimes Blackstone the magician, sometimes even Sherlock Holmes."

"Oh, my. Multiple personalities?" Caroline was worried.

"Nah. More like multiple people. He's harmless, and we all go along with it. Besides he's really good at it. Sorta scary."

Benny put a hand on the glass door. "Wait here. I'll get Peter to come inside."

"While you are talking to Peter, I'll see if Grace has anything to remove that stuff from your eyes. I will meet you in the lobby."

"Okay."

"Here I'll give you the license number." She dug the little notebook out of her purse, tore off the page with the number and handed it to Benny.

Caroline turned and walked off.

Benny pushed open the glass door, and stepped outside. Petersen's voice could be heard all over the swimming pool area.

"A man came up to me the other day and said, 'Do you see a cop around here?' I said, 'No.' He said, 'Stick'em up.' "

"This guy is talking to a friend on the phone. The friend says, 'I've got an awful headache.' The guy says, 'You know what I do for a headache? I lay my head on my wife's bosom, and after a while the headache goes away.'

"The next day he gets a call from his friend. 'You know,

it worked. You know you have a nice apartment?' "

Benny caught Peter's eye and signaled him to come inside.

Peter nodded, and got up from the lounge chair.

Petersen continued without taking note of Peter's leaving. "Once I was going to become an atheist. But I changed my mind. They have no holidays."

"Hi, Benny," Peter said. "Everything okay?"

"Yeah. C'mon inside." Benny pulled open the glass door, and Peter walked through. Benny followed, closing the door behind him, shutting out Petersen's voice. Benny indicated the coffee alcove and they took a seat at one of the tables. As Peter was sitting down he noticed the dark smears around Benny's eyes behind the sunglasses.

"What happened to your eyes?"

"It's nothing." Benny waved away the question.

"Is Mildred all right?"

"Yeah. She's at her exercise class right now. We're going back to pick up on her when the class is finished." Benny leaned in and spoke in lowered tones. "Mildred's right, there is a guy following her. We got his license number." He handed the piece of notebook paper to Peter.

Peter looked at it, and nodded. "I will take this to Ardley now."

"There's something else."

"What?"

"I know the guy who's following her," Benny said.

Peter looked up from the notepaper and raised his eyebrows in surprise. "Really?"

Benny nodded. "I saw the guy at the bar the other night when we went with Mildred to meet her computer man."

"You sure?"

Benny nodded. "Yep. He was at the bar giving Mildred and us the eye. He was wearing a fancy belt buckle. I couldn't see if he was still wearing the buckle, but I did get a good look at his face in the car today. The same guy."

CHAPTER 11

Sitting behind the desk, Ardley did not look happy to see Peter and Eleanor. But then, Peter thought, Ardley never looked happy—period. Peter had wanted to come alone, but Eleanor had insisted on coming with him. He couldn't deny her.

"Please sit down." The way Ardley said it, there was no courtesy in the statement.

There was only one empty chair in the office, and Eleanor sat in it.

"I'm hoping you came here to tell me something about the killings at Coral Sands."

"No," Peter said. "I'm sorry."

"Me, too," Ardley said, with a sigh. "I still haven't found anything useful in even coming up with a motive for the killings. Damn exasperating." He leaned forward, folding his arms, his elbows on the desk. "Why do you think these men were killed?"

"Well," Peter said, "we came to see you about something else."

"I'd still like to hear your opinion."

"Have you found anything in common between the two men?" Peter said.

"No. At least not yet. We've gone through Mike Coswell's files, but he never did any work for Yamaguchi or his sons. From what we know the two men's lives never crossed. They had some interests that were similar, though. They both liked to gamble—the dog track, mainly. Maybe they were into some loan shark for a lot of money, and the loan shark decided to cut his losses, and put pressure on the others who owed money. It's a stretch, I'll say that. But that's where we are right now.

"The only other things the men had in common were where and how they died." Ardley shrugged. "Which leads me back to someone in Coral Sands. Possibly someone unbalanced."

Peter was getting apprehensive. In his experience with the police, they never revealed this sort of information about a case to a civilian. He wondered where this conversation was leading. "That should narrow down your suspects a trifle," Peter said flippantly.

For an instant Ardley gave Peter a hard look. Flippancy, Peter thought, wasn't the right move.

Then Ardley said, "A crime without a motive is the hardest to solve. But we do have one clue, if you want to call it that. The medical examiner said both men were stabbed by the same knife, and in the same way. Whoever did it, knew just where to insert the knife to hit the heart. Which narrows the field to someone with medical training, or"—he hesitated for effect—"someone with military hand-to-hand combat training."

"Back to the crazed veteran theory," Peter said.

"Let's widen that a bit. Back to an unbalanced mind with medical or combat training."

Time to take the bit in the teeth, Peter thought. "Why are you telling us this?"

"Yeah, why?" Ardley said. He sat back in his chair and ran a hand hard over his face. "Why? It's because I'm desperate for a lead, and I'd really like you to maybe do a little digging into the people at Coral Sands. I need someone who can recognize aberrant behavior in any of the residents and tell me about it."

"I was given the impression you had enlisted the aid of Benny for that purpose?"

Ardley shook his head. He was annoyed. "I figured he tell you, damn it. I had asked him not to tell anyone. He assured me he would keep his mouth shut and his eyes opened."

Peter felt foolish. He had been walked into a trap with *his* eyes opened. Ardley was too good at this. Peter was glad he had never run into the man during the years when he was skirting the law. If he had, he would surely have spent time in prison. Peter felt doubly foolish because he had been maneuvered into this slip of the tongue in front of Eleanor.

Ardley sighed. "Well, the harm has been done. Instinctively I knew Mr. Ashe was the wrong person to ask to cooperate with the police. Next time I'll pay more attention to those instincts." Ardley once again leaned forward with his arms folded, his elbows on the desk. "Nonetheless, I would consider it a favor if you would let me know of any resident you think might be a possible candidate for these crimes."

Peter nodded.

"And, please," Ardley said, "do not tell Mr. Ashe or anyone outside this room that you are communicating with me."

"You have my word."

"Fine. Now what can I do for you?"

"We were in here yesterday about a woman who was being stalked."

"Yes, I remember."

"Well, today we obtained the license number of the man's car." Peter handed Ardley the piece of paper with the license number on it.

Ardley looked at the number. "So, he was following her again today?"

"Yes."

"And what do you want me to do about it?"

"Stop him," Eleanor said.

Both men looked at Eleanor. This was the first she had spoken since entering the room.

Ardley took a deep breath, then spoke with that patient tone only policemen have. "Ms . . . ?"

"Call me Eleanor." She shrugged. "It's my name."

Ardley nodded. "They call me Ishmael." Then he dropped the smile. "Sorry. Touched a bit of old memory with that line. Anyway, Eleanor, there is not much I can do to stop the man until he actually causes trouble, unless he harasses this woman, or attempts to abuse her."

"But . . . !"

"Please, Eleanor"—Ardley held up his hand—"let me finish. I can have an officer approach the man about this. Let him know the police are involved. Then''—Ardley shrugged—''he might think twice about continuing what he is doing.''

''We would appreciate any help you can give us,'' Peter said.

''Now let's see what information this license plate will give us.'' Ardley turned to the computer on his desk, and punched the keys. ''It will take a moment.''

Peter and Eleanor watched Ardley looking at the computer screen, and they waited.

''Ah, there it is.'' Then Ardley shook his head. ''No help. It's a rental. Alamo. Let's see.'' He peered closely at the information on the screen. ''The airport here in Sarasota.''

Ardley turned away from the computer and picked up the telephone. He punched in a few numbers, then looked at Peter. ''If he's from out of town, the rental agency will have his home address, not where he's staying here. Won't be much help.''

Ardley turned his attention to the phone. ''Yes. This is Detective Ralph Ardley of the Sarasota Police Department. I need some information on an automobile rented from your location. Yes. The manager would be fine.'' He paused a moment. ''Yes. You're the manager? Okay. I'm Detective Ralph Ardley of the Sarasota Police Department. I need to know who rented an automobile from you, license number SF4-H42.'' He listened. ''No, sir. There has been no accident, and the vehicle has not been involved in a crime. This is a routine investigation. We think the man may have witnessed a crime and we'd like to get in touch with him.'' He listened. ''Yes, I'll wait.'' Ardley tapped his fingers on the desk, looked off in the distance, and waited. A few very long moments went by before he turned his attention back to the phone. ''Yes. George Esterman, 5715 Peach Grove Road, Macon, Georgia. Any record of where he's staying in Sarasota? I see. Thanks. Goodbye.'' He hung up the phone, and looked at Peter and Eleanor.

''No record of where he's staying. Sorry.''

''Now what?'' Peter said.

Ardley held up his hands. ''If I don't know where he is, I can't help you at all.''

''You mean,'' Eleanor said, ''that we should follow him to where he lives?''

"However you get the information," Ardley said. "I can't do anything until I know where he is."

Eleanor didn't want to accept that answer. "Can't you have your policemen looking out for the car and pick him up?"

Ardley took a deep breath and let out a long sigh of patience. "The man is not a wanted criminal, that I know of. I can not put out a request for his detention without some evidence of his committing a crime. The offer I made to you was done as a favor, not as official police procedure. Please try to understand."

Ardley began busying himself with papers on his desk as a way to dismiss them. "My offer still stands. Find where he lives, and I'll do what I can. Now, unless there is anything else, I have two murders to solve."

Peter thanked him for his time, and Peter and Eleanor left. In the car on the drive back, Peter said, "If we had known of this possibility, Benny could have followed the man home today."

"It just makes me mad that the police can't do anything to help," Eleanor said.

"I'm sure Walter would have something appropriately cynical to say about this." After a moment of thoughtful silence, Peter said, "Tomorrow, I think it best if you and I follow Mildred. Benny said he knew the man in the car. He recognized him from the bar where Mildred was to meet her computer friend. That means the man may have recognized Benny. If he again sees Benny tomorrow he may become suspicious, and not let Benny follow him home. Is that all right with you?"

"Yes," she said, "I'd like to see this creep myself."

Mildred had been trying to sign on to the Microsoft Network for fifteen minutes without success. The network's busy time was early in the evening, but she usually got through after a minute or two. Tonight's delay was exceptional. She gave up and made herself a cup of tea. At twenty after seven she tried again. This time she got through. When she arrived at Beach Blanket 2F chat room, Timothy was still there.

FineLace has entered the conversation

Shy-Guy: Good Evening Mildred. { }

Oh, my, she thought. That's the first time Timothy has given me a hug.

FineLace: Sorry I'm late, Timothy. { }
Shy-Guy: I was worried you would not show.
FineLace: The Network is very busy tonight. I couldn't sign on.
Shy-Guy: Kids probably have off from school tomorrow. It is always the way.
FineLace: How long would you have waited for me?
Shy-Guy: Until you came. You are worth waiting for. <g>
FineLace: Seriously. There may be a time when I can not get on. I don't want to think that you were here waiting.
Shy-Guy: Fair enough. From now on I will wait one hour. If you don't show I'll try the next night.
FineLace: An hour seems a long time for you to wait.
Shy-Guy: Not when I'm waiting for you.
FineLace: Flirt. <g>
Shy-Guy: Thank you. <g>
FineLace: lol.
Shy-Guy: How was your day?
FineLace: Busy.
Shy-Guy: You are evasive.
FineLace: I do a lot of volunteer work. Makes the time go by. Makes me feel I'm contributing.
Shy-Guy: Anymore killings? That question sounds like something out of a comic book mystery.
FineLace: Yes, it does. <g>
FineLace: No more killings. All Quiet on the Western Front. <g>
Shy-Guy: Police arrest anyone yet?
FineLace: From what I've heard they don't have a clue.
Shy-Guy: No motive?
FineLace: Not that I know. They had a policeman patrolling the grounds last night. Nothing happened.
Shy-Guy: Sounds like they expect more killings.
FineLace: God, I hope not.
Shy-Guy: Please be careful. Do you need a bodyguard?
FineLace: You want to guard my body?

Shy-Guy: Now who's flirting? <g>
FineLace: <looks innocently around to see who's flirting>
Shy-Guy: No one else here. <g>
FineLace: <eyes downcast—smiles> Guess it was me.
Shy-Guy: <smiles> Let me take with me the flattering memory of that flirting. Talk to you tomorrow. Nite, dear lady :*
FineLace: Goodnight Timothy :*
Shy-Guy has left the conversation

Mildred smiled at the screen. He had kissed her goodnight, and she had kissed him back. Another first. Maybe he's getting brave enough to arrange another meeting? Maybe she'll test the water tomorrow night?

Funny, she thought, how at first she was reluctant to meet Timothy. Now the situation was reversed. She wanted to meet this man, and he was the one who was cautious. Oh, Timothy, what could I say that would give you the courage to come to me? She'd have tonight and all day tomorrow to work on that before they talked again.

With a sigh, Mildred saved the chat history, and turned off the computer.

"Don't lose him now," Benny said.

"There's nothing wrong with the way I'm driving." Peter's tone was patient.

Peter wished now that he had not let Benny talk him into allowing him to come along instead of Eleanor. If things got rough, you don't want Eleanor to get involved, Benny had said to him. Peter admitted he was right. Eleanor didn't like the idea, but Peter convinced her that it was best if Benny came along. Benny could identify the man, should the man leave the car, or be in a different one. With that they ended up taking Benny's car, and Peter offered to drive.

"We have been following that blue car all day, and not once have I let him get out of our sight." It was after four in the afternoon. Mildred had returned to the Home, where the blue sedan had stopped following her and went on its way. Peter and Benny continued following the car driven by the man they assumed was George Esterman. At this point there was no way of knowing for sure whether the driver was the same man who rented the car.

"Now ain't the time to make that mistake," Benny said.

After riding with Benny the whole day, Peter's patience was severely strained. To top it off, Benny had been humming the same tune over and over, until it grated on Peter's nerves. Peter had turned on the radio hoping to give him another tune to hum, but Benny had turned it off. He said it distracted him. Too much togetherness can be very bad, Peter thought. It was a wonder that policemen, who drove together all the time, didn't kill one another.

"I hope you know where we are." Peter said. "It would be impossible for me to tell Ardley how to get wherever it is we end up."

"Don't worry," Benny said. "After all the years I've been here, I know where every street is."

The blue sedan turned onto Route 41 going north.

"This is North Tamiami Trail," Benny said. "In Sarasota its got a north and south end to it. It once was a major road here in Florida before the new Interstates were built. You go south it'll take you all the way to Miami. This end of the trail in Sarasota is motel row. The motels are strung out along both sides of the road like highway trash."

"I guess, then," Peter said, "that our man is headed for a motel."

"Let's hope that's so. It would be better than him staying in a house with friends. Won't have to drag anybody else into this."

Peter drove past a number of motels of all sizes, shapes, and conditions—from sleaze to luxury. Then the blue sedan turned across the traffic and into The Flamingo Colony Motel, a pleasant looking string of rooms set back from the street, and fronted by a pink stucco wall. Royal palms, their fronds swaying gently, were strategically placed around the office, and here and there they towered over the rooms. Table umbrellas poked above the wall where, Peter assumed, the swimming pool was. Most of the motels they had passed had outdoor swimming pools.

"Go in after him," Benny said. "We gotta see what room he goes into."

"We could simply ask for his room number from the registration office," Peter said.

"Unless he used a different name," Benny said.

"A good point." Peter pulled up, waited for a break in the traffic, then drove across and into the driveway of the motel. He guided the car past the registration office and into the parking area in front of the rooms. The blue sedan was parked at the end of the string of rooms, and the man was getting out of the car.

"There he is." Benny pointed to the man. "Same guy. Hey, take a look at the belt buckle, like I told you. A fancy cowboy belt buckle."

Peter could see a large, shiny silver buckle on the man's waist as he turned toward the rooms. From that distance, Peter could make out no details on the buckle. As they neared the blue car, the man dug a key out of his pocket and walked up to room 21.

"That's it. We got him," Benny said.

"Now to find a phone," Peter said. He drove on past the room and back onto the road. Then he rode up to the entrance and drove back inside to the parking lot.

"I hope Ardley's in his damn office."

Peter parked the car off to the side of the motel office, where room 21 was visible in the distance.

"If not," Peter said, "there'll always be tomorrow. At least we know where he lives." Then he said, "There's a diner across the street. They must have a phone. I'll call Ardley, and you keep an eye on that room. We don't want to lose him." Peter got out of the car, then looked back in at Benny. "Now, don't do anything rash. And whatever you do, don't confront him. If he should leave before I get back, follow him, and I will meet you back at the Home."

"You know me, Slick," Benny said, as he slid across to the driver's seat.

Yes, Peter thought, *I know you, and that's what worries me.*

Peter stepped across the street to the Mel-o-dee Diner. The afternoon heat was rising off the pavement and Peter immediately started to sweat. Inside, it had the familiar warm homey feel of those diners that served good food and lots of it. The telephone was on the wall to the left of the entrance. Peter fed in a quarter and dialed Ardley's number.

"Detective Ardley," the man answered on the first ring.

Thank God, Peter thought.

"Peter Benington here. We followed that stalker." Then Peter realized he didn't know where he was to give Ardley directions.

Ardley's sigh was audible over the phone. "Okay. I was just getting ready to go home. But, this shouldn't take long. Where is he?"

Peter peered out the window at the sign over the motel. "The Flamingo Colony Motel. It's on Route 41. He's in room 21. How soon can you get here?"

"That's it? Where on Route 41? It goes all through the state."

What had Benny said? "Tamiami Trail. North. I don't know the street."

"All right, I'll find it. Give me fifteen minutes." Ardley hung up.

Ardley was true to his word. Fifteen minutes later a patrol car drove into the parking lot of the Flamingo Colony Motel. Peter flagged the car down. Ardley rolled down the window on the passenger's side. There was a uniformed patrolman driving the car.

"What room number again?" Ardley asked.

"Room 21." Peter pointed toward the other end of the parking lot. Just then, the door to room 21 opened, and the man stepped outside, shutting the door behind him. "That is him leaving now!"

Ardley motioned to the driver and the patrol car leaped forward, coming to a skidding stop behind the blue car as the man was about to unlock the car door.

Peter and Benny watched the action. They were close enough to hear what was being said.

The man in the motel office stepped outside to see what was going on. And an elderly couple who were heading for their car, also stopped to watch.

"Just a minute, sir," the policeman behind the wheel said out of the car window to the man, while Ardley was already getting out of the car.

The man froze, his key poised above the lock on the door of the blue sedan. He frowned a huge question at Ardley and the uniformed cop.

"We'd like a word with you, sir," Ardley said, as he stepped up to the man. Out of long habit Ardley sized the man up. In his fifties, the man appeared to be fit, with a slight paunch pushing at the fancy Western belt buckle. He was wearing a plaid short-sleeved shirt tucked into the pants, and dark trousers with no apparent bulge of a gun.

"What's this all about?" the man demanded.

"Do you have any identification, sir?" Ardley said. The uniformed patrolman had stepped up next to Ardley.

"Yep, I do. But are you going to tell me what this is about?" This time there was a hard edge to the man's voice.

"In a minute, sir. But first I'd like to see some identification."

The man mumbled something angry under his breath, extracted a wallet from his back pocket, opened it, and handed Ardley a driver's license. Ardley looked at it. A Georgia license in the name of George Esterman.

"Now, how about you telling me what's happening here?"

Ardley handed the driver's license back to George Esterman. "Mr. Esterman, we've received reports that you are harassing a woman over at Coral Sands Retirement Residence."

"What! You must be crazy! I've never been near that place." George Esterman snapped the words out.

"Oh," Ardley said. "You know where it is."

"Hell, I don't know where it's at. But I sure as hell know I ain't never been there. Don't you have crimes to solve or something, instead of annoying us tourists?"

Ardley's voice became calmer. He didn't like this man's attitude, and from Ardley's experience, he knew he was dealing with a man who had a short fuse. "That is exactly what we are doing, sir."

"Hell," George Esterman said in a smart mouth tone. "It ain't no crime to drive around the streets. That right? The streets are for everybody."

"Interesting, sir," Ardley said, "but I don't remember mentioning driving around. Perhaps you could tell us why you were following this lady for the last three days?"

"You cops are all the same." Esterman raised his voice, he was having trouble holding down his anger. "You looking for trouble where there ain't none. I've done nothing wrong that you should be bothering me now. Whyn't you go on about your business and leave me be?"

Ardley did not want to get into an argument out in the open with other people around, whether it be a street or parking lot. It was clear Esterman was going to do just that—create a scene. The procedure here was simple—quickly remove to an area of control. Ardley gave a curt nod to the patrolman, but kept his eyes on Esterman. "Maybe we should discuss this down at the station, sir."

"I'm not going to no station." Esterman turned to the door of his car and inserted the key in the lock. "You got no call to arrest me. I know my rights. No crime's been committed, now." He turned the key in the lock.

The handcuffs snapped around one of Esterman's wrists, and the patrolman pushed Esterman against the door, yanked the other wrist behind the man, and slipped on the second cuff. It happened so fast that Esterman didn't have time to resist.

"What in hell you doing!" Esterman yelled.

Ardley grabbed Esterman. "I know my rights!" Together with the patrolman, Ardley pulled him over to the back door of the patrol car. "You got no call to do this!" The patrolman threw open the door and they pushed Esterman into the backseat. "Goddamn dumb cops! You bastards think you can push people around!" Ardley shut the door on Esterman's hollering.

"Let's get out of here," Ardley said to the patrolman as Ardley walked around the car, and got into the front passenger's seat.

Peter and Benny watched as the patrol car drove off.

"That Esterman is an arrogant stupid jerk," Benny said. "Now what, Slick?"

"I guess we will follow Ardley to the police station. He might need us to make a statement about this guy following Mildred. And I'd like to know what Esterman is up to."

At the station, Peter and Benny asked for detective Ardley. The policeman behind the desk spoke to Ardley on the telephone, then asked them to sit on the bench and wait for Ardley to come out to them. Forty-five minutes went by, during which time Peter went to the watercooler, drew a glass of water, and downed a beta-blocker—he had missed taking the pill at three that afternoon. Benny had visited the men's room twice, and together they had stood outside while Peter smoked a cigarette. In general, they paced and spoke little.

Finally Ardley came out, escorted them back to his office, took his seat behind the desk, and motioned for them to take a seat. This time there were two chairs, and Benny and Peter both sat down.

"I want you to know that we're going to hold on to Mr. Esterman for twenty-four hours," Ardley said. "We fingerprinted him, and sent the prints to Georgia to see if there are any outstanding warrants. Hopefully we'll get something back from them by tomorrow afternoon. The twenty-four hours will give Mr. Esterman a chance to cool off. And your woman friend won't have to worry about being followed around tomorrow." Ardley shrugged. "It's the best I can do."

"It was more than I expected," Peter said. "Mildred will be relieved."

"Have either of you seen this guy around Coral Sands before this woman noticed him following her?"

"No," Peter said.

"I saw him at the Beach House bar once," Benny said.

Ardley raised a questioning eyebrow.

"Mildred was supposed to meet some guy she'd met on the computer. She had never seen him before. I went with her. And there at the bar I saw Mr. Belt Buckle."

Ardley nodded pensively.

"There's one thing I'd like you both to do, and that is, give us a statement on who, what, where, and how. If I don't get back an answer from Georgia by tomorrow afternoon, then on the basis of your statements, I may be able to hold him another day."

"No problem," Benny said.

"That officer over there"—Ardley pointed to a uniformed policeman behind a desk in the sea of desks outside Ardley's office—"will take your statements." Then he stood. "I, for one, am going home. It has been a long day."

Peter and Benny stood.

"Thank you, again," Peter said.

Ardley waved him away. Then he turned and left the office.

When Peter and Benny finally left the police station it was going on seven o'clock. As they came out the front door, Benny looked at his watch.

"Well, the dining room at Coral Sands is closing by now. We'd better go someplace to get a bite to eat."

"That sounds good to me," Peter said. "Since you know your way around Sarasota, you pick the place."

"You know," Benny said, stopping at the car, "I'm wondering if this guy might be involved with the two killings? Seems too much of a coincidence, his showing up like this right after."

Peter opened the car door. "I am sure Ardley is thinking the same thing."

FineLace has entered the conversation

It was seven o'clock and Timothy wasn't in the chat room. Strange, Mildred thought. He was always there before her. She sat there not knowing what to do. It was not like a real room, where she could go to the door and look down the corridor or check out the window to see if his car was parked outside.

Mildred had been apprehensive about chatting with Timothy this evening, because she had made up her mind to broach the subject of their trying once again to meet in the real world. She didn't know exactly how she would do this, but, somehow, she would bring it up—tactfully. Tact was most important. She didn't want to scare off Timothy. He seemed like such a fragile personality that scaring him off seemed a probable outcome of too aggressive an approach.

Now she was apprehensive because he was not waiting for her in the chat room. Something may have happened to him. The world was not a safe place.

Shy-Guy has entered the conversation

Shy-Guy: <panting hard> Hi Dear One. Sorry I'm late. Rushed here as fast as I could. <pant, pant>

Mildred smiled with relief. "Thank God," Mildred said aloud. She was glad to see him.

FineLace: You had me worried there for a moment. You're always on time.

Shy-Guy: Delayed a bit. Always a first time, I guess. Sorry I made you worry.
FineLace: Are you all right?
Shy-Guy: Never felt better.
Shy-Guy: So, how's murder row?
FineLace: Oh, Timothy, let's not talk about such depressing things.
Shy-Guy: You're right. We have more important things to discuss—like when we are going to meet.

Mildred's heart skipped an excited beat. *He* had broached the subject! Her hands began shaking.

FineLace: Yes. Do yu thnk

She giggled to herself. The excitement she felt had her trembling hands fumbling over the keyboard. She focused on typing slower.

FineLace: Do you think you are ready to try again?
Shy-Guy: I'm so ready I could bust. <g>

This was more than she had hoped for! All day she had rehearsed the things she was going to say to convince Timothy to try another meeting. Now he had taken the initiative, and it made her feel that it would happen at last.

FineLace: Really?
Shy-Guy: Really.
FineLace: That's wndrful! When shsll we dy ths?

She laughed when she saw what she had typed.

Shy-Guy: Somebody rearrange your keyboard? <g>

Mildred laughed.

FineLace: lol Having a bad vowel day <g>
Shy-Guy: lol. I'll lend you a couple—aa oo ee ii uu
FineLace: That'll help. <g> Let me try again.

FineLace: That's wonderful! When shall we do this?
Shy-Guy: How about now?
FineLace: Now! Are you serious?
Shy-Guy: Strike while the urge is hot. <g>
FineLace: <smiles>
Shy-Guy: I might have second thoughts if we wait. Meet me at the Beach House Bar, now.
FineLace: This is so sudden.

Why did I write that? she thought. She was the one who had intended to push for a meeting tonight. Why was she suddenly hesitant?

Shy-Guy: Time's a wasting, Dear One.

Oh, what the hell, she thought. What's wrong with being a little impulsive? She could feel the excitement like electricity in her veins.

FineLace: I'm changing my clothes right now. <g>
Shy-Guy: Yeah! My feet are pulling me to the door. See you there in fifteen minutes?
FineLace: Twenty minutes is the best I can do if you want me dressed. <g>
Shy-Guy: lol. Dear One, don't tempt me. For propriety's sake, I'll give you twenty minutes.
FineLace: See you then. <smiles excitedly>
Shy-Guy: Twenty minutes, now. <smiles>
Shy-Guy has left the conversation

Mildred quickly saved the chat history, signed off the MSN Network, and turned off the computer. Twenty minutes was just enough time to refresh her makeup and get out the door. The Beach House was a good fifteen minutes away.

She was smiling and humming as she went into the bathroom, took a brush to her hair, and touched lipstick to her lips. She ignored the wrinkled, aged face that looked back at her in the mirror. Nothing was going to dampen her spirits. She felt young and excited, and she enjoyed the feeling. Life was holding out to her another adventure.

CHAPTER 12

When Peter and Benny returned to Coral Sands it was a little past eight. They entered the lobby and saw a large group being entertained by Mr. Petersen.

"It's Blackstone the Magician." Shirley smiled. She was standing behind the counter. "He always draws a big crowd."

Peter raised a questioning eyebrow at Benny.

Benny shrugged and smiled. "You haven't seen him do magic. He is really great at this. C'mon."

They walked toward the crowd. Peter spotted Eleanor sitting on a sofa in the front row along with Betty and Walter and Caroline. Many people were standing behind them. Applause broke out and Petersen bowed.

"Thank you," he said as Peter and Benny stepped past to join the standing crowd. "Ah, just what I need, a volunteer." Petersen stepped over and laid a hand on Peter's arm.

Peter stopped and looked at Petersen.

"Would you please join me center stage?" Petersen motioned to where he had been standing in front of the sofa.

Peter smiled. "Certainly," and moved over with Petersen to 'center stage'.

Petersen produced a deck of cards from his pocket, held them up and fanned them open for everyone to see. "A normal deck of cards, as you can see." Then he shuffled them with impressive dexterity, and fanned them out face down to Peter.

"Now, good sir, would you please choose a card."

Peter slid one card out, and looked at it—the three of clubs.

"Now, please, hold it up so the audience can see the card, but do not let me see it." Petersen turned away.

Peter held up the three of clubs for everyone to see, then brought it down close to his chest. "You may turn around now."

Petersen turned around. He then shuffled the cards, and fanned them face down to Peter. "Now, please insert your card into the deck."

Peter carefully pushed the three of clubs into the deck, off to one side of center.

Petersen squared the deck, and went through an elaborate array of shuffling techniques. "Now, please pick a number from one to ten."

Benny yelled from the crowd, "Thirteen."

Petersen smiled. "There is always a doubter in the audience. Thirteen it shall be. And to insure that I am an honest magician, I shall shuffle the cards again to ease your mind that they are not mixed up enough." He shuffled the cards a few more times, then held them out to Peter. "Please, one last task. Cut the cards."

Peter took a portion of cards off the deck and placed them in Petersen's other hand.

Petersen, then put the bottom half on top of those cards, holding the entire deck now in one hand. He then raised the empty hand high over the audience. "An illusionist uses all sorts of trick boxes and gimmicks. A true magician uses only his ability to create magic." Then he turned to Peter. "I am sorry, but it seems you do have one more task to perform. Please hold your hand open."

Peter extended his right hand, palm up.

"Now, please correct me if I am wrong. My short term memory has not been very good. The number was thirteen, is that right?"

"Yes," Peter said.

Petersen began counting aloud as he took one card at a time off the top of the deck and placed it in Peter's hand. ". . . ten, eleven, twelve." He held onto the thirteenth card. "Now, this is card number thirteen. And this is your card, the card you had chosen from the deck." He held the card up for all to see, and it was the king of spades.

"Wrong!" Benny yelled. "That ain't his card."

Petersen, with a puzzled look on his face, turned the card to look at it himself. "But this must be the card. It is the . . . oh, yes. I warned you about my short term memory. The card we are seeking is the one *after* the thirteenth card." He placed the king of spades in Peter's hand. Then he took the next top card off the deck and held it up. The three of clubs.

Everyone smiled and applauded, and Petersen took a deep bow.

"Thank you. You are an appreciative audience."

"So, how'd you do it?" Benny yelled.

Petersen smiled. "It is not the usual practice for a magician to reveal his secrets. But, I will say this—magic is the art of using the assumptions people make. Assumptions, I might add, that are always wrong when it comes to magic. Assumptions such as this being a normal deck of cards, because it appeared so and because I said so." He feigned a sheepish look. "Sometimes I lie." The sheepish look disappeared. "Also, you assumed that my shuffling the deck actually mixed up the cards. Another mistaken assumption. So, my advice is this—every time you make an assumption, all you can assume is that you are wrong." He smiled. "And that is all I will reveal." He bowed again. "Thank you, and good night."

Everyone applauded as Petersen stepped away and disappeared into the first floor corridor.

Eleanor and Betty and Walter rose up from the sofa and came over to Peter and Benny.

Eleanor smiled and kissed Peter on the cheek.

"You were a wonderful stooge," Walter said with a straight face. "Not everyone is able to do it. It requires a certain talent."

"Oh stop that, Walter." Eleanor smiled.

"Ah, the fair damsel coming to the defense of her knight. In this case, her stooge." This time Walter couldn't help but grin a little.

Benny stepped up beside Peter. "I told you he was good."

"Yes." Peter nodded. Petersen never ceased to amaze him.

"We were worried about you two," Eleanor said. "You were gone so long."

"Did you get the police after that man who was following Mildred?" Betty asked.

"Yes, we did," Peter said. "Let's go to the sofa group over there in the corner where we can talk without all these people around."

They got up, walked across the lobby, and settled into the corner area.

"So, tell us what happened," Eleanor said to Peter.

Benny jumped in. "That cop, Ardley, scooped him up and chucked him in the can for the night.

"He arrested him?" Walter said. "On what grounds?"

"The guy smartmouthed Ardley, and the next thing the guy knew he was wearing cuffs and riding in the back of a patrol car. And eating peanut butter and jelly sandwiches for supper."

"Did the man say why he was following Mildred?"

"No," Peter said. "Ardley said that he will hold him for twenty-four hours. Ardley is also checking the man's fingerprints to see if he is wanted in Georgia."

"Well," Walter said, "if the man was up to no good, this little tussle with the police should change his mind."

Peter shrugged. "Let's hope so." Then Peter glanced around at the people still in the lobby. "Is Mildred around? I'd like to tell her what happened."

"I didn't see her here for the show," Eleanor said.

Betty added, "The last time I saw her was around six-thirty. We had dinner together. After that she went upstairs."

"Well," Peter said, "let me have Shirley call her. I would really like to tell her what happened. I'll be right back."

Peter turned and walked across the lobby to the front desk. Shirley was seated behind the counter at the desk doing a crossword puzzle.

"Yes?" Shirley looked up as Peter leaned on the counter.

Peter noticed Shirley's hair was done up nicely—the gray had been changed to a soft blond, and she wore makeup and a nice dress. Trying to impress somebody, Peter thought. "Would you please call Mildred Perkins? I have something to tell her, but don't want to barge in on her if she is indisposed."

"I'll try," Shirley said, picking up the phone. She ran a finger down the residents' list taped to the desk in front of her. She stopped, peered at the list then punched Mildred's room number into the phone. "I didn't see her come back. She must have come in the back way." The phone rang at the other end.

"Come back?"

Shirley nodded, the phone ringing again at the other end. "I saw her leave here"—she glanced at the clock on the desk—"about an hour ago." The phone rang once again. Shirley shook her head. "No answer. She must not be back." Shirley hung up the phone.

"Thanks," Peter said. "Guess the news will have to wait until morning."

"Any time." Shirley smiled, and went back to her crossword puzzle.

Peter turned to walk away.

"You wouldn't happen to know a five letter word for a corner occupant?" Shirley asked.

"Dunce," Peter said over his shoulder, and he went to join the others.

At ten to nine, they were all sitting in the coffee alcove looking out at the lighted swimming pool. It had been a very warm day, and hadn't cooled down much. The night was steamy. Too hot and humid to sit outside. They were trying to cheer up Betty, who's hearing was two days away, assuring her they would all be there to give her support.

Shirley crossed the lobby and came over to them.

"Mr. Benington, there's a phone call for you."

Peter frowned. "Who would be calling me at this hour?"

"Maybe a desperate girlfriend." Eleanor smiled playfully.

"It is a Detective Ardley of the Sarasota police," Shirley said.

Benny raised his eyebrows. "Something's up."

"Excuse me," Peter said to the group. He stood and followed Shirley back to the desk. There he picked up the phone.

"Yes, Detective?"

"It would give me immense pleasure to have you and Mr. Ashe and the woman who said she was being followed, join me right now at the police station." Ardley did not sound happy.

"What happened?"

"Our overnight guest has decided to talk. I'd like you all down here to listen to what he told me."

Peter went back to the group, got Benny and they went looking for Mildred.

When Benny and Peter arrived at the police station, Ardley was sitting at the front desk drinking a cup of coffee with the policeman manning the desk. The desk stood just behind a wood railing that stretched wall to wall.

Ardley watched them come in, and when they stepped up to the railing he frowned in annoyance. "Where's the woman this guy was following?'

"She was not at home," Peter said. "She left earlier in the evening and has not returned."

Ardley sighed heavily. "Everyone gets to enjoy their evening but me." He put his coffee cup down on the desk, grabbed the arms of the chair, and pushed himself up with a grunt. "Okay. Let's get this over with." He pointed to the gate in the railing. "Follow me."

Peter and Benny went through the gate and followed Ardley down a short corridor to a windowless room with a table and half dozen chairs. The table and chairs were a heavy wood. The top of the table was worn and scarred. It had seen better days.

"This is where we beat them up. Nobody hears their screams."

Peter wasn't sure Ardley was entirely joking.

"At eight your guy decides to talk, and"—he shook his head in frustration—"wants to talk only to me. So, here I am on my time off."

Peter didn't know what to say to that.

"Have a seat over there." Ardley pointed to the chairs off to the side. "I'll bring in Mr. Esterman." Ardley left the room and Benny and Peter sat down.

A few moments later the door opened and George Esterman came in, followed by Ardley. Esterman was in handcuffs. This was the first time Peter had seen the man up close. His skin was like worn leather and his hands had the ground in grease of a mechanic.

Benny elbowed Peter and nodded at Esterman's belt buckle.

"Like I told you." The buckle looked to be silver and had a longhorn steer's head in three dimensions across the expanse of the buckle.

Ardley brought Esterman to the other side of the table, sat him down in the chair, and locked the handcuffs to a chain on that side of the table. This was normal procedure with potentially violent prisoners. Ardley had seen a sample of the man's temper and decided to be cautious until he got the report back on the fingerprints.

Esterman pulled at the handcuffs. "Is this here really necessary? I am no murderer or anything."

Ardley ignored the man's question. "Suppose you go over what you told me earlier?"

"Who're these fellas?" Esterman indicated Peter and Benny.

"People interested in your story," Ardley said. "Now, unless you want to go back to your cell, let's get on with it."

"Oh, yeah. I know you." Esterman was looking at Benny. "I saw you at that bar the other night. Thought you looked familiar."

"Yeah, that was me," Benny said. "So, you're the guy from the computer."

"Yep. I'm Timothy. Always liked the name better'n my own. If I had any say in naming myself, Timothy's what I would'a chosen."

"So, what's this bullshit all about?" Benny said. "You agree to meet her, then stand her up, then follow her around. What the hell are you after?"

"I was real sorry that I didn't own up in that bar. When push came to shove I was too scared to meet her. Didn't know how she'd take it, my coming back into her life after all those years."

"She knew you before?" Peter said.

Esterman nodded.

"Then," Benny said, "how come she didn't recognize you that night in the bar?"

Esterman shrugged and gave them a sad grin. "Been over forty years. I've done a lot of changing in that there time."

"You've been talking to her for a month on the computer," Peter said.

"Yep."

"You never told her who you were?"

"Scared to. Her past catching up to her like that, she might never talk to me again. But I really liked her, after all that talking. She's a real nice lady."

"How did you find her?" Ardley said

"Hired a private detective specialized in finding people. Took him a while, and cost me some money. But I don't know how he did it. Them fellas have their ways."

"I don't understand?" Peter said. "What made you want to contact her after forty years?"

"Well," Esterman said, "to shorten up the story a bit—she's my mama."

"What!" Benny said, more angry than surprised, ready to leave his chair.

Ardley gave Benny a cold hard look, and Peter placed a restraining hand on Benny's arm.

"Yep," Esterman said. "She abandoned me when I was just a tyke. Left me waiting in a hospital waiting room while she left town. Hell, I was sitting there for hours 'fore somebody asked me what I was waiting for." Esterman gave an easy shrug. "Was the last time I saw her."

"Until when?" Ardley said.

"Saw her for the first time a couple days ago at that bar in the Beach House."

"If your private detective found her, then you knew where she lived."

"Yep."

"So, why didn't you go directly to Coral Sands and talk with her?"

"It didn't seem like a good idea. I walk in and ask for her, she comes down and I say, 'Hi, I'm your son.' I thought it best to get to know her some before I approached her."

"Did you go to Coral Sands at all before you made contact with her?"

"Yep. Went to see what kind of place it was. I was real glad to see it was a nice place to live. Never went inside. Just walked around the place."

"Excuse me," Peter said to Ardley. Then he turned to Esterman. ''How did you know where to contact her on the computer?''

''That private detective gave me all that information: what her E-mail address was, what her computer handle was. I just roamed the chat rooms until I found her. Didn't take long.''

''Can you prove,'' Benny said, ''that she's your mother?''

''It was the private detective that found her. He was convinced. But I'm sure a DNA test would be proof enough. And I'd gladly take such a test.''

''What hospital did she leave you at?'' Ardley asked.

''I don't know the name. It was in Elizabeth, New Jersey. That's all I know about it.''

''You're from Georgia?''

''Yeah. After years bouncing from foster home to foster home, I finally came of age. When that happened I left the North as quickly as my legs would carry me. Got a job in Macon, Georgia, in a garage fixing cars. Macon was big enough a town where they didn't shy away from Northerners.'' Esterman shrugged. ''When the owner retired eight years later, he gave me the business. Been there ever since.''

''You know something?'' Benny said. ''I think you're full of shit.''

''I'm sorry you feel that way. All that I've told you can be checked.''

''Yes,'' Ardley said, ''I'd like to check out your story, so that we all can be satisfied that it's true. Perhaps you can give me the name of the private detective you had hired?''

''Certainly. His name's William Robert Torrence. I have his card in my wallet, which you confiscated when you brought me in here.''

Ardley looked at Benny and Peter, then back to Esterman. ''I think that will be all for this evening.'' Ardley stood.

''You going to let me go now?''

''Not until tomorrow, Mr. Esterman.'' Ardley stepped over to the man and unlocked the handcuffs from the chain.

''But I didn't commit no crime.''

''Let's just say, if your story checks out, we'll drop the charges of resisting a police officer.''

• • •

"I don't know," Benny said. "There's something fishy about all of this bullshit the guy was throwing around."

They were in Benny's car driving back to Coral Sands. Benny was driving, and from what Peter could see, Benny's night vision wasn't very good. In fact it was downright dangerous. Fortunately, most of the roads had reflectors on the center line. The few they drove on that didn't had Benny wandering up on the shoulder, keeping Peter's heart in his mouth.

"He did know about Mildred on the computer," Peter said.

"You really think Mildred is that guy's mother?" Benny looked to Peter and away from the road as he spoke. Peter searched with his foot for the brake he wished was on his side of the car.

"Stranger things have happened," Peter said, staring hard out the windshield, hoping Benny could see the traffic.

"How are we gonna tell Mildred about this?"

"I don't know. It's probably best if we wait until Ardley is satisfied and releases the man. It's still a possibility that he is a wanted man, and may be shipped off to prison."

"Yeah, that's good. If he is a crook, and they send him away, then she doesn't have to know anything about this." Benny turned away from the road again. "We'll keep this to ourselves for now."

"Agreed," Peter said, through clenched teeth, averting his eyes from what he anticipated to be a pending collision with a car in front of them stopped for a red light.

Benny saw the look on Peter's face and quickly looked back at the road. He hit the brake hard, tires screeching and the car swerving to a rocking stop. "Geez. I gotta watch what I'm doing here."

"I would greatly appreciate it," Peter said.

When they arrived back at Coral Sands it was nearing ten-thirty. Eleanor, Caroline, and Walter were waiting for them in the coffee alcove.

"So, what happened?" Eleanor asked.

"Nothing much." Benny shrugged. "The guy babbled away, but didn't say anything."

"He talked?" Walter said.

"If you want to call it that."

"Has Mildred returned?" Peter asked Eleanor.

"I haven't seen her."

"I guess it can wait until morning. I just wanted her to know the man is in custody, at least through tomorrow."

"Yes." Walter nodded. "It should relieve her mind some."

"I don't know about anyone else here"—Peter sighed, he was tired—"but I have had a long day. I'm going to turn in." He gave Eleanor a hopeful look.

"Good idea," Benny said. "C'mon, Caroline, I'll take you home."

The mind could feel the dark of the tropical night as if it had substance. The heat was oppressive, the air sticky with humidity, and the mosquitoes whined relentlessly for blood. Every night the same, every night a torture. But the night brought something worse. Hunger.

The daylight hours were spent in stumbling, weary labor—carrying exhaustion like a huge weight on the back, in constant fear of beatings and death. The mind was consumed with thoughts of survival, of making it through one more day. There was no time to dwell on the hunger.

Until night came, and one sat alone in the dark. Then the hunger was all pervasive. It was impossible to think of anything else. The mind tried every night to push the thought of food aside by concentrating on the world before the prison camp, on the loved ones somewhere out there, on the civilized life that was once all the mind knew, on God and religion, on anything. But thoughts always turned toward food. Fantasies of memorable meals, of foods once savored with a thrilling joy, occupied the night.

At times the hunger was all-consuming and drove out the civilized soul, giving full freedom to the animal within to fight and kill for food. Grown men cried when precious bits of food, hoarded to deal with the night, were stolen. And grown men died when their wasted bodies could no longer survive on the meager rations given out by the Japanese to the prisoners.

The mind once enjoyed the night, before the War. But it knew that the night would never again be a time of pleasure and peace.

• • •

"She's his mother!" Caroline said.

She and Benny were sitting at the dining table in Caroline's mobile home having a cup of coffee. They were both dressed for bed, Caroline in a nightgown that hung badly on her bent body and Benny in full pajamas.

"That's the story the guy told us," Benny said. "But you can't tell anybody. Slick and I . . . Peter and I agreed not to tell anyone until Mildred knows for sure, one way or the other."

"I won't tell a soul. But it is something that could be a terrible tragedy for the dear woman."

"Tragedy?"

"To be forced to abandon a child must be a terrible thing. The poor woman must have suffered such guilt. Now, after all those years of putting that guilt behind her, to have it come back into her life, will be tragic."

"He's her son!" Eleanor sat upright in bed, the soft orange glow of the night-light making her naked body barely visible in the darkness.

"So much for my ability to keep a secret from a woman," Peter said. He was lying in bed next to her in his apartment.

"God, that's going to be a terrible shock to Mildred."

"If it's true."

"It sounds like this man knows it's true."

"Yes, it does."

"Why come looking for her after all those years?"

"Some people can not feel whole until they know their roots."

Eleanor was silent for a moment, thinking. Then, softly, she said, "I hope that's all it is."

CHAPTER 13

The ringing was dragging him from the comfortable, warm darkness. He fought it, trying to squash the sound that grated in his mind, that irritated like fingernails on a blackboard. But he didn't have the strength to drive it away. With his eyes still closed he reached for the sound of the ringing. When his hand closed on the telephone, he picked up the receiver, and the ringing stopped. Thank God, he thought.

The bedroom light went on with a blaze that penetrated his eyelids and hurt his eyes. "What is it?" Amanda said close to him.

Ardley, keeping his eyes closed, put the phone to his ear. "Yeah?" It came out more a croak than an intelligible word. He listened to the voice at the other end, and knew he could not hide in sleep anymore. "Yeah, I'll be there." Ardley grunted and hung up the phone.

"I'll make some coffee," Amanda said, throwing off the light sheet and getting out of bed.

Ardley stretched and yawned wide enough to hear his jaw crack. Finally, he opened his eyes, and the light stabbed into his brain. He squinted at the light to keep the pain to a minimum. God, he needed more sleep. He threw his legs over the side of the bed, pulled himself up to a sitting position and squinted at the clock radio on the night table next to him. 4:20 A.M. Damn.

Fifteen minutes later, hurriedly dressed and shaved, he came into the kitchen. Amanda, wearing a silky nightgown, was pouring coffee into a thermos, and there was a cup of steaming coffee for him on the table.

"Instant," she said over her shoulder. "Best I can do on short notice." Amanda, short and slender with dark hair and dark eyes, was one of those women who, without working at it, would always retain her beauty. The beauty would grow old, would mature, take on a softer power with time, but would never disappear.

Ardley enjoyed watching her.

"I'm glad this doesn't happen too often." She put the cap on the thermos, turned, stepped over to the table, and placed the thermos on the table in front of him. "Want to talk about it?"

He gulped some of the coffee from his cup. It was hot, and it felt good going down. "They found another body at that retirement residence. Since it's my case, I gotta go." Then he stood up, leaned over and kissed her on the forehead.

"Coral Sands?"

"Yeah." He straightened and put the thermos under his arm.

"I thought you had some patrolmen watching the place?"

"That's who found the body," he said over his shoulder as he headed for the door.

"I didn't hear or see anything," Patrolman Jerry Otis said to Ardley. They were standing on the grounds outside of Coral Sands a little away from the scene. It was still dark, and the area around the body was lit with police floodlights. Ardley preferred to remain in the darkness, the floodlights too painfully bright for Ardley's sleep-deprived eyes. Crime-scene tape had been stretched around the area. A half dozen people were standing around, including two men with a gurney waiting for the medical examiner to release the body. The medical examiner was kneeling next to the body and carefully probing the corpse.

"Got any idea of the time this happened?" Ardley was drinking the coffee directly from the thermos.

"I went for one last walk around, then took a break about two or so. I was sitting inside having coffee with Shirley and with Jimmy Ernest—he roams the halls at night. Got some kind of insomnia problem. Shirley says she thinks he's a vampire.'' Jerry Otis grinned, but immediately wiped it off his face when Ardley did not react. ''I went back outside about two-thirty or so. Walked the grounds a couple times before I found the body. That would put it around three, maybe.''

''Good guess then is sometime after two?''

''Best guess.''

''Thought Hartford was supposed to be on the second shift tonight?''

Jerry Otis shrugged. ''We switched. He said he couldn't sleep before midnight, which meant he was up all night when he had the second shift. Me, I can sleep anytime, anywhere.''

''Well, it looks like you won't be needed anymore tonight. You know the drill. Write it up before you go off duty.''

''Yes, sir.''

Ardley left Jerry Otis and walked over to the edge of the circle of light around the body. The harsh light from the floods made the scene look stark and unearthly, with deep shadows like something out of a grade B horror movie. Maybe, he thought, that's what life was—a grade B horror movie.

He called to the medical examiner, Pat Curtain, who was crouched over the body. Pat was a skinny man with dark hair that needed combing and had that disheveled look of being roused from bed and dressing quickly. ''What have you got?''

''Well, for one, she's dead.''

''That's what they pay you the big bucks for?''

''At this hour you want more?'' Then he leaned back on his heels and looked over at Ardley. ''Wasn't killed here. With all those knife wounds, the ground would have been soaked with blood, but there's nothing around here. With this St. Augustine grass it's hard to tell if the body was dragged here, which is my guess. One other thing. The way the body is covered with blood, it's a good guess the killer got a lot on him.''

''Any ID?''

''Not found by me.''

''Thanks,'' Ardley said. ''Let me know when you're finished so I can check out the body.''

''Be a few minutes yet. Almost done.''

''Okay. I'll be inside,'' Ardley said. At a distance, out of the lights, Ardley paced around looking at the whole scene. This time the body wasn't tucked beneath the bushes. Instead it was stretched out in front of them. Where the body lay the grass was too thick to give up any footprints. Well, he thought, time to ask around inside Coral Sands, see if he could get anyone to identify the body.

"Hello Shirley." Ardley managed a weak smile. "We met the other morning. You got me coffee."

"Yes," Shirley said with no enthusiasm.

"Sorry we had to meet again under these circumstances."

Shirley nodded sadly. "All this death," she mumbled to herself.

They were seated in the coffee alcove, where Ardley had asked Shirley and Jimmy Ernest to wait while he finished up outside.

He turned to Jimmy Ernest. "And we've met before. The man who can't sleep at night since the War."

Jimmy Ernest nodded solemnly.

"Did you go outside at all?" Ardley looked at Shirley when he asked this of Jimmy Ernest. Her reaction would tell him if she knew he was lying.

"No. Too damn buggy out there. Mosquitoes eat you alive at night."

"Didn't hear anything strange? A noise, or something from outside?"

"No. Spent much of the time talking with Shirley, here."

"Yes. We were working a crossword puzzle together," Shirley said.

"Then that cop came in for a cup of coffee, and we chatted for awhile."

Pat Curtain came in. "It's all yours," he said, then turned and left.

"Thanks," Ardley said to the man's back. Then he looked at Shirley and Jimmy.

"Would you both mind coming outside and taking a look at the body? See if you can identify who it is?" Ardley looked at Shirley's ashen face. He wasn't sure she'd hold it together when she viewed the corpse.

After Ardley had finished with Jimmy Ernest and Shirley,

and released them it was going on five-thirty. At that point Jimmy Ernest went around knocking on doors to tell everyone what had happened. Within a half hour the entire household was aware of the news. Dazed and sleepy, yet concerned and anxious, they stumbled down to the dining room. By that time Shirley, with two shots of "medicinal" whiskey in her, had recovered from the trauma of viewing the body, and she arranged for coffee and tea to be served.

At a little past six-thirty Ardley was seated in the dining room at the same table as Eleanor, Peter, Alice, Walter, and Betty. Benny had spent the night at Caroline's, where Eleanor had telephoned him a short while before to break the news. He was on his way back to Coral Sands.

"Did any of you see or hear anything unusual last night?" Ardley said. He had made the rounds of most of the tables, asking the same questions of everyone. He had a notebook in front of him, ready to jot down answers.

Each of them at the table said no.

"Things certainly have been unsettling around here lately," Walter said. Considering the recent events, it was a huge understatement.

"What a terrible thing to happen." Eleanor was very upset. "Who would do such a monstrous thing to another human being?"

"Poor, poor Mildred," Betty sighed. "Shirley said Mildred was happy and excited when she left here last night."

"Anyone know where she was going? Or who she went to see?" Ardley looked hopefully at the faces around the table.

Heads shook no.

"If I didn't know better," Peter said, "I would have nominated Timothy, her computer friend. But being in jail all night has given him the perfect alibi."

Ardley nodded. "Did any of you see anyone outside yesterday or last night who you didn't recognize? Or see a strange car? Or notice if she was picked up or took her own car?"

"Is her Toyota in the parking lot?" Eleanor asked.

Ardley shook his head as he wrote in the notebook. "Doesn't mean she wasn't picked up, then later on came back and went out again."

Then Ardley took a Polaroid photograph from his pocket

and passed it around. "Anyone see this guy hanging around over the last month or so?"

One by one they took the photo, looked at it, then shook their head.

When Peter looked at the photo he saw it was a mug shot of George Esterman. "How could he be implicated in this? He was in jail all night."

Ardley took the photograph from Peter. "There have been two other murders. Possibly he was involved, or knows something about them."

"Sounds like you're grabbing at straws."

"Straws are all I have at this point. And this man is the only visible element added to this environment the past month. Besides"—Ardley looked at the mug shot—"there's something not straight about Mr. Esterman."

"Didn't the same man kill all three people?" Walter leaned forward on his cane.

"Possible, but I'm not sure. There were differences between this killing and the others. This one was more brutal and bloody. The other two were clean surgical strikes with one stroke of the knife." Ardley shrugged. "Though it wouldn't be the first time someone has killed a number of people to hide the real victim."

Betty started to cry. She dug a handkerchief from the sleeve of her dress, and daubed at the tears. Then she stood up. "All this terrible talk about blood and knives. This is our friend Mildred you are talking about. Couldn't you be more respectful?" With that, she turned and left the dining room.

There was a moment of embarrassed silence around the table. Then Eleanor turned to Ardley. "She's been under a lot of pressure lately. Her son is trying to have her declared incompetent. The hearing is scheduled for tomorrow, and she's very worried."

And Betty has a right to be worried, Peter thought. Even with all the support she'll get from Eleanor and the others.

Eleanor saw Benny and Caroline coming into the dining room. She raised her hand and waved at them. Benny was wearing his NY baseball cap.

"The curse of the elderly is the young that hover around

like vultures waiting to pick your bones,'' Walter said. ''Some are too impatient to wait for you to die.''

Benny and Caroline came over to the table. Caroline sat in the chair Betty had vacated, and Benny pulled a chair over from another table.

''Sorry I had to call you with such bad news,'' Eleanor said.

''It's all right,'' Benny said unconvincingly. ''So, how did he do it?''

''She was brutally stabbed,'' Peter said.

''No, I mean how did that Esterman guy arrange it?''

''He had the perfect alibi. He was in jail all night.''

''That don't mean he ain't behind the killing. I mean he's got the best motive in the world—Mildred's money.''

Ardley sat there listening to them.

''Who is this Esterman person you keep referring to?'' Walter asked.

Benny turned to Walter. ''He's the guy that's been following Mildred around and talking to her on the computer. Says he's her son.''

Walter's expression became thoughtful. ''Her son.''

Alice's eyes widened. ''Her son! She never mentioned anything to me about having a son.''

''Says she abandoned him when he was a kid.''

''Can he prove that?''

Peter looked at Ardley. ''Are you going to have a DNA analysis performed on Mildred's blood?''

Ardley nodded. ''Already ordered it. Will take a few days. I'll get a sample from Mr. Esterman when I get back to the station. That should settle his lineage. But I do suspect Mr. Esterman would not have raised the issue of DNA if he wasn't confident she was his mother.''

''Yeah,'' Benny said, ''but kids kill their parents all the time for money. Young kids and old kids. And what is this guy—an auto mechanic. Can't have a lot of bucks put away. He probably tracked his mother down to get whatever money she had.''

''Darling man, you are so suspicious of everyone,'' Caroline said.

''Well, it's just too damn much a coincidence, him showing up and her getting killed. I don't believe in coincidences.''

''Well,'' Ardley conceded, ''you are right about the motive. He's the only one in the picture so far that has a good motive. And you may be right about him arranging this with someone else. But, my investigation has only started. I'm sure there are suspects in the wings just waiting to be discovered. It is interesting to see what comes out of the woodwork once the police start asking questions and investigating a person's life.''

Walter said, ''As to this newly discovered son, I believe the real question is: Can he make a claim on her estate? She undoubtedly has a will, which may have directed her assets to someone else. In fact, if he is mentioned at all in the will, then he has no grounds to contest its distribution formula.''

''Good point, Doctor,'' Ardley said. He was glad he had sat with these people. With only a few hours sleep, his mind had yet to get into full gear. What he had settled on doing was simply gathering information. He would do his thinking later when he got back to the station. But these people had done much of his thinking for him, and had given him a jump on what he had to do next. ''After I finish interviewing the rest of the people here, I guess the next person to see is Ms. Cummings.''

''She's around somewhere,'' Benny said. ''I saw her when I came in.''

And she's probably in a lousy mood, Ardley thought. He stood. ''If you people should remember anything that may be useful, please contact me. Thanks for your time.'' He walked away and sat at the next table of people.

''That poor man looks so terribly tired,'' Caroline said sympathetically.

''Yeah,'' Benny said, ''and his workday is just starting.''

Caroline shook her head sadly. ''No man should be burdened with such gruesome work.''

It was well after nine when Jessie Cummings found them sitting out by the swimming pool. The morning was cool and pleasant, with a soft breeze to stir the fronds on the palm trees. None of this was able to dispel the dark feelings surrounding them by Mildred's death. Peter saw Jessie coming and thought that she looked terribly in need of sleep.

What Jessie needed more desperately than sleep was a vacation. She was tired of dealing with all this death and the problems that came with it. She'd been on the phone to Jacobson, who stopped just short of blaming her for the murders that were going to ruin his business. Next was to fend off the press, getting the police to help her keep the newspeople at bay, and out of the Home. All she needed was to have the residents hounded by frantic reporters, getting them all worked up and worried, it would be enough to give a few residents a stroke. Then she had had Mildred's room secured, checked Mildred's file and contacted the lawyer listed there. There was no next of kin or other contact person in Mildred's file. She asked the lawyer about funeral arrangements. He called her back and gave her the name of the funeral home that would be coming for the body, once the police released it. The body was to be shipped north to be buried next to her husband. Then he mentioned Benny.

"Benny," Jessie said, "I just got off the phone with Mildred's lawyer. He wants to see you as soon as you can get there."

Benny gave her a questioning look. "Me? Why?"

"He told me you are the executor of Mildred's estate. He wants to confer with you about it."

"You're the executor?" Caroline said, a little jealousy creeping into her tone.

"Yeah, that's right," Benny said. "I forgot all about it. Mildred asked me, God, must be years ago. She didn't trust lawyers. Figured they'd churn the money out of her estate until there was nothing left for the people she wanted to give it to."

"But why, dear man, did she ask you?"

Benny shrugged. "Guess she thought I could be trusted. She didn't have anybody left in her family to ask."

"That still doesn't answer my question," Caroline said, frowning at Benny.

"Caroline, I must be the executor for a dozen people here in the Home. I know everybody here, and they trust me, I guess." Then he turned to Peter. "What do you say, Slick? I'd like it if you came along. You're as slick as any lawyer. And you know, me, I'll just get pissed and holler a lot."

Peter looked to Eleanor.

She nodded. "Go ahead. I think he needs you there."

"Okay," he said, but he couldn't imagine a situation where Benny would ever need help.

They went in Benny's car. This time Benny drove. Fortunately, Benny's day vision and his reflexes were good, and Peter relaxed in the passenger's seat. It was after ten when they found the lawyer's office and pulled into the parking space near the front door of the building.

"Do you know this lawyer, Carter Collins?" Peter asked.

"Nope. Never met him. Have no idea what he's like."

They got out of the car and went inside. The waiting area was small but elegantly modern. Behind the reception desk sat a perky little girl who appeared to be no more than fourteen. She looked up when they came in.

"Can I help you?" she said. No smile. Totally disinterested.

"My name is Benny Ashe. Mr. Collins is expecting me."

"If you will have a seat, I'll tell him you're here." She recited this like a machine, and returned to working on the papers on her desk.

Benny remained standing at the desk watching the girl. After a few moments, she looked up again.

"Is there something else?" An edge of annoyance beneath the tone.

"No. I'm just waiting for you to tell him I'm here."

She gave Benny a look that was supposed to freeze him solid. "I *said* I would tell him you're here."

"Look, lady." Benny's temper was becoming visible, and Peter began to worry. "Collins called me down here. Said he wanted to see me as soon as possible. Now, my time is as important as his, and I got no intention of sitting here cooling my heels while he's chasing his secretary around the desk and you're working on your math homework. If you don't tell him now that I'm here, I'm going to walk in there and tell him myself."

She looked at him a long time. Peter figured she was trying to decide what to do with Benny. Then, she picked up the phone and pressed a button. "What did you say your name was?"

"Besides being rude you got a bad memory. Benny Ashe."

Her eyes blazing now on Benny, she said into the phone,

"Mr. Benny Ashe is here." There was a pause as she listened. "Yes," she said and hung up the phone.

She took a deep breath, and said unemotionally, "Go through the door." She nodded at the door next to the reception desk. "And it's the first door on the left." Then she looked down and began working on the papers on the desk in front of her.

Benny gave Peter a knowing grin, and together they went through the door. "I hate people like that," Benny said. "She'da had us cooling our heels until she felt like getting off her ass." They went into the first office on the left.

The man behind the desk was dapper in a fastidious way. He seemed excessively neat and polished, his suit without a wrinkle, his dark hair combed flat. His office was a reflection of him, neat to the point that it appeared to be unused. The man stood when they entered the room, smiled, leaned across the desk, and extended a hand to Peter. "Mr. Ashe, I'm happy to meet you."

"This is Mr. Ashe," Peter said, pointing to Benny in his NY baseball cap. Peter watched the sudden surprise on Collins's face as it was replaced quickly by the same smile he had offered Peter.

"Mr. Ashe." He extended his hand to Benny.

Benny shook the man's hand.

"And I am Peter Benington," Peter said, and extended his hand. "I'm a friend of Mr. Ashe. He asked me to come along."

"Well," Carter Collins said, shaking Peter's hand, "you are welcome here if Mr. Ashe has requested it."

Then they all sat down.

"So, what do you need to talk to me about?" Benny asked.

"Ms. Cummings at Coral Sands telephoned me this morning with the sad news of Mildred Perkins's death. I extracted her file and saw that you are the executor of her estate." He reached for the only file folder on his desk, brought it in front of him, and flipped it open. "As executor you must approve of all expenses charged to the estate. Her will has some instructions that you should be made familiar with. When I saw this, I immediately telephoned Ms. Cummings and asked her to have you come see me so we can straighten out expenses and procedures before they become a problem. At such sad times emotions can run high and create problems that could be averted with a little up-front communication.''

"Before we go any further,'' Benny said, "I gotta see your fee schedule for handling the estate settlement.''

Peter looked at Benny. The man never ceased to surprise him.

Carter Collins took a hard look at Benny. "Yes. Certainly.'' He reached over and punched a button on the telephone. "Kathy, bring in the papers to sign for estate settlement.''

"Who do you want them made out for?'' The receptionist's voice came out of a microphone in the phone.

"Bring in a set of blanks. We'll take it from there.''

"Okay.''

He pressed the button again, turning off the communication. To Benny, "You'll find my fees are competitive and I have an excellent reputation for handling the settlement of estates.''

Benny nodded. "You know I gotta protect the assets of the estate.''

"Yes,'' Carter Collins said.

The telephone buzzed, and Collins pressed the red button. The receptionist said, annoyed, "Mr. Collins there's a policeman coming into your office.''

Before Collins had a chance to react, Detective Ardley came through the door.

"Well, well, well,'' he said to Benny and Peter. "Seems you guys are everywhere. With the three of us after him, Esterman doesn't stand a chance.''

"We got a right to be here,'' Benny said.

"Yeah, yeah. Ms. Cummings told me.'' Ardley pulled out his badge and flashed it at Collins. "Detective Ralph Ardley of the Sarasota Police. I'm here to talk to you and these gentlemen about Mildred Perkins's will.'' Then to Benny, "So, what did you find out?''

"We weren't here for that,'' Benny said. "But now that you mention it''—he turned to Collins—"tell me about Mildred's will.''

"That was what I was trying to do, Mr. Ashe,'' Collins said indignantly. He picked up a set of papers from the open folder, but looked at Benny when he spoke. "Mildred Perkins specified in her will, that an attempt must be made to locate her children. That will entail the expense of contracting with a private investigator, and . . ."

"Children!" Benny, Peter, and Ardley said it at the same time.

"Why, yes," Collins said. "And such a search can be expensive. That is what I wished to talk to you about, Mr. Ashe."

"What children?" Ardley said.

Carter Collins referred to the papers in his hand. "It says here that 'a reasonable effort must be made to locate my two boys.' " He looked up from the papers. "This normally would be privileged information if she were alive, but it appears that Mildred Perkins abandoned her twin sons when they were . . ."

"Twins!" Again Ardley, Peter, and Benny spoke at the same time.

"Shit," Benny said, "there are two of them."

CHAPTER 14

"So, this other twin, Paul, killed her," Benny said. Ardley, Peter, and Benny were outside the lawyer's office standing by Benny's car.

"Easy, Mr. Ashe." Ardley's tone was controlled patience. "I know the emotions that surround a death can be very heated, but it is wrong to jump to such conclusions and make accusations without foundation."

"Well, I think that Esterman guy is a bum." Benny was angry, and it showed in his face and his tone of voice. "There's something very fishy about him, and I think he killed Mildred. He or his damn twin. God, two bums."

"I'm not fond of Mr. Esterman, but until I have proof that he's involved in this killing, there is nothing I can do. And there is nothing that you should do. I don't want you stirring up trouble for yourself. You leave this investigation to the police."

Peter just listened and watched the two men. There wasn't anything he could add to what Benny had said, nor contradict anything Ardley had said. But he had his own ideas on what they should or shouldn't do, and they pretty much concurred with Ardley's view—stay out of it.

"You gonna hold him until you can investigate all this stuff?" Benny said, more as a challenge than a question.

"I can only hold him twenty-four hours. It's all the law allows. Hopefully, by this afternoon I'll have something from Georgia telling me he's a wanted man. Then I can hold him indefinitely. Otherwise, he's on the street this evening."

Ardley saw the angry look in Benny's eyes. ''He'll be on the street, but not out of sight. I'll have someone watching him all the time. And I don't want you going near him. Don't make me lock you up for doing something stupid. We all want to find Mildred Perkins's killer, but nobody else should be hurt while we're finding him.'' Benny stood there and said nothing while Ardley talked. Ardley could see the man was not really listening, but was feeding off his own anger. Ardley added power to his voice, and frowned hard at Benny. ''Do you understand what I'm saying! I don't want to have to lock your ass up! But you screw around, and I will!''

''Yeah. I gotcha,'' Benny said reluctantly. ''But . . .''

''No 'buts.' Stay out of it.''

It was time for Peter to jump in before Benny talked himself into trouble. ''So, how do you go about finding out who did this?''

''I got a picture of Mildred Perkins from Ms. Cummings. We'll have men with copies of that picture going around to all the places she might have been last night. We find someone who saw her, we may find someone who saw who she was with. That's the start. Meanwhile we go looking for the other Mr. Esterman. When we find him, we ask him where he was last night.''

''Are your men going to have George Esterman's picture with them as well as Mildred's?''

''Yes,'' Ardley said. ''Now I suggest you two go home and enjoy your retirement and leave the police work to me.''

Peter dragged Benny away, and they drove home in silence with Benny stewing in his own anger.

When they arrived at Coral Sands, Petersen—as Henny Youngman—was entertaining Eleanor, Caroline, and Betty in the coffee alcove. Peter and Benny walked over to join them.

''A tourist saw a loafer leaning against a post and said to him, 'Why don't you get a job, save your money, then invest your money? Then when you become rich you won't have to work anymore.' 'Why should I go through all that trouble? I'm not working now.'

''Americans are getting stronger. Twenty years ago it took two people to carry twenty dollars worth of groceries. Today a five-year-old can do it.

"A priest is sent to Alaska to start a new parish. He is there a whole year and nobody hears from him. A bishop goes to investigate. He asks the priest, 'How do you like it here in Alaska?' The priest says, 'If it weren't for my rosary and two martinis a day, you could keep Alaska. Bishop would you like a martini?' The bishop nods, and the priest hollers, 'Rosary, get the bishop a martini!' "

As they sat down with the women, Benny was laughing uncontrollably, which made the women laugh all the more. Eleanor made room for Peter next to her and he sat down. She smiled and put her arm in his.

Henny Youngman continued, "Betcha you can't tell me why they call the English language 'the mother tongue?' It's because father never gets a chance to use it."

"How did it go?" Eleanor whispered.

"Not so good," Peter said in a low voice. He indicated Petersen with a glance. "What we really need is Sherlock Holmes, not Henny Youngman."

Suddenly, Petersen stopped talking, and stood straighter. Peter, shocked, swore the man changed physically somehow. Petersen stepped over and sat in a chair opposite Peter. Everyone stopped laughing, and stared at Petersen.

"What can I do for you, Mr. Benington?" Petersen said.

Peter didn't know what to say. He didn't know what was going on.

Petersen put a slight tilt to his head. "You said you needed my help, and here I am."

"Is that you, Mr. Holmes?" Eleanor asked.

Petersen nodded deferentially.

Eleanor turned to Peter. "Well, tell him how he can help."

Peter looked at Eleanor as if she were crazy.

Eleanor prodded him with her elbow. "Go on. Tell him," she insisted. When Peter hesitated she said, "You asked for his help. Now tell him, for God's sake."

She was serious! Peter couldn't believe it. He didn't know what she was up to, and he didn't want to embarrass her or Petersen by arguing with her there in front of everyone. But they were going to have to talk later. Peter looked at Petersen who sat there quietly waiting for Peter to speak. He looked back at Eleanor. She, too, was waiting for Peter to speak. He saw no other way out of this, and turned back to Petersen.

"You know about the deaths that have occurred here?" Peter asked. He felt like an idiot talking like this to Petersen.

"I have not lived in isolation, Mr. Benington. But tell it to me as if I know nothing of it. Your own views may reveal things to me I have not seen myself."

Peter looked at Eleanor, who nodded at him to continue. So, Peter took a deep breath and told Sherlock Holmes the whole story about the deaths of Yamaguchi and the private investigator and Mildred. He also told him about the sudden return of Mildred's abandoned twin sons. When Peter finished, Sherlock Holmes sat back in the chair.

"You realize that I can not get involved unless the police request my assistance?"

Peter nodded, and listened intently.

"I will, of necessity, require some time to contemplate all you have told me. But, rest assured, I will employ my utmost effort in solving this mystery." Petersen stood. "I will call on you in due time."

"Thank you, Mr. Holmes."

Petersen nodded to everyone, turned, and left them.

Peter needed a drink. He had just participated in the most bizarre conversation of his life—talking to Sherlock Holmes, for chrissake. God, what was happening to his mind? At one point he actually felt he *was* talking to Sherlock Holmes instead of poor delusional Petersen. Worse, Peter had gone along with the conversation. He'd been at Coral Sands hardly two months and he was getting as crazy as the rest of the residents.

That evening they were at dinner in the dining room. Charlie and Alice were at the table along with Eleanor, Peter, Walter, and Betty. Benny and Caroline had left earlier to have dinner alone somewhere. In the middle of dinner, Shirley called Peter away to the phone.

"Yes?" Peter said.

"This is Detective Ardley, Mr. Benington." To Peter the man sounded weary. Peter checked his watch—6:10 P.M. Detective Ardley has had a long day.

"What can I do for you?"

"I just want you to know I had to release George Esterman. Nothing came down from Georgia."

"Did you locate his brother Paul?"

"Not yet. What I want you to do is keep a reign on Mr. Ashe. He's not the type to take no for an answer."

"I'll do my best," Peter said, but he knew Benny wasn't going to like this. "And thanks for your concern."

"Have a good night, Mr. Benington."

"You, too."

Peter hung up the phone. The longer he could keep this news from Benny, the better it would be. Peter didn't understand why Benny was so unreasonably hung up on George Esterman being responsible for Mildred's death. Peter sighed. Benny would probably stay the night at Caroline's, so hopefully he could keep this from him until morning.

A sudden crash and a chaos of screams and shouting came from the dining room. Peter, followed by Shirley rushed back to the dining room. Alice came running out to meet them.

"Call 911! Charlie's had a heart attack!"

Shirley turned right around and ran back to the phone. Peter went back into the dining room with Alice.

"The damnedest thing," Alice said to Peter. Her voice was shaky, nervous. "We were joking and laughing, and suddenly Charlie broke out in a sweat and fell off the chair just like that."

When they got back to the dining room, there was a small crowd clustered around Charlie, who was lying on the floor. Walter was seated on the floor next to Charlie. Betty was standing a little ways off, her hands to her mouth, her eyes wide. Everyone else remained at their tables, stunned, looking at each other, not sure what they should do. Peter and Alice pushed through to Walter and Charlie.

"How is he?" Peter said.

"Holding on." Walter did not look up. Walter spoke in a soft, easy tone.

Charlie was sweating badly, and his breathing was labored, as if he couldn't get enough air.

"Is there anything I can do?" Peter wanted to help somehow.

"Everything is under control." To Charlie, "Just relax. We're right here with you."

Eleanor came back from somewhere with a cold, wet cloth and handed it to Walter. Walter gently swabbed it over Charlie's forehead and face.

"That feels good. I don't know what hit me." Charlie's voice was hoarse. "Felt funny in the chest and started sweating. Next thing I'm on the floor."

"Sometimes it happens like that," Walter said. "You're having a heart attack. Not a serious one, but one just the same."

Peter wondered when a heart attack was *not* serious.

"Heart attack. That must be what this awful pain is in my chest." Charlie put his hand over his breast pocket.

"No," Walter said. "That's where I hit you."

"Hit me?"

"Well, your heart needed a little coaxing to get back its beat."

"Jesus, you sure must've hit me hard."

"Hard is what it takes, but it's all right now. The important thing to do is relax. Everything will be all right as long as you stay calm and lie here until help arrives."

"Stay calm, he says." Charlie chuckled in a hoarse whisper. "That's not easy lying here looking up at all your faces looking at me."

"It isn't often one gets such attention," Walter grinned.

"Got the darnedest luck. I didn't even get to eat my apple pie," Charlie smiled.

Walter smiled. "I'll have the waiter save it for you. Wouldn't want you to go without the pie."

"Having trouble getting enough air."

"Don't worry, you're getting enough. It's just that your blood pressure is a little confused right now. Relaxing will give it a chance to straighten out."

"Okay. I'll try to relax." He grinned. "You gonna stay here on the floor with me?"

Walter laughed softly. "I have to. With my bum leg I can't get up without help."

Charlie smiled. "Maybe we should start a card game while we're waiting? Everybody's here."

Walter chuckled. ''With the way you play? I don't think that's advisable. You're blood pressure would really give you trouble.''

Charlie laughed softly. ''Maybe you're right.''

Peter turned at the sudden movement to his right and saw Betty rushing from the dining room, her hands still over her mouth. Then Peter felt Eleanor next to him, her arm slipping around his. He looked in her eyes and knew what she was thinking. Peter was sure it was the same thing he was thinking—the same thought that was on the mind of everyone in the dining room. Time was catching up, and each person knew that it could be them on the floor.

The ambulance arrived a few minutes later. Shirley came into the dining room with two paramedics, who immediately rushed to Charlie's side and began working on him. Peter helped Walter to his feet and out of the way of the paramedics.

''We'll see you at the hospital,'' Walter said to Charlie. ''Just relax. These people know what they're doing.''

''Don't forget my apple pie.'' Charlie grinned.

Walter smiled and nodded. ''Not to worry.''

One of the paramedics was an attractive young woman. Walter, still looking at Charlie, nodded in her direction. ''And you keep your hands off that woman.''

Charlie glanced in her direction and chuckled, then gave Walter a look of wide-eyed appreciation. ''My blood pressure is already getting erratic.''

Walter laughed.

Within a few minutes the paramedics had Charlie on a stretcher and were wheeling him out of the dining room. Everyone watched in silence. They were seeing themselves one day.

Eleanor rolled over on her side to face Peter. She could just make out his features in the soft orange glow from the night-light plugged into the wall socket. ''If you don't get to sleep, I'm going to go back to my room and my own bed,'' Eleanor said. ''Tomorrow's Betty's hearing and I'm supposed to testify. I need my rest.''

''Sorry,'' Peter mumbled. He was lying on his back staring at the ceiling. ''The mind refuses to shut down. So much going on here. In two months there have been seven people killed, Betty is going on trial for incompetence, and Charlie just had a heart attack. God, I can not believe this is the peaceful retirement everyone dreams about."

"You want peaceful, you get a cabin in the mountains, or a deserted island in the tropics. Otherwise, you're still part of the world, and the world is not peaceful."

"Maybe that's what Betty should have done." Peter was half joking.

"I don't think it would have helped. Greedy families have a way of finding your money wherever you are."

Peter nodded at the truth of that. "Does it ever quiet down around here?"

"Yes. But as Murphy once said, 'If you're feeling good, don't worry. You'll get over it.' "

He grunted a laugh. "So right. I guess there is always something coming just around the corner."

"Besides"—she smiled and sidled close to him—"you'd get pretty bored with peaceful all the time."

He turned to look in her eyes, and smiled warmly. "Being in the world has certain advantages." He reached over to her.

CHAPTER 15

It was a little past nine the next morning when they got in Benny's car and started for the courthouse. Besides Benny, who was driving, there was Betty, Eleanor, and Peter. Walter had headed to the hospital to see Charlie, and would show up at the courthouse later. Peter was in the front seat next to Benny.

Peter noticed that Betty was exceptionally excited, but in a pleasant and positive way. He wondered what happened to change her mood. Betty was wearing a dress of a silky material that was predominantly blue with a tiny irregular pattern in light blue, a plain gold chain hung from around her neck.

''Charlie is going to be all right,'' Betty smiled. ''Eugene said he would recover fully.''

So, that's what it was, Peter thought, she'd been hearing good things from Eugene. Eleanor looked absolutely gorgeous in a tan skirt, a blouse of muted pastels, and a tan scarf around her neck attached to her blouse by a gold pin in the shape of a bird. Her hair was styled expertly and she wore small hoop earrings in gold. Her eyes were hidden behind sunglasses with soft brown lenses. Even Benny had dressed for the occasion in a blue silk shirt and tan slacks, and he had left his NY baseball cap at home. Peter looked at them all and thought that they didn't look like a group prepared to do battle, but more like they were going to dinner.

''Did Eugene happen to mention how things were going to go today?'' Benny asked. The car behind them honked, and

Benny looked back. A young woman behind the wheel smiled and waved at him. He had no idea who she was.

"Oh, yes. Things will be just fine."

"That's it?" Benny said. "No clue what to do? Just everything'll be peachy?"

"He said to trust in my friends." She took on a happy glow when she said that. "And I do."

"That's what friends are for," Eleanor said.

"Oh boy," Benny groaned. He glanced at Peter and rolled his eyes. "All the pressure's on us." There was more honking from the car in the back. Benny looked over his shoulder. It was a different car with a couple of young men laughing.

Peter smiled at Benny's remark, but he desperately wished Benny would keep his eyes on the road.

The car behind bolted into the left lane and pulled up parallel with them. It was a small pickup truck with oversized wheels. The guy in the passenger's seat was hanging out the window. He was shirtless and tattooed and his long blond hair was blowing madly in the wind. He was laughing and pointing at the rear of Benny's car. He gave Benny a thumbs-up, then he turned and said something to the driver, who was also laughing. The pickup sped away.

Benny frowned. "The loonies are out today," he said more to himself.

"Don't worry," Betty said. "Eugene is never wrong."

Well, Peter *was* worried for Betty's sake. If she came out of this hearing all right, he felt it would be nothing less than magic.

"Eugene didn't happen to mention anything about Mildred's murder?" Peter said.

"Yes he did," Betty said. "But I don't know what it meant."

"Lay it on us," Benny said, again glancing at Peter and rolling his eyes.

"Well, he said the detective would solve it with horns. Something like that. I don't remember exactly. But I felt better that her murderer won't get away with it."

Benny giggled. "Do they have booze where Eugene is? Sounds like he's on the sauce." Then Benny said to Peter, "You know what's gonna fry my ass? As her executor I'm gonna have to give them sleazy twins her money.''

Peter nodded. ''I do not envy you.''

They stopped for a red light. There was more honking from the back of them. This time when Benny looked around, there was an old couple behind in a car as big as Benny's. They were smiling at him.

''What the hell is going on?'' Benny was annoyed.

''Something wrong with your car?'' Eleanor said.

''I don't know.''

The light changed. Benny drove the car through the intersection, and pulled it to the curb. He opened the door, got out, and walked to the back. The rest watched him from inside the car. As soon as Benny reached the rear of the car, he started laughing. Then he reached down, out of sight. When he stood upright he had what looked like a bumper sticker in his hand. Still laughing he came back into the car.

''The Mad Joker's been at it again,'' he said, chuckling. He held the bumper sticker up for everyone to see. ''This was taped to the bumper.''

It read HONK IF YOU LIKE PEACE AND QUIET.

They pulled into the parking lot across from the courthouse. The courthouse sat on the corner property and dominated the area.

''That's it?'' Peter said.

''Yep,'' Benny said as they got out of the car. ''Built in 1927 when they had the land boom down here in Florida, and Ringling was settled in Sarasota with his circus.''

It didn't have that look of authority found in most courthouses. Peter speculated that John Ringling had had a hand in its design. A U-shaped white building, two stories high, with wrought-iron balconies and barrel-tiled roof in earth tones. There was a large ornate belltower in the center that gave it a Spanish Mission look. Too pretty a structure to house the machinations of the law.

They walked across the street and tentatively entered the front doors of the courthouse. Inside was a sharp contrast to outside. It was gray and dreary with black and gray terrazzo squares on the floor, dark wood doors, and wrought-iron lanterns hanging from a vaulted ceiling. There was a small hall that led to a small rotunda with a ceiling that vaulted two stories. There they found Bill Fresno sitting on a dark wood bench. He got up, and walked up to them.

"Good morning. Everybody ready for this?" He seemed more composed and neater than they had seen him in his office. He had a leather briefcase that was stuffed to overflowing with papers.

"I'm ready," Betty said cheerfully.

"Yes," Peter said. "I guess we are ready to face this today."

"Okay. Just one thing."

They all looked at him.

"Don't volunteer information. Just answer my questions, and the other attorney's questions as briefly and directly as you can. If you go off on your own, you may say something that will jeopardize the case. Understand?"

Peter and the others dutifully nodded.

"I don't think the hearing will go on too long. We've got Judge Maria Jackson, and she's not one to waste time. Which may be to our advantage."

Peter heard him, but didn't see how someone quick to judgment would be an advantage.

Then to Betty. "We'll be all sitting on one side of the courtroom. Your son and his attorney will be on the other side. Do not say anything, or even acknowledge his presence. This is a time to keep your cool."

Betty nodded.

"Okay. Let's go. It's almost ten, and the judge should be coming in soon."

Bill Fresno smiled at Betty and offered his arm. "Don't worry. We'll slay the dragons."

Betty took his arm. "Eugene told me there was nothing to worry about. Everything would be all right."

They walked ahead, Eleanor holding Peter's arm followed along with Benny. They all went down a few steps into a hall that looked more like a basement. There a guard stood before the arch of a metal detector which they had to pass through. Beyond the metal detector were elevators. Once in an elevator, Bill Fresno pressed the button marked two, the elevator doors closed, and they rose slowly to the second floor.

They stepped off the elevator. The hall there was equally gray and dreary. Bill Fresno opened a large wood door and escorted Betty into the courtroom. The courtroom was a welcomed contrast to the halls. Warm wood covered the walls, and made up the tables, chairs, and the judge's bench. For all its warmth there was the sense of authority in the room, which made one feel it necessary to speak in whispers.

There were two tables beyond the railing separating the spectators from the judge's bench and the tables set before the bench. There were people already seated at the table on the left. Fresno signaled Peter, Eleanor, and Benny to sit in the first row of spectator chairs along the railing. Then he guided Betty to the long table to the right beyond the railing, and they sat down. He hoisted his heavy briefcase onto the table, and started removing some papers and folders.

After they had seated themselves, Peter looked over at the opposition. Besides a tall, intense man who, by the papers in front of him, Peter assumed was an attorney, there was a slender man with thinning gray hair and skin that was very white and mottled with a red rash. Looking at the man, Peter realized he didn't know his name.

He turned to Eleanor and whispered, "What is the name of Betty's son?"

"Andrew," she whispered back.

A court recorder came in from the rear of the courtroom, went through the railing and sat before the judge's bench. She set up her recorder and waited.

Moments later a bailiff came through a door in the far wall, followed by an imposing black woman in a black judge's robe.

"All rise," the bailiff said.

Even as they got to their feet, the Honorable Maria Jackson had already reached the bench and waved them to be seated, then seated herself.

"Is everyone present?" Judge Jackson said, in a voice that was powerful and confident.

They agreed that everyone was there.

"For the record, and with the court's approval, William Fresno is the attorney representing Elizabeth Jablonski.

"This hearing is to determine to what extent Elizabeth Jablonski is able to handle her own affairs. I have before me, as do both counsels, a report from the committee appointed by the court to examine Elizabeth Jablonski. In the opinion of that committee, she is not capable of complete rational awareness and should not be trusted to manage her own affairs.

"I also have in front of me a petition from Mr. Fresno in contradiction to the findings of the committee. Included in that petition is a psychiatric report finding Elizabeth Jablonski to be mentally sound and completely rational.

"This puts the court in the position of establishing support for the findings of the committee. In that regard I will hear further testimony from both sides before I render a decision."

"Your Honor?" It was Andrew Jablonski's lawyer who stood up.

"Yes, Mr. Attenboro?"

"I am dismayed that the court would give credence to Mr. Fresno's petition, in light of the findings of the committee appointed by the court."

"I'm sorry to hear that you are upset, Mr. Attenboro. However the court's duty is to seek the truth here, and that is what I intend to do."

"Yes, your Honor." Attenboro, unhappy, sat down.

Judge Jackson turned to Bill Fresno. "I understand, Mr. Fresno, that you have some witnesses you would have testify on behalf of Mrs. Jablonski?"

"Yes, your Honor."

"Not too many, I hope?"

"Just three, your Honor. However, one of the witnesses is presently at the hospital visiting a friend who had a heart attack last night. I hope he will arrive shortly."

"I hope so, too, Mr. Fresno."

Bill Fresno turned to Eleanor and signaled her to come up to the witness stand. Eleanor stood, stepped up to the railing, opened the gate, strode confidently to the witness stand, and stood there.

"You may sit down," Judge Jackson said warmly. "This is a hearing. It is more relaxed than a trial. We don't swear you in. We assume you will be honest in your replies."

Eleanor sat down in the witness chair.

Bill Fresno stepped up before her.

"State your name for the record, please."

''Eleanor Carter.''

''And you are a resident of Coral Sands where Elizabeth Jablonski lives?''

''Yes.''

''How long have you know Elizabeth Jablonski?''

''A little more than three years.''

''Are you and she friends?''

''I consider myself her friend.''

''Have you, in all the years you've known Elizabeth Jablonski, seen her in a position where she was incapable of making sound decisions about herself and her life?''

''No.''

''No strange behavior?''

''No.''

So much for honest replies, thought Peter.

''As you perceive her, Elizabeth Jablonski is a normal adult in every way. Isn't that right?''

''Yes.''

''As a friend you would certainly be aware if she acted strangely, or exhibited tendencies in her behavior that would be obviously abnormal. Isn't that so?''

''Yes.''

''And you have witnessed none of those tendencies?''

''That is correct.''

''Have you ever seen Mr. Andrew Jablonski before?'' He pointed to the man with thinning gray hair and mottled skin sitting at the other table.

''Not that I remember.''

''In the three years you have known Elizabeth Jablonski you never once saw her son visit her?''

''Not that I recall.''

''Doesn't sound like a son interested in his mother's welfare, does it?''

''No.''

''Thank you, Mrs. Carter. You may step down.''

Eleanor was made to rise when Attenboro stood up. ''Excuse me, Mr. Fresno. But I would like to ask the witness a few questions.''

''Certainly.'' Bill Fresno went back to the table and sat down next to Betty.

Attenboro stepped before Eleanor. "Please don't be nervous."

"I'm not nervous."

"And please remember that we all have Elizabeth Jablonski's interest at heart."

Eleanor nodded.

"I have just two questions for you. Have you ever been with Elizabeth Jablonski when she gave money away?"

"Gave money away? I don't understand what you mean?"

"When she encountered a panhandler or two on the street and gave them money?"

"Well, yes. I was with her a few times when that happened."

"And how much did she give these beggars—a quarter, a half dollar?"

Eleanor hesitated. "Twenty dollars."

"Twenty dollars!"

"Each," Eleanor added.

"Each! Twenty dollars to each beggar she sees! You consider that rational behavior?"

"Well, I . . ."

Attenboro held up his hand and smiled. "You need not respond. It was a rhetorical question.

"Now my other question is this: Who is Eugene?"

Here it comes. Peter groaned. Poor Betty.

Eleanor looked to Fresno for help. He nodded his head.

"Betty's husband."

"By Betty, you mean Elizabeth Jablonski. Is that right?"

"Yes."

"Have you ever seen Eugene Jablonski?"

"No."

"And why do you think that is?"

"Because he died before I met Betty."

"Isn't that strange. I've heard that she talks to him frequently. That she always seeks his advice before she makes any decision. Have you heard that?"

"Yes."

"In other words she communicates with her dead husband. Is that right?"

"Yes."

Attenboro threw up his hands. "And you said before that she is normal in every way."

"Well, I . . ."

He cut her short with a wave of his hand, and shook his head. "That is all the questions I have for you," and walked away.

Bill Fresno stood. "I would like to hear what you were going to say, Mrs. Carter, before Mr. Attenboro cut you short."

"I would, too," Judge Jackson said.

"What I was going to say, is that Betty is not incompetent. She's just different. If she were a younger person, she would be called a psychic, not abnormal. When I was much younger, and a person claimed to be psychic they were looked at rather funny, and considered to have some loose things rolling around in their attic. Today they are not. And Betty is not abnormal, either. She cares for herself, dresses neatly, tends to her health needs, and is a good friend to many of us.

"That is all I have to say."

"Anything else for this witness, Mr. Fresno?" Judge Jackson asked.

"No, your Honor."

"Mr Attenboro?"

No questions, your Honor."

"You may step down, Mrs. Carter."

Eleanor stood, left the witness stand, and returned to sit next to Peter.

"Some loose things rolling around in their attic?" Peter whispered to Eleanor. "I love it."

"I think," Judge Jackson said, "that I would like to hear from Elizabeth Jablonski next, Mr. Fresno."

"Your Honor, I did have two other witnesses I would like to present first?"

"Let's hear from Mrs. Jablonski, now."

"Yes, your Honor." He turned to Betty and gently took her hand. Betty stood, and Fresno guided her over to the witness stand where she sat in the chair.

Judge Jackson leaned toward Betty. She spoke in a low gentle tone. "You are Elizabeth Jablonski?"

"Yes," Betty said, in her tiny voice.

"Are you aware of what is being decided today?"

"Yes. My son wants control of my money."

And that's the truth, Peter thought.

"What we are trying to decide today is whether you are capable of handling your own affairs. That does include your handling of money. You understand that?"

"Yes. Andrew is trying to say I am incompetent. But that's not true."

"Do you regularly give twenty dollars to beggars on the street?"

"Of course."

"Why do you think it is right to do that?"

"Have you ever begged for money on the street?"

Judge Jackson smiled. "No, I have not."

"Well, Eugene thinks that it is a terrible indignity to hold your hand out and ask for money. And then people give these poor souls a dime, a quarter. What can you buy with a dime or a quarter? Eugene told me to always give them twenty dollars, to show how serious you feel their trouble is. And that way they have enough money to buy food, or something to wear. It was his way of giving back to people some of his good fortune."

"I see." Judge Jackson nodded.

It was then that Eleanor stood up, leaned over the railing, and whispered something to Bill Fresno. He listened, then nodded encouragingly. Eleanor returned to her seat next to Peter.

"What was that all about?" Peter whispered.

"You'll see soon enough."

"You mentioned Eugene," Judge Jackson was saying to Betty. "Tell me about him."

"Please don't humor me," Betty said, annoyed.

Judge Jackson pulled back at Betty's remark.

"I know what everybody thinks," Betty continued. "What you want to know is do I talk to my dead husband? And the answer is yes."

Peter saw Attenboro and Andrew Jablonski exchange satisfied glances. Well, Peter thought, looks like they have the right to be satisfied now.

"But why is that so bad?" Betty was speaking directly to

Judge Jackson. "Isn't there supposed to be life after death? Don't you believe that?"

"We are not here to discuss what I believe, Mrs. Jablonski." Judge Jackson kept her tone even and soft.

"Well, I believe it. And Eugene is the proof. He talks to me every night. He tells me what to do. He advises me on what clothes I should buy." Betty smiled. "I don't want to wear anything he dislikes. I like to please him."

"Do you see him when he speaks to you?"

"Of course not." Betty said it as if it was the silliest thing she had ever heard. "I talk to him through the Ouija board." She shrugged. "It's slow. So we don't have much time to talk."

"You say he picks out your clothes?"

Betty nodded. "Actually, I pick them out. But if Eugene says he doesn't like them, I return them to the store."

"Are there things you do for which you do not ask Eugene's advice?"

Betty frowned in thought. "I can't think of anything."

"I see." Maria Jackson sat back in her chair, and turned her attention to Attenboro. "Mr. Attenboro, is there anything you would like to ask Mrs. Jablonski?"

"No, your Honor." He had a small grin on his face.

"Mr. Fresno?"

"I have one question. Betty, did you ask Eugene about these proceedings today?"

"Yes."

"What did he have to say?"

"He said that he didn't like what Andrew was doing. It was shameful. Love and family should come before money."

"Thank you, Betty." Then to the judge, "I don't have anything further to ask Mrs. Jablonski, your Honor. But I would like to ask for a delay, so that I might contact another witness."

"I have a very tight calendar, Mr. Fresno." Her tone was now official. "And I don't see the need to delay these proceedings for another witness. I think the court has heard enough to make a decision."

"Your Honor, please. Mrs. Jablonski's life, her freedom is at stake here. You are being asked to judge her because she is different. But humans, by nature are diverse. It would be a very boring world if we all thought and acted alike. It is diversity that enriches our lives with new discoveries, new philosophies, new attitudes. Einstein was criticized for his odd behavior. And by my standards, and many others, that was true. But my standards are not the only guidelines for living. Nor are the standards of Mrs. Jablonski's son. The woman is here today with friends who also feel her standards are different. But they accept them, as I feel the court should. Mrs. Jablonski does handle her own affairs successfully. She does pay her bills, and is not irrational in her lifestyle. She is not a danger to herself or to others. And, I'm sure that if Mrs. Jablonski did not possess a good deal of money, we would not be in this court today.''

''Are you through, Mr. Fresno?'' Judge Jackson's tone clearly said that he *was* through.

''All I'm asking is the court give me the opportunity to present one witness who I feel is important enough for the court to hear.''

A still silence settled heavily over the room as Judge Jackson looked hard at Bill Fresno. To Peter it seemed like minutes ticked by, but he was sure it was just a few moments. Then Judge Jackson signaled to the bailiff, who turned and went through the door behind him.

''I have a very busy calendar, Mr. Fresno. So I won't be able to give your witness much time.''

Peter saw Attenboro throw his hands up in frustration.

The bailiff returned with a black appointment book, and handed it to the judge.

''Thank you,'' she said to the bailiff. Then she began flipping through the pages. ''How much time do you need to bring your witness to the court, Mr. Fresno?''

''No more than a day.''

''Well, the best I can do for you, Mr. Fresno, is four days. I have an opening in my calendar for an hour this Friday at one o'clock. Is that sufficient?''

''Yes, your Honor,'' Bill Fresno said.

''And you, Mr. Attenboro and Mr. Jablonski? Is that all right? Can you return this Friday at one?''

Attenboro let out a long breath of exasperation. ''Yes, your Honor. We shall be here.''

''Then it is settled. We will return back here in this courtroom at one on Friday.'' She rose.

''All rise,'' the bailiff said.

Judge Maria Jackson was already through the door and gone before they stood up.

Bill Fresno turned to Eleanor. ''Eugene better be right.''

CHAPTER 16

The two men stood before the desk sergeant at the police station. To the sergeant they looked like bookends, identically dressed, identical fancy silver belt buckles and Western belts, the same haircut, the same big hands with ground-in dirt. No way to tell which one was which.

"We're here about our car," the one on the right said. "It's a damn rental, and we're paying for it while you guys are screwing around with it."

"We want to know what you're doing with it, and when we can get it back?" the left side said.

"You'll have to talk with Detective Ardley about that," the desk sergeant said. He looked young for his age, and his muscles fit tightly into his uniform.

"Then, kindly let us speak to this detective," left side said.

"He's not in his office at the moment."

"Well, where is the great detective?" right side said, sarcastically exaggerating the "great."

The sergeant wondered whether there was some agreement between them that each would take turns speaking.

"I'm expecting him shortly." Actually, Ardley was in the back at his desk. But he had asked the desk sergeant to stall the twins.

"Well, then, I guess we'll just wait here for the great detective," the left side said. The two men turned and took seats on one of the benches in the lobby area.

Ardley was talking on the phone to one of the technicians at the garage. "Nothing? No blood traces?"

"Nothing," the technician said. "Did find some semen stains, but they were very old. Probably from a former renter. We did vacuum up some fibers. Could come up with a match to her clothes. But that'd take a while."

"How long a time is that?"

"Couple days, a week, I guess. Other than that, the car is clean. If he did her in a car, it wasn't this one."

"Shit," Ardley said, and hung up the phone. He knew in his heart one of these guys killed Mildred Perkins But he couldn't find any evidence to point to them. His men had been all over the streets with the pictures and turned up nothing. "All old people look alike," one of the bartenders had said, when they showed him the pictures.

Ardley had their rental car impounded and all the techs he could find pored over it for the past two hours looking for anything he could use. They also tossed the apartment at the motel. Only the computer in the room linked them with Mildred Perkins. There was a small piece of notepaper taped to the monitor. On it was *FineLace*, Mildred Perkins's computer handle. All that showed was they were communicating with her, and they had admitted that. Actually, George Esterman had admitted that. Which was probably the only thing he told them the other day that was the truth. He had carefully given them the impression that he was alone, the only son. It worked long enough for the twin brother to kill her, that Ardley was as sure of as he had been sure of anything in his life. If Ardley had known there was a twin, he would have advised Peter to have Mildred Perkins watched. He's sure that would have saved her life.

He picked up the fax he had received that morning from Georgia, and looked at it again. Nothing there to give him an edge. There were a couple convictions for fraud in connection with the garage they owned. Bilking some people for repairs they never performed. Fines and suspended sentences. Nothing jail worthy.

The only hope Ardley had left was Mildred Perkins's car. They hadn't found it yet. What he suspected now was they killed her in her car, and then they had abandoned it. Find the car, and it should hold the evidence he needed to nail these guys.

He threw the fax on the desk. There were some days he really hated his job.

Martin Berrins, a large bony man, poked his head into Ardley's office. "Paulie, at the desk, says to tell you the Bobbsie Twins are still waiting on you."

"Thanks," Ardley said. He picked up the phone, and punched in two numbers.

"Sarasota Police Department," the voice said at the other end.

"Paulie, this is Ardley. Would you show my guests into the conference room? I'll be there in a minute."

The conference room was really one of the interrogation rooms. This one had slightly better furniture. When he entered the conference room, the two men were standing before the one-way mirror, smiling and making faces at their reflections. They turned to Ardley.

The one on the left smiled an insincere, greasy smile. "Just trying to give your boys on the other side of the glass a few laughs."

The one on the right said, "Detective, I want you to meet my brother, Paul."

"I'm not Paul! You are."

"No, you are."

Then they both gave Ardley a smile like a sneer. "Well what do you think, Detective? Which one of us is Paul and which is George?"

"You know, it really doesn't matter. All I have to do is nail one of you smartasses, and you both go. An accessory to a murder gets the same electric charge as the actual killer."

The smiles faded on the faces of the twins. "We came for our car. Are you through with it?" This from the one on the left.

"We're paying for that rental, and we can't get around this place without some transportation," the man on the right said.

"We got places to go, things to do," the left side said.

"Why didn't you tell me about your brother the other day when you were here?" Ardley directed his question to the man on the right.

The man on the left said, with a tone of artificial innocence, "Because I didn't want to create trouble for him. I love my brother."

The man on the right said in the same innocent tone, "And I figured you'd just harass him, like you were doing me. Didn't seem to make sense to do that to him."

Shit. Ardley's temper grew instantly hot. He hated to be toyed with by a couple of hick bastards. It took all his willpower to keep his temper under control. He took an invoice out of the folder he was carrying, scribbled his signature on it, and handed the invoice to the man on the right. "The car is in a garage on Fruitville. Show the guy that, and he'll release the car to you."

"Thank you, Detective," said the man on the left, in an exaggerated sweet tone.

"Yes, thank you, Detective." The man on the right smiled arrogantly.

They walked past him on either side. He turned and watched them leave the room. He knew he had better nail those guys or he was not going to be fun to live with for a long while. Well, all the avenues of investigation hadn't been exhausted yet. They hadn't found Mildred's car, and he was still waiting to hear from that private detective the twins had hired, William Robert Torrence. Might be some thread there to start pulling on. William Robert—Billy Bob. Figures, he grunted to himself.

When they were leaving the courtroom, they met Walter limping toward them and turned him around. Bill Fresno had questions for Betty and took her away in his car. The rest of them returned to Coral Sands. The mourners lunch buffet for Mildred was well under way. Whenever a resident died, Jessie Cummings arranged a luncheon. Not too many people who died in Florida had their funerals in Florida. There was a big business in shipping bodies "home," somewhere in the north, to be buried. So, the luncheon was a way all the residents could mourn the death, pay their respects, share memories of the deceased, and then put it behind them. Jessie had a caterer come in and set up the buffet table. A photograph of Mildred sat in the center of the table.

They had gathered food together from the buffet table, and were sitting at one of the tables in the dining room. Alice joined them in the dining room, and they briefed her on what had happened in court. She shook her head when they told her how bad it looked for Betty, about how the judge had seemed convinced and ready to make a decision, until Bill Fresno had talked the judge into a postponement.

"Damn. Poor Betty."

"The sad thing," Eleanor said, "is she's got such faith in Eugene that she didn't seem worried at all."

Peter looked at Eleanor. "So, are you going to tell us what you said to Betty's lawyer back there in the courtroom?"

"I didn't say anything important to the lawyer." Eleanor was insistent.

Benny shook his head. "Whatever it was, Bill Fresno jumped up and went into action."

"All right, all right." Eleanor surrendered. "All I said to the man, was he'd better do something quick, or Betty was lost."

"Then why did he turn to you and say that Eugene better be right?"

"I told him that Eugene said to delay this to another day and things would be all right."

"You lied to him?" Peter said.

"I couldn't think of anything else to do. Poor Betty was in serious trouble. I thought, maybe if things were postponed, the judge might have a change of heart. And maybe Mr. Fresno would have a chance to come up with something, now that he knew the way things were going in the court." She poked her fork into the potato salad on her plate. "Now, let's drop it. And don't tell Betty what I told the lawyer."

"Are you going to see Caroline today?" Walter asked.

"Yeah," Benny said. "I told her I'd call her when I got back from court. Didn't know how long we'd be there." Then he frowned at Walter. "Why?"

"I just think she's a charming lady, and I enjoy talking to her."

"Uh-oh." Alice laughed. "Better watch out for him, Benny."

"Hmm. Maybe, I better stop bringing her around."

Walter chuckled. "You need not worry, Benny. I am a man of honor. I would not attempt to move in on you."

It was then that Grace came into the dining room and walked over to their table.

"Benny, Jessie sent me to get you. There are a couple of guys want to go through Mildred's things."

"Jesus," Benny said, and stood up.

"You need company?" Peter said.

Benny nodded.

When Benny and Peter walked out of the dining room and into the lobby, they passed Petersen who was standing off to one side, looking intently at the twins across the lobby. He did not acknowledge Peter or Benny.

"Sherlock Holmes at work," Benny said to Peter, in a low voice.

"I wish he was the real Sherlock Holmes. We could sure use him," Peter whispered back.

The Esterman brothers were standing by the front desk with Jessie Cummings. She did not look happy.

"What's the problem?" Benny said, as he walked up to them.

"These gentlemen," Jessie said, "want to go through Mildred's things. They say they are her sons, and have a right to them."

"Ah, yes," the man on the left said. "You are the two gentlemen from the police station the other day."

"I'm, sorry," the man on the right said, "if I upset you then. I would have preferred this all to turn out differently."

"We didn't meet formally," the man on the left said. "I'm George Esterman." He stuck out his hand to Benny.

Benny made no move to take it.

"No, dang it," the man on the right said. "I'm George. You're Paul."

"I don't think so," the man on the left said. "But then I'm not sure."

They grinned at Benny and Peter.

"I don't care which one is which. Grace says you want to go through Mildred's stuff. No way."

"And what right do you have to stop us?" the man on the right said.

"I'm the executor of Mildred's will. I have the right."

"But we're her rightful heirs." The man on the left dropped the smile and toughened his tone. "We have a legal right to her possessions."

"I don't know who you are. You gotta prove that to somebody."

The man on the right looked Benny and Peter up and down. "You two *tough* guys gonna stop us here?" His voice was hard and mean. He stepped closer to Benny, and looked hard into Benny's eyes. He stood six inches over Benny's head. Benny didn't move an inch, nor did he flinch. Peter saw Benny's hands begin to curl. *God, he's going to fight them!* Peter thought.

"I'm sure the police will be glad to oblige you gentlemen," Peter said. Then he nodded at Jessie Cummings, who picked up the telephone and began to dial.

The two brothers looked at each other, and backed off.

"We will be back another day," the one on the left said.

"Guess, we'll get ourselves one of them fancy lawyers," the other one said.

"Be seein' you," they both said, with a smile that made Benny even angrier. Then they left Coral Sands.

"Damn." Benny's anger was clear to everyone there. "Those guys really get me pissed."

Peter laid a hand on Benny's shoulder. "Why don't you call Caroline and spend the afternoon relaxing with her. I think you should get your mind off this for awhile."

Peter returned to the dining room. To the questioning looks he said, "Benny's going over to Caroline's. The twins took off to get a lawyer."

"Benny's really uptight about this whole thing," Eleanor said. "I worry he'll have a stroke or a heart attack or something."

"Speaking of heart attacks," Peter said to Walter, "how's Charlie?"

"He'll survive," Walter said. "They were prepping him for surgery when I left."

"Surgery!" Eleanor exclaimed.

Walter nodded. "Bypass. They did an angiogram early this

morning. Three blocked arteries. They're going to operate on him this afternoon."

"From what I know," Alice said, "those operations are like an appendectomy. They knock'em out one, two, three."

Walter nodded. "The miracle of modern medical science."

"All this depressing stuff," Alice said. "Where's Henny Youngman when you need him?"

"We just saw him in the lobby. I think he's still in his Sherlock Holmes mode."

"That's no fun."

"Well," Peter said, "I hope he's good at it. Because it looks like the police are going to need some help solving these killings." Three killings, Peter thought, and shook his head.

Peter turned to Eleanor. "Would you care to accompany me for a stroll around the grounds?"

"Love to." Eleanor smiled.

"You will excuse us?" Peter said to Alice and Walter, who both nodded. Then he stood up and pulled Eleanor's chair out. She stood and together they walked toward the glass doors leading to the swimming pool area.

When they stepped outside the air hit them like a hot wall.

"Ooh. It is hot out here," Peter said.

"But very pretty." Eleanor sighed.

They strolled down toward the gazebo.

"Yes. Florida has more than its share of pretty days."

"I think people live longer in Florida because you don't have those terrible depressing periods of winter like you have in the North. Here people feel better just admiring the day."

"They live longer as long as they stay out of the line of fire." Peter grunted.

"I'm sure there are no more killings here than in other places in the country."

"By 'here' do you mean Coral Sands?"

Eleanor gave him a look.

As they approached the gazebo they saw that Tweedledee and Tweedledum were in their usual positions, sitting in the chairs and looking out over the lake.

Peter nodded in the direction of the two men and guided Eleanor closer to the gazebo.

Sailor Hat's T-shirt read: IF I'M NOT SUPPOSED TO EAT ANIMALS, WHY ARE THEY MADE OF MEAT?

"Who you gonna vote for?" Sailor Hat said.

"Miss Mississippi," Gray Hair said.

"I mean for President of the United States."

"Me, too."

"Maybe you're right. She can't do anymore harm than the politicians, and she's nicer to look at."

"Would her husband be called the First Man?"

"That title's been taken."

Peter and Eleanor walked away chuckling.

"I needed that." Peter grinned. "Those guys are always good for a laugh."

"Sometimes laughter *is* the best medicine." Eleanor smiled.

When Benny showed up at Ardley's desk, Ardley groaned. Benny had told Peter he was going to see Caroline, but he never mentioned he was going to stop at the police station first. Ardley could see the anger in the man. Ardley sighed and leaned forward, his hands clasped on the desk.

"What can I do for you, Mr. Ashe?" He said it with a patience developed from years of dealing with angry people.

"You can get those bums off the street." He spat the words out between gritted teeth.

"I'm doing everything I can, Mr. Ashe."

"What you ain't doing is putting those guys behind bars."

"I can not simply arrest people because I suspect them of a crime. It's not the way the system works." Although, Ardley thought, there were times when he wished it didn't work that way.

"How come you ain't out there digging up evidence, instead of sitting here with your feet on the desk?"

Ardley took a deep breath to quiet his own anger. "I have not stopped investigating, if that's what you're trying to say. We impounded the Estermans' car and went over it with a magnifying glass. Nothing. We took apart their motel room. Nothing. There was no trace evidence to suggest Mildred Perkins was ever in the car or the motel room. I can't even prove either one of them was with her that night."

There was too much anger and frustration building in

Ardley for him to hold it all back, and he snapped at Benny. "I've been going over the report from the P.I. they hired." He picked up two sheets of paper, and waved them at Benny. "Just got the damn fax from him. He tells me everything I don't want to hear. How the 'boys'—that's what he called them, do you believe it?—how the boys were looking for their mama. Wanting to find her and see if she was all right. And, here's the juicy part"—he looked down at the papers in his hand, and read from them—"and wanting to help her if they could. Take her in, provide for her"—he threw the papers on the desk—"and all that crap.

"I asked him if he had any suspicion, any at all, that the boys had any other intent in finding their mother." He picked up one of the papers and searched it, then pointed at it. "Here. He says that all he saw was goodness in their motives." He threw the paper back down on the desk, and threw himself back against the chair. "You believe that? Those guys don't show any goodness saying hello, for chrissake."

He looked at Benny, and realized he was taking his frustration out on the old man. "I'm sorry I lost my temper. But I'm doing the best I can. Now, believe me, if there's anything or anyone that can put one of those guys with Mildred that night, I'll throw them in jail quick as you can spit."

Benny said, "You gotta do something quick. Those guys are gonna get a lawyer and push to get at Mildred's money. It's gonna give me a stroke to turn over her money to them."

Ardley nodded, and sighed. "I know. I won't be nice to be with, either, if that happens. I do this job because I want to put bastards like those guys away. Get them off the streets and out of the faces of good people. I let them get away with this, how am I going to look my wife in the eye?"

Ardley rubbed his hand over his face, trying to rub away the frustration he felt. "Look, Mr. Ashe. Go home. I'm doing my job the best I can. You trust in that. It's the best I have to offer."

Benny nodded. "Okay." But he didn't feel okay. If the cops couldn't stop them, then somehow he would stop them.

CHAPTER 17

"I'm worried about Benny," Peter said. He and Eleanor were stretched out in lounge chairs by the swimming pool. The sun was going down, and the sky was filled with smears and clusters of the garish colors of a Florida sunset. There was a soft breeze, and the fronds of the palm trees were whispering restfully. Peter and Eleanor had been there for close to an hour. Peter felt he could sit there forever. So nice, restful. It would have been perfect except Peter could not get out of his head the image of Benny ready to hit one of the twins at the front desk.

"Benny can take care of himself," Eleanor said in a lazy voice. Her eyes were closed and she was relishing the soft wind on her face.

"He has a problem with his anger."

Eleanor chuckled. "Yes, he does. And he's managed to live with it all those years."

"You weren't there when he confronted those twins at the front desk. I am sure he was about to resort to his fists."

"Well, he didn't, did he?"

"No. But he is furious about having to give the twins Mildred's money. I'm afraid he might do something rash."

"Like what?"

"I don't know. I like Benny, and I wouldn't want to see him in any trouble over this."

"Life's not fair."

"Yes. And sometimes it is difficult to accept unfair situations that do not go your way."

They sat in silence for awhile, then Eleanor said, ''What do you think we should do?''

''I don't know that, either. But I feel we should do something.''

They settled quietly into their own thoughts. The sky grew steadily darker, and the colors of the clouds in the sky shifted to soft tones going to gray. The world seemed to get quiet around sunset.

''Stay close to him,'' Eleanor said. ''Maybe stop him before he does anything crazy.''

''Yes. That is all I could come up with, too.''

''I stopped off at the hospital first thing before breakfast, and Charlie's still in intensive care,'' Walter said. It was the next morning and they were all seated in the dining room at breakfast. Benny had brought Caroline, and Peter noticed Benny appeared to be in a very good mood.

''Is there a problem?'' Alice said.

''Well, it seems Charlie's high blood pressure could create some problems right after such an operation. The doctor decided another day hooked up to the machinery of modern medicine would be best.'' Then Walter grunted. ''More a formality brought on to cover his ass against litigation.''

''Is he conscious?'' Eleanor asked.

Walter shrugged. ''He's his old self. Grabbing the nurses and laughing. Of course, with tubes sticking out of him everywhere and not being able to eat normally, he is annoyed. But that will be only for a day or two at the most.''

''When can he have visitors?''

''I'll check tomorrow on his status. Once he's on the cardiology floor he should be able to have visitors.''

''Is he in any real danger?'' Peter asked.

''Well, there is always the danger of blood clots and a stroke after open heart surgery. The body is struggling to get things back to normal, but it is sometimes clumsy in its efforts. And high blood pressure increases his chances of something going wrong.''

''He'll be just fine,'' Betty said with absolute certainty. ''Eugene told me Charlie would be okay.''

''Maybe you should ask Eugene how I can stop those twins

from getting Mildred's money?'' Benny said. Peter saw the good mood vanish, and Benny's face grow tight with anger.

''I'll ask him tonight.''

''Ask him to give those guys a heart attack or something.''

''Now, Benny,'' Betty scolded, ''he can't do any such thing, and you know that.''

''You told me Eugene said the detective was going to solve Mildred's murder?''

''Yes. Something about horns.''

''But he didn't say when?''

''No.''

''Damn,'' Benny said, and pushed back into his chair.

''Did Eugene say anything more about your hearing?'' Walter said.

She shook her head. ''No. He told me the other night that everything would turn out just fine, and I believe him.''

Walter looked at Peter and raised a quizzical eyebrow. Peter returned a slight shrug. Eugene, at least took the worry off Betty's shoulders. But, Peter thought, unless Eugene could pull off a miracle, Betty's outlook in the hearing was grim.

''Well, guys,'' Alice said. ''I gotta go get ready. Another kids party to go to.'' She pushed back her chair and stood up. ''Benny, if you need some guys to break a few legs, let me know. I stay in contact with a lot of people from the circus who are very good at that.''

Jesus, Peter thought, *that's all Benny needs to hear.*

''Alice,'' Benny said, ''that's the best idea I've heard. I'll let you know.''

Peter saw Benny's mood suddenly brighten, and he worried all the more.

The rest of the morning went normally. A lazy kind of day. When the telephone call came, Peter was playing a game of chess with Walter out by the swimming pool. Walter had set up the game, and now Peter was sorry he had admitted to knowing how to play the game. Peter was having serious trouble holding his white forces together against Walter's onslaught with black. In the tension of the combat, Peter had already smoked two cigarettes and was on a third—well ahead of his quota of ten cigarettes a day. Eleanor, Caroline, Benny, and Betty were sitting in deck chairs talking and generally enjoying the milder temperature and sunny weather.

"Benny," Grace called across the pool. "Telephone."

Benny gave Grace a questioning look.

"He said his name was Collins, an attorney."

Peter looked over at Benny.

Benny frowned, stood up, and followed Grace.

"Mr. Ashe," Carter Collins said, "I have in my office two gentlemen who say they are Mildred Perkins's children and rightful heirs."

"Tell 'em to prove it," Benny snapped.

"They are accompanied by their attorney, a Mr. Thompson. They have presented me with their birth certificates identifying them as George and Paul Esterman. Esterman was Mildred Perkins's name at the time the children were born."

"Well, I think you better check on those birth certificates. Today you can get any ID you want for a few bucks."

"They want to accompany you on an inventory of Mildred Perkins's apartment."

"I know what they want."

"You are aware they do have a certain right to be there?"

"Yeah. But I think you'd better check with the police. They were doing some DNA stuff that should tell if these guys are really her sons. If that checks out, call me back." And Benny hung up the phone without saying good-bye. "Bastards," he said to the phone. Then he thought of Alice.

It was nearing three when the telephone call came for Peter. By that time Peter had given up playing chess after two serious losses to Walter, and the group had moved inside. Benny and Caroline had left, and Betty had gone upstairs to take a nap. Walter, Eleanor, and Peter were in the coffee alcove sipping on strong coffee. Although, for Peter, decaffeinated coffee never tasted quite like real coffee. Peter had told Walter that they were worried Benny might do something rash to the twins.

"I'll do what I can," Walter said. "Benny has a strong spirit, though."

"Nicely put," Peter said wryly.

Grace called to Peter from the front desk. Peter got up, walked over, and picked up the phone.

"It's Detective Ardley, Mr. Benington," the voice said at the other end of the phone.

"Yes, Detective?" Peter said.

"I want you to know that we just got back the DNA results on the Esterman brothers and Mildred Perkins. There's no doubt she was their mother."

"Damn," Peter said.

"I'm telling you this, because, as we discussed once before, I want you to keep an eye on Mr. Ashe. When he finds this out, he's liable to do something he shouldn't, if you know what I mean. I would really hate to see him in trouble."

"Are you going to tell him?"

"Only if he asks, but I'm sure he will ask."

"Thank you, Detective."

"You're welcome. Good-bye."

"Bye."

Peter hung up the phone. Damn, he thought, and Benny's not around.

Benny didn't show up at the Home until after lunch the next day. When he and Caroline came into the lobby, Peter and Walter were in the coffee alcove once again playing chess. Peter had decided to give Walter another chance to let Peter win. But Walter wasn't cooperating. Benny and Caroline went over to them.

"Oh, chess," Caroline said. "My daddy was so fond of the game. Played it often. I'm sorry I never learned the rules of the game."

"So what's up?" Benny said.

"You mean besides the slaughter taking place here on the board?" Walter said stoically.

"Where are the girls?"

"They went for a stroll about the grounds." Peter did not take his eyes from the chessboard. "They should return soon." Then he carefully lifted a white pawn and moved it on the board.

"We visited Charlie this morning," Walter said. It was his turn to concentrate on the chess game.

"Oh yeah? How is he doing?"

"Good. Should be back home in a few days." Walter dragged a black bishop across the board and snagged a white pawn. He dropped it in the wood box with the other chess casualties. "There was a telephone call for you a few minutes ago. Grace took the message."

Benny left Caroline in the coffee alcove with the two men, and went to the front desk.

Grace came out from Jessie's office. "Benny, that lawyer, Collins, called. Wants you to call him back ASAP." She retrieved a pink telephone message slip from the desk and handed it to Benny.

"Thanks, Grace." He took the pink slip and looked around for a telephone with a little privacy.

Grace guessed what he was after. "You can use the one in Jessie's office. She's out for a couple hours."

Benny nodded, went into Jessie's office, sat behind her desk, and dialed Collins's number. He sat there listening to the ringing and waiting for someone to answer at the other end. He knew what Collins wanted, but he didn't know what to do or say. He'd agonized all night about it, but the only thing he'd accomplished was to get little sleep.

The secretary answered the phone, pronouncing a string of lawyers' names that Benny didn't understand.

"Let me talk to Collins. This is Benny Ashe."

There was a click, a moment of silence, then. "Mr. Ashe. Good of you to return my call."

"Let's not dance around Carter. Get to the point."

Carter Collins cleared his throat. "I had another visit from the Estermans and their lawyer. This time they presented to me the results of the DNA testing by the police. It definitely confirms Mildred Perkins as the mother of these two men."

Shit. Benny's mind burst to red with an explosive urge to strike out. He slammed his hand on the desk, and he bit down hard, and the red slipped away. His hand stung.

"They want to know when they can witness the inventory of Mildred Perkins's apartment. They also requested that some of the money due them be turned over now, before probate."

"No money," Benny said. "Not yet."

"It is customary, with such a large estate as Mrs. Perkins's, and with as simple a will as hers, to advance the heirs some of the money. My figures show her estate to be in the eight-hundred-thousand range. Most of which is in stable assets. It is not unreasonable to turn over a hundred thousand dollars at this time.''

''No!'' Benny shouted in the phone. ''Not a dime! Not yet.''

''When can they witness the inventory?''

Benny took a deep breath, finding it hard to think straight. ''Tomorrow afternoon. Four o'clock.'' It was a random time that he blurted out without thought.

''I will inform them. Good-bye, Mr. Ashe.''

Benny slammed the phone down. Damn, damn, damn. What the hell was he going to do? He had to stop them somehow. But how? Then on sudden inspiration he dialed Ardley's number. Give the cops one last chance before he talked to Alice.

''Detective Burns.''

''I want to talk to Detective Ardley.''

''Sorry, he's out to lunch right now. Can I take a message?''

Benny hesitated then jumped in with both feet. ''Yeah. Tell him to be at Mildred Perkins's apartment at Coral Sands at three o'clock tomorrow.''

''Whoa!'' Detective Burns said. ''You'll have to give me that a little slower.''

Benny repeated the message slowly.

''Tomorrow afternoon at three. Mildred Perkins's apartment. Coral Sands,'' Burns read back to him.

''Right.''

''Your name, please?''

''Benny Ashe. And thanks.'' He hung up the phone.

When he returned to the coffee alcove, Peter and Walter were putting the chess pieces in the wood box. Eleanor, Betty, and Alice had returned from their walk and were sitting having coffee with Caroline. Peter looked up and saw the expression on Benny's face.

''What's the matter?'' Peter asked, and everyone turned to Benny.

Benny looked at the group, his gaze meeting the gaze of each of his friends one by one. ''I need your help.''

CHAPTER 18

The next day Ardley showed up at a little past three. Benny was waiting for him in the lobby. One look at Benny, and Ardley saw a man who hadn't slept well, and who was under a tremendous strain.

Benny came over to Ardley. "Glad you came."

"I'll tell you how I feel about it once you tell me what's going on."

"Upstairs. I'll tell ya upstairs."

Ardley sighed. He was a patient man, he kept telling himself. However, there were times when he didn't believe it.

Benny turned to Grace. "You let us know when those guys arrive. Okay?"

Grace nodded. "I'll buzz you in Mildred's apartment."

"Let's go," he said to Ardley, and led him across the lobby to the elevator.

"Who are 'those guys' that you're expecting?"

"The twins," Benny said.

Ardley frowned.

They rode the elevator up to the third floor. When the doors opened, Benny stepped out quickly. Ardley followed at a sedate pace. Benny stopped in front of room 309, opened the door, and stepped aside. Ardley went into the apartment and was surprised to find it filled with people. He turned to Benny, who had stepped in behind him and closed the door.

"Okay, what's going on?"

"Come here." Benny put a hand on Ardley's arm and led him into the group.

Ardley didn't know all their names, but he knew all their faces, except for the kid at the computer. When he saw Alice, he turned to Benny, and said, "If this is a gang rape, I want her last."

Alice laughed aloud. "I'd be last because everybody after me would be spoiled for you."

Ardley couldn't help but laugh. "All right, all right. What's going on here?"

Peter pointed to the kid at the computer. The computer sat on a desk that protruded out into the room. "His name is Artie, and he just may be able to prove that Mildred saw one of the Esterman twins the night she was murdered. That's what you said you needed, right?"

Ardley stepped up to look over the kid's shoulder at the computer screen. Artie was clicking the mouse, and the screen was changing.

"It'll be simple," Artie was saying to Walter, "if she saved her chat. You see, the ISP . . ."

Walter turned to Ardley. "That's Internet Service Provider."

Ardley shrugged. He had no idea what they were talking about.

". . . doesn't keep a record of the chat. But the people in the chat can save it for themselves." While he was talking, Artie was changing screens and searching the information that came up on the new screens. "Yeah. That looks like it." He moved the cursor to what looked like a small file folder, clicked on it, and a list of the folder's contents appeared on the screen. He smiled proudly. "Yep. That's it."

Artie turned to Walter. "See. The list shows the chat name, you know, the chat room and the date and time."

"Yes," Walter said, looking intently at the screen. "The last entry is for the thirteenth. That's the night Mildred was killed." He looked at Artie. "Can we see that?"

"Sure." Artie moved the cursor to that entry and double clicked. The screen changed to:

Shy-Guy has entered the conversation

Shy-Guy: <panting hard> Hi Dear One. Sorry I'm late. Rushed here as fast as I could. <pant, pant>

"What am I looking at?" Ardley said.

"The conversation Mildred had online the night she died," Walter said, his eyes scanning down the screen. "The conversation started at seven."

"So who the hell is this Shy-Guy character?"

"That's gotta be one of the Esterman twins," Benny said.

"Here," Walter said, pointing at the computer screen. "He says he wants to meet her." Then Walter took the mouse from Artie's hand and clicked on the bar at the right to skip to the next screen where the conversation continued. He scanned the dialogue. "There she says she's ready to try again." He clicked on the bar again, and the screen rolled up once more. "And there he says he wants to meet her again at the Beach House. Now, he says." He clicked the bar again. The screen changed. "Ah. And there she says she's going to meet him in twenty minutes."

Walter stood straight and turned to Ardley. "There's your proof that she saw one of the Esterman twins that night."

Ardley shook his head. "Look. I'm as anxious to nail these guys as you all seem to be. But I don't know who this Shy-Guy is. It could be anybody."

"Well," Artie said, taking the mouse from Walter. "Let's see what he put down on his profile." He clicked the screen off, and a sign-on screen for the Microsoft Network came up. It showed Mildred's handle, FineLace, and the box for Remember My Password was checked. "Good. Her password is already there." He clicked on Connect. "Everyone's got a profile on the network that tells you who they are."

They all hovered over the computer waiting. The connection was made, and Artie started clicking on the screens, changing them as fast as they would change. "See," he said at last, "this is what a chat screen looks like. Now we can go into the profiles area and search for Shy-Guy." He typed on the keyboard, and clicked. A small screen laid over the larger one. It was a layout for name and address and other personal information. For Shy-Guy what it said on the name line was simply "Timothy." There was no other information entered.

"That don't look like any help here," Ardley said.

Artie looked up apologetically. "Well, you don't have to

put your real name in here or anything. You can put whatever you want.''

''Great.'' Ardley threw up his hands. ''You guys are wasting my time and yours.''

''Wait,'' Peter said. Then to Artie. ''Somehow these people are billed for their time. So there must be a connection between this name and their real names at this Microsoft Network. Isn't that correct?''

''Yeah,'' Artie said. ''But that information ain't available to us. It's secured.''

Walter leaned in, his face next to Artie's. ''My boy, I know you are very good at this. Is there a way you can—how do you say it?—break in to that information?''

Artie looked nervously up at Detective Ardley. ''It's illegal to do something like that.''

Walter looked at Ardley.

Ardley shrugged. ''I ain't the FBI. Not my jurisdiction.''

Walter turned to Artie. ''Go to it, lad.''

Artie hesitated a moment, then picked up the case of diskettes he brought with him, and began searching through them. ''It might take a while.'' Artie pulled out a diskette and inserted it in the drive on the computer.

''We aren't going anywhere,'' Walter said, straightening up. Then to Ardley, ''I'm sure if Artie is unsuccessful, you can obtain that information from these people at Microsoft Network.''

Ardley nodded, made a face. ''It'd take some doing. Red tape and all that, but yeah, I could get it. Maybe a couple days.'' Then he looked down at Artie. ''But if I had it now, then I could act on it now.''

Ardley looked around the room. ''I've met you all before, but I'm not so good with names.''

Benny introduced him around to Eleanor, Betty, and Alice. Eleanor went to the kitchen area and returned with a coffee pot and some cups.

Ardley turned to Benny. ''So, why'd you invite the twins here?''

''I didn't. They're anxious to witness the inventory of Mildred's things. That's what they're coming for. And I gotta let them in.''

For the next twenty minutes they milled about and drank coffee and waited, while Artie worked the computer incessantly. Ardley looked at the kid and wished he had the kid's ability to stay so focused.

Suddenly the hall door opened.

"What the hell we got here, a convention?"

Surprised, everyone turned to see the Esterman brothers coming into the apartment.

"Looks like a convention of the Misfits of America," the one on the left said, and laughed.

"The Confused and Addled," the one on the right said. He, too, was laughing.

Petersen came in behind the twins and closed the door. He saw the question on Benny's face. "I met these gentlemen downstairs in the lobby and told Grace not to bother calling you, that I would gladly escort them here."

The one on the left looked at Benny. "Sorry we showed up early and busted in on your party."

Benny looked at them and felt he had been caught with his pants down.

The brothers were dressed in identical outfits: light yellow sport jackets, white shirts, and dark pants being held up by Western belts with the longhorn belt buckles.

"So, what's all happening here?" the one on the right said. Then firmly to Benny, "This ain't right. These people shouldn't be here messing with my mama's things."

"I'm in!" Artie said, oblivious to what had been going on around him.

Everyone moved to the computer, peering over Artie's shoulders.

"Say, what have we got here?" one of the Esterman twins said. "Playing around with Mama's computer? Now that's not decent."

The computer screen was filled with a list of names and addresses and their associated computer handles. Artie searched the screen, then clicked, and clicked again, bringing up screen after screen of lists. "There," Artie said pointing at the screen. "Shy-Guy! And the name with that is George Esterman of . . ." Artie went wide-eyed. The screen had wiggled and wobbled and slipped away. They were staring at a blank screen.

"My, my, my," said one of the Esterman brothers with a smirk. "Looks like some sort of computer bug, sonny."

"Possibly a systems crash, kid. Too bad." The other brother also smirked.

"I don't understand?" Artie frowned. "I never saw a computer do that."

"Maybe you never saw one with a magnet on it's case," the one brother said, and smiled. "Like that one there."

The other brother was pointing at the four-inch heavy horseshoe magnet stuck to the side of the computer case. "Such a thing could just wipe everything outta your system. Just like that." He snapped his fingers. Then he put on a sad face. "Everything gone. Just too bad."

Everyone was shocked.

Artie helplessly looked to the others.

"Can't you do something?" Walter said.

"No." Artie's voice was sad, disappointed. "The computer stores everything magnetically. All the data on the disks, everything. A magnet just scrambles it all."

"The chat history?"

"Everything. There's nothing left."

"Shit," Benny said in a sudden rage. "That's why you wanted to come here! You knew there might be something on her computer to nail you guys!"

"Mr. Ashe," one of the brothers said mocking a hurt tone, "how could you accuse us of such a terrible thing?"

Ardley facing Benny, stepped between Benny and the twins. He put his hands on Benny's shoulders. "Easy, now. Just take it easy. They may have won this round, but the war isn't over. Just don't do anything stupid." He was holding tightly to Benny's shoulders, keeping him from moving.

Furious, his mind in an explosion of hot rage and screaming hate, Benny struggled against Ardley's grip. Desperately, Benny searched the faces of his friends for help. There was no support there to see, until his eyes met Alice's eyes. She gave him a small nod.

"You gotta do something?" Benny pleaded with Ardley.

"I will," he said softly. "But now's not the time."

Petersen stepped up to Ardley. "If you will permit me, Detective, I would like to speak with the two gentlemen."

Ardley, still holding Benny at bay, said, "I don't think this is a good time to continue this . . ." Peter's hand was suddenly on Ardley's arm. He turned to Peter.

"Let him talk," Peter said in a soft voice.

Ardley looked at Petersen, a thin balding man with glasses. The quiet harmless type. Ardley shrugged.

Petersen turned to the twins, who were standing together wearing smug expressions.

"If I may make a few observations, gentlemen," Petersen said.

"Another nutcase," the one on the right said with a grin.

"Squirrels all in a cage." The one on the left returned the grin.

All eyes were on Petersen and the twins.

"I couldn't help but notice that you are dressed exactly alike. It makes it extremely difficult to tell you apart. Do you always dress alike?"

"Yep." From the one on the left.

"We enjoy confusing the hell outta people." From the right.

"I must say here that I admire your Western belt and the silver buckles."

"Yeah, they are nice, aren't they?" From the right.

"Gifts to us from Edgar when he retired and turned over the gas station to us." The one on the left.

"In a way that man was the only real father we ever had."

"Wear them all the time."

"I know this may sound peculiar," Petersen said, "but do you wear each other's clothes?"

"Geez, no. Give us a break will you?" The one on the right said.

"Nope. We have them marked." The one on the left smiled. "We have our own little code. So don't think you can tell us apart by the markings on our clothes."

"I'm sure you are carrying identification that would tell you apart."

"Sure," the one on the right said, with a slick smile. "But you don't know if I'm carrying my identification or his."

"That is true." Petersen spoke gently and evenly. He took

a small black cylinder from his pocket and began to absently play with it in his hands. "And that makes for an interesting puzzle. One of the more interesting of my career."

Ardley gave a peculiar look to Peter. Peter signaled Ardley to wait and see.

"What kind of career is that?" the one on the left asked.

"Well, as Sherlock Holmes, I've had many puzzling . . ."

Both twins laughed aloud.

"Sherlock Holmes!" From the one on the left.

"Oh, boy. The squirrels are loose." From the one on the right.

Petersen continued as if the men had said nothing. "You see, I thoroughly love such a challenge to the intellect as your position poses." Petersen took the metal cylinder in one hand and used it as a pointer while he spoke. "The one thing that had me puzzled was the context of the murder act itself. For instance, if you murdered Mildred Perkins, there is the question of the weapon used."

"I heard it was a knife." The one on the right grinned to the other. They were having a grand time of this.

"Yes, definitely a knife. But, as intelligent as you gentlemen are, I don't think you would have worn a hunting knife when you met Mrs. Perkins in a rendezvous. That would have been too stupid, and obvious. And, I do not think you went out and bought a knife to use for this killing. There would be the sales receipt, and the memory of the sales clerk to contend with. Therefore, the knife had to be something on the order of a simple kitchen knife. Possibly a small carving knife, because it would cut deeply and cleanly, without a danger of it slipping from the hand. That means it was a knife with no scabbard." Petersen began pacing back and forth as he spoke, always waving the black cylinder.

"So, I asked myself, where would you hide such a knife? Obviously, on your person, to be sure it was handy when the right moment came to use it. You see, I believe this act of killing was not thoroughly planned in advance. It was more a grasping of opportunity. So, you would use this small carving knife, and you would have concealed it. But where? Let us assume you wore a light sports jacket, similar to the one you are wearing now. You could put it in a pants pocket or a jacket pocket. But in either case there would be the danger of the naked blade poking through the material unexpectedly. It would also produce an obvious distortion of the pocket which would be noticed by anyone. Including Mrs. Perkins.'' Petersen stopped pacing and looked at the two men.

The twins just watched Petersen and grinned, enjoying their superior position. Everyone else was mesmerized by the unassuming Petersen's performance. Peter could have sworn he was looking at Sherlock Holmes himself.

''So, I have eliminated most places on your person. What is left? Where would the knife be hidden where it would not be noticed and yet be ready for use?'' He pointed with the black cylinder. ''Where else but tucked in your belt in the back. Obvious, when you think of it. The jacket would hide the knife well. And you could easily reach around with one hand and pull the knife out when you were ready to act.'' He resumed his pacing.

''The next question is what do you do with the knife when you are finished using it on Mrs. Perkins? Do you toss it away? I think not. You are too clever for that. You want to be sure it is disposed of properly, where it wouldn't be found. The police finding no weapon is a more secure situation, than them finding a weapon and doing some of their magical analysis of it and pointing an accusing finger at you.'' He kept pacing and looking down in thought.

''So, it seems clear that you would have returned it to your belt to dispose of it later, where it would never be found.'' Petersen stopped pacing and looked at the two men. But he spoke to Detective Ardley. ''Detective, I think if you examined their belts you will find one that has a few nicks in it from the knife, along with some microscopic traces of Mrs. Perkins blood, which you should be able to detect and type with some of your advanced equipment.''

The one on the left, reflexively looked down at his belt. While the one on the right, equally reflexively looked at his brother. Before anyone could react, Petersen reached out with the black cylinder and ran a black mark across the back of the hand of the man on the left.

''Your killer, Detective, is the man marked with this permanent marker.''

The twins bolted. One of them shoved Ardley who stumbled back against Benny, and Benny and Ardley fell to the floor, people scattering to get out of their way. Noises, shouting. The other charged at Petersen, who stood between them and the door. Petersen nimbly stepped aside and tripped the man as he rushed past, the man stumbling and sprawling to the floor in front of the door. The second man moved at Petersen to shove him away. Petersen twisted his body, the shove only a glancing blow, and grabbed one of the man's fingers, pushing it back so severely, the man screamed and fell to his knees as Petersen continued to apply pressure. Peter had jumped over the scrambling figures of Ardley and Benny on the floor, and got to the door as the first man got to his feet and tried to open it. Peter punched the man in the kidney, the man jerking upright with the pain, then Peter kicked him in the back of the knee, the leg collapsed. The man went down, landing hard on the one knee, and letting out a cry of pain. Walter had stepped up to the struggle between Petersen and the other man, as the man was about to hit out at Petersen with his free hand. Walter swung his cane like a man chopping wood, and hit the twin between the neck and the shoulder, knowing he would cause a great deal of pain. The man's face screwed up with the pain, and he collapsed to the floor, the fight gone from him. With the cane held like a bat, Walter stood over the man. Peter stepped away from the brother by the door, who stood, holding a hand over his knee. Benny came up past Peter and punched the Esterman brother in the face, the man's head jerked back and bounced off the door, then he slid slowly back to the floor. And it was over. Everything suddenly calm and under control.

Ardley stepped up and dragged the two brothers together on the floor. Then he put his handcuffs on them, left hand of one to the left hand of the other. "If I had known about this, I would have brought two sets of cuffs."

Walter limped over to Benny who was rubbing his right hand with his left. "You have to watch that sort of thing. Bones get brittle with age. It would not surprise me if there were some broken bones in your hand."

"Doc"—Benny grinned—"I don't care if it's shattered in little pieces. I never felt better."

The two brothers sat on the floor, moaning and rubbing their wounds.

"I told you it wouldn't work!" the man on the left snapped at his brother. "We should have stayed with the plan."

"It was your idea to make her death look like another victim of this killer! You said the setup was made for us. It would be simple." He shook his head. "Shit, simple."

"Don't blame it on me, now! You were the one anxious for her money. We could have waited a while before we killed her! No, not you. You wanted her money now!"

"You killed Mildred for money, your own mother!" Walter was astonished.

"What mother!" The one on the left snapped. "What did she do for us? The bitch gave us life, and dropped us when we became inconvenient. What kind of mother does that?"

Walter shook his head in despair. "A desperate one, no doubt."

"This kind of mother," Ardley said. He took a folded paper from his pocket. "This is a copy of the letter her lawyer was to give to you both when he found you." He unfolded the paper, and read from it.

"Dear George and Paul,

I sincerely hope Mr. Collins finds you. When you read this my life will be over. I'm so sorry I had to leave you both when you were so little. It hurt me so to walk away from you. Believe me, when I tell you, that I did it for you. My life was in shambles. A single woman with children, living on the edge of the world, I didn't stand a chance. Not then, not in that time. What the drugs didn't suck from me, poverty did. I couldn't give you the care and the future that you both deserved. I tried with all my heart to find another way. I loved you both so much, too much to condemn you to the horrible life I was able to give you. It tore my heart out to give you up, but it was the only way I could give you a chance in life. There was no chance with me. I knew someone would help you, and take care of you, and give you the things I could not.

There were times when I ached to find you, and see

how you turned out. But I didn't try. By then you were grown men, and had lives of your own. I would have been an unwelcomed nuisance, interrupting the lives you had made for yourselves.

I know you've grown up to become wonderful people. My beautiful boys could be nothing else.

All I can hope for now, is that someday you will forgive me. I love you both.''

Ardley looked up from the letter at the two men. ''She signed it—'Your Mother'.''

Petersen shook his head. ''It is sad that her sacrifice was wasted on you both.''

CHAPTER 19

"Well, Benny is happy," Eleanor said.

It was past midnight and she was in bed with Peter. The only light in the room was from the yellow night-light. The orange bulb had burned out, and the only replacement Peter could find was yellow.

Peter smiled. "I thought he was going to dance a jig when they put those twins in the police car, and took them away." He sighed. "What an amazing day." Then he chuckled. "Retirement is certainly exciting."

"What horrible men the twins are. Poor Mildred."

"There was a lot of hate in them. The terrible slashing of Mildred's body was a sure sign of that."

She turned on her side and snuggled up to Peter. "I was proud of you. The way you jumped right in and stopped that man from getting away."

"Shucks, ma'am. T'weren't nothin'," he said in his best John Wayne imitation.

Eleanor giggled.

They stayed like that for awhile, quiet in their own thoughts; Eleanor looking at Peter's profile, Peter looking at the yellow light on the ceiling.

Peter said, "There are still two killings unsolved."

"I was just thinking about that."

Peter chuckled again. "That Petersen is a remarkable man. It was fantastic the way he reacted so calmly to their attack and fended them off."

"And Eugene was right again. He said the detective would solve it."

"Who knew he meant Sherlock Holmes, the Great Detective? And Betty couldn't remember what he said about the horns, but it probably referenced the longhorn cattle on the Estermans' belt buckles."

"Mr. Petersen certainly makes a good Sherlock Holmes. His reasoning was astounding."

"He's also a pretty good Henny Youngman, and that magician. What's his name?"

"Blackstone."

"Yes, Blackstone." Peter frowned. Then he suddenly brightened. "Yes, Blackstone! What he said about assumptions people make!"

She smiled. "Something about when you make an assumption, the only thing you can assume is you're wrong."

"That has to be it!" Peter sat up. "The killings. Both times the men were gardening. Digging in the dirt. That's what no one saw!" He threw off the top sheet, stood up and, hopping, slipped on a pair of shorts.

Eleanor sat up in bed. "Where are you going?"

Peter went into the kitchen, turned on the light, and rummaged around in a drawer. "Has to be something here I can use." He was talking aloud to himself. "Ah!" He pulled out a penlight. "This should do. I found my way through many a dark bedroom with this light."

"Peter, what the hell are you doing?" Eleanor called from the bedroom.

He hadn't heard her. He was already out in the hall, rushing toward the elevator.

Eleanor sat there in the bed thoroughly confused. One minute they were talking quietly, the next the man had dashed off and left her alone in bed. And in the middle of the night no less.

She got out of bed, slipped on a light robe, and left the apartment. Out in the hall she saw no sign of him. Peter sure was fast, she thought. Her bare feet silently stepped over the red carpet as she headed to the elevator. She rode the elevator down to the lobby. Sitting in the alcove having coffee were that handsome policeman, Jerry Otis, and Shirley. Shirley looked rather nice tonight, Eleanor thought.

"Did you see Peter go by here?" Eleanor asked.

Jerry Otis pointed to the glass doors leading out to the swimming pool area. "Some guy in shorts just went outside."

"It was Peter." Shirley nodded.

"Thanks," Eleanor said. She went to the glass doors, pushed them open and walked out onto the concrete deck around the pool. In the distance, back toward the rear of the building, she saw a tiny light bobbing along probing the shrubbery. Eleanor stepped off the concrete deck onto the cool grass.

The bare feet walked on the coarse St. Augustine grass, but the mind felt the hard dry earth of another time. The mind saw the night, but not the night of Florida. With one step, the world of Coral Sands and Sarasota had dissolved into the Japanese prison camp, and the night sky of bright stars in a cloudless sky of many years ago. Hidden creatures chirped and squawked and sent shrill cries to tear at the darkness—sending terror into those who heard them. The mind was not afraid. Those creatures were the lesser fear. The night was a time of refuge for the prisoners. The guards were lax and sleepy, the darkness was a place to hide. It was the time to dig in the ground and unearth the treasures. The mind chuckled at the thought of treasures. Trinkets in another world, the money of life in this, the gold of bribery for survival.

Bribery kept them alive. One learned quickly which guards were willing, which were cheats, and which would turn you in. The learning was painful: beatings for trying to bribe an honest guard, good jewelry traded for nothing or next to nothing. Most of the prisoners survived on the few possessions they had smuggled with them into the camp. Possessions they quickly buried from the others. Watches, bracelets, rings, money—all bought food. A simple egg could go for three dollars worth of bribes.

For some, had the War been shorter, their possessions would have lasted. With the money of life used up, the only recourse for survival was to steal from those who still had things to trade. Steal, then hide them where no one knew, and guard that hiding place with your life, for those things were life itself.

The guards searched for newly turned earth, looked for the stash the prisoners kept hidden. When they found one and cleaned it out, a prisoner's life was forfeited to sure starvation.

The mind looked down at the bamboo knife the hand was carrying. Not much of a weapon, not a knife at all. A pointed sliver of bamboo. Hard as steel, but only good for one thrust. One thrust of force was all the mind needed, for it knew the body, and knew just where to puncture the body to cause death.

Once in a while a Japanese soldier was found dead with a puncture wound in the back. No one was accused of the crime. The Japanese did not have the forensics to track down the killer, but the camp was punished as a whole—shorter rations, harder work. Then time passed and life went on as miserably as before, the struggle for survival continued, the dead guard forgotten.

To kill was a desperate effort, for the mind had been trained to save life, not extinguish it. But the killing was the lesser of evils weighed against the welfare of the children. The children could not survive without food, without nourishment. The mind's responsibility was to those children, to keep them alive, to see that, of all the people in the camp, they survived. Without the responsibility of the children, the mind knew it would have surrendered to death long ago. So, the children kept the mind alive, and the mind kept the children alive. And it killed to do it.

The mind saw the guard moving about in the darkness with a tiny flashlight. He was searching, and the mind knew what he was searching for. The mind wanted to cry out to stop the man, to stop the madness of survival, to stop the cruelty and the suffering, to stop the insanity that life had become. The mind was tired of it all, tired of the constant struggle to live in a world that was unlivable, to survive for the sake of being able to take another breath of the foul air, to exist in a horror that was inhumanly cruel. But the lives of the children were at stake if the greedy bastard found the buried treasure.

The mind couldn't let that happen, wouldn't let that happen. Not so long as there was a breath left in its body. No Jap bastard was going to kill the children while the mind lived. With a heart pounding with fright, and thoughts hot with hate, the mind kept to the deep shadows and watched the search. Nervously the hand tightened and loosened and tightened again around the sharpened bamboo stick. The fingers were dry, there was no sweat. The body had been drained of its sweat, worked too hard, fed too little until there was nothing left to sweat.

As the guard moved on, so did the mind, keeping out of sight, moving silently over the ground, staying in the darkest shadows. There was the hope that the guard would not find where it all had been buried, that his search would be futile, and the guard would give up and leave. The mind prayed for that. Prayed to a God the mind knew wasn't listening, but the mind prayed anyway.

It wasn't that the mind feared killing. It hungered for the killing. The hate that raged inside lived for the killing, lived to strike back at the sadistic people that destroyed the value of living. What the mind feared was discovery, and the sure death that would come from it. With the mind dead, the children would die. The children were all the hope that was left for the world. So, the mind prayed the guard would leave empty-handed and alive.

But he didn't. The mind saw the guard stop, then crouch down, flashing his little light under the large bush. The guard then went to his knees and leaned forward to more closely examine the dirt beneath the bush. Oh, no, the mind whispered its plea. Please, no. The guard began digging in the dirt with his hand.

The mind grabbed its fear and shoved it aside, filling its thoughts with hate, hot and bright. The fury surging through the body like a raging fire. The hand tightened hard around the pointed bamboo, hard as it could hold it. The hand must not slip. The hand must be strong. It must not waver, must not bend with weakness, must not give way. The bamboo knife must be guided firmly. The hate gave the body strength where it had no strength. The mind crept forward, silent and focused.

Each step was carefully placed and noiselessly executed. The mind was totally focused, an animal intent upon its prey. Each quiet step brought the mind closer to the guard, brought death closer to the man. The guard was focused on his find, digging in the soil to claim the treasures. He did not hear, was not aware of the nearness of his death. The mind had stepped to stand barely two feet from the guard. The steel strength of hate brought to every muscle of the arm, the hand, the shoulder, the power that would bring death, the body tight with the raw energy of a coiled spring ready to be released.

"Peter!" the woman screamed, startling the mind, causing it to hesitate a moment. Then the arm shot forward toward the back of the guard. The man twisted his body, dropping down, and throwing his arm backward, knocking the knife off target, the knife running across the man's back, tearing out a line of flesh.

Peter could feel the point dig out a streak of the skin along his back after he blindly swung his arm up and hit some part of his attacker. He rolled onto his back, as the dark figure stood over him, and he kicked out, again connecting. The figure grunted and stumbled back. Another dark figure lunged into his attacker, knocking the attacker to the ground. Peter quickly picked up the penlight and flashed it at the two wrestling figures. Eleanor! The penlight flashed off a knife flying around in the struggle. He jumped in, keeping the light on the figures, and grabbed at the hand with the knife, missing it at first, then getting a good hold on the wrist, forcing it down against the ground. With that, the hand released the knife, and suddenly stopped struggling. Eleanor straddled the figure and sat up.

Breathless, she said, "I thought for sure you were dead."

Peter shone the penlight on the body on the ground. Elaine Singleton was weeping silent tears that glinted in the tiny light.

"Elaine!" Eleanor said.

"Jesus," Peter said.

The paramedic was cleaning the blood from the wound on Peter's back. Frowning in concern, Eleanor stood over them watching, her arms folded tight against her body, her robe dirty and torn. Walter, in a blue robe, was standing next to her, leaning on his cane. Peter was sitting sideways in a chair in the alcove trying not to show the pain he was feeling as the paramedic cleaned his wound. Half the house was up, milling around in the lobby. The police had Elaine in handcuffs, and were leading her through the front door to the patrol car outside. A sorry figure in her soiled nightgown, she was still weeping quietly. She hadn't said a word since the confrontation. She just hung her head and let the tears trail down her face. A sleepy Ardley finished talking with Patrolman Jerry Otis, and walked over to Peter and Eleanor.

"That was a dumb thing for you to do, Mr. Benington."

"Thanks. I needed that," Peter said without humor, and winced as the paramedic applied an antiseptic to the slash on his back.

"Lucky for you . . ."—Ardley squinted at Eleanor—"Eleanor, isn't it?"

Eleanor nodded.

"Lucky for you Eleanor followed you, or we'd be zipping you in a bag right now. I think you'd better lay off the heroics for awhile." He leaned against a table. "What made you go out there in the first place?"

"It occurred to me quite suddenly that it was assumed the men were killed for a motive directed at them. No one gave a thought to the fact that they both were digging in the ground. And it just might be that the real motive lay buried."

Ardley nodded and looked at the small bundle he held in his hand. The bundle was wrapped in a soiled rag.

"You could have waited until morning. At least that way I would have gotten a decent night's sleep for a change."

"What did you find in the hole out there?" Peter said.

Ardley pulled away the top pieces of the rag. There sitting in his hand was a silver gravy boat in which was a small collection of jewelry.

"My brooch!" Eleanor said, and moved her hand to pick it out of the gravy boat.

Ardley moved his hand out of her reach. "Not now. I'm sorry."

"But it's mine."

"In due time. Right now it is all evidence." Then to Peter, "Have any idea why she had this stuff buried out there?"

Peter shook his head. He stiffened and winced as the paramedic bandaged the wound.

"Any idea why she'd steal it in the first place?"

''No.''

Ardley looked at the others. ''Anyone?''

Both Eleanor and Walter shook their heads.

''But,'' Walter said, ''we would appreciate it if you could tell us what you find out.''

Ardley nodded, and folded the rag back over, covering the gravy boat and jewelry. ''It's times like these—when I see that frail, sick old lady being taken to jail—that I hate this job.'' He sighed, then looked up to see Jessie Cummings coming through the front door. No makeup, and her hair barely combed, she was dressed in slacks and a light top, and her face wore a tight scowl.

''If you will excuse me,'' Ardley said to the group. ''I must tell Ms. Cummings what happened.'' He looked over at Jessie Cummings. ''Seems she didn't get a decent night's sleep, either.''

CHAPTER 20

As it was, no one got a good night's sleep. Peter, however, got no sleep. The wound on his back hurt like hell and kept away any chance of sleep. That and the fact that, when he closed his eyes, he saw the dark ominous figure with the knife in hand leaning over him, and he immediately opened his eyes. It seemed that each time his eyes closed the figure appeared larger and his fear greater. Finally around four in the morning he got out of bed and made a pot of coffee—regular, not decaf. If his heart acted up he'd take two beta-blockers instead of one. He had to keep his eyes open to keep the monsters away. Eleanor, on the other hand, slept soundly. He envied her that.

He turned on the television, keeping the sound low in order to not disturb Eleanor, and searched the channels for something interesting to watch.

At seven he shaved and dressed and went down for breakfast and more coffee. He was sure he looked worse than he felt. The need for sleep had a way of retreating when he put up a good fight against it. The dining room was filled, and the talk was all about Elaine Singleton and the killings. He ate lightly, a full stomach would make him sleepy. He marveled at dinner functions where the food was served first, then the speakers spent the rest of the time trying to keep the diners awake. After he finished breakfast and two cups of coffee, he went for a walk in the cool morning air.

It was eight-thirty when Eleanor found him squirming in a lounge chair by the swimming pool, trying to find a position where the wound would not hurt. She looked well rested.

"You up to going to Betty's hearing today?" she asked.

"Yes."

"How's your back?"

He shrugged bravely. "Fine. As long as I don't have to lean back against anything." Then he looked directly in her eyes. "Did I thank you for saving my life?"

"A hundred times." She smiled. Then she gave him a seductive look. "But you can thank me much better when your back is healed."

Peter chuckled. "It's a deal."

Ardley called at ten. Grace came out to the swimming pool area to get Peter.

"He wants to speak to you," she said.

Peter struggled out of the chair. His body was getting stiff, and the wound in his back was hurting worse with each movement he made. Moving slowly didn't help, but he moved slowly anyway because he was afraid to open the wound with quick motions.

When he finally reached the front desk and picked up the telephone, Ardley said, "You sure took your time getting to the phone."

"The walking wounded walk slow," Peter said.

"I just finished talking to Elaine Singleton's son. He was very upset. I called you because I said I would let you know anything I learned about her. He told me she used to be a nurse, and she was in a Japanese prison camp for three years during World War Two. She had two children with her. Him and his sister, mere babies at the time. The sister didn't make it. But Mrs. Singleton managed to keep him alive. He said his mother would bury things in the camp so the Japanese soldiers wouldn't get them. Jewelry and things like that."

"Well," Peter said, "that explains the thefts. But it doesn't explain why she stole the things, and why she killed Yamaguchi and that private detective."

"Her son said it was all right to tell you this. She's dying of syphilis. Picked up from the Japanese in the prison camp. Seems she and the other women were raped regularly. The syphilis wasn't diagnosed or treated until long after she was freed from the camp. Too long. She's been fighting it for years, but it was too far gone. She's losing the battle. Her son said that on their last visit to the doctor, the doctor said he didn't expect her to live out the year. In her case the syphilis is now attacking her brain.

"When I spoke to her earlier, she's talking as if she's still in the prison camp." Peter could hear Ardley's sigh over the phone. "Hell of a way to spend your last days, reliving the worst part of your life."

"Thanks," Peter said, and hung up the phone. He didn't know what else to say. He felt terrible for Elaine, and what she must have been going through. Sometimes justice didn't work. The real killers here were the Japanese. They gave her the disease and the ugly memories that ended in the killing of two more casualties of the War.

Walter was wrong. The War doesn't end when the last soldier dies, it ends when the last victim dies.

It was one o'clock and they were all back in the courtroom. Andrew Jablonski and Attenboro, his attorney, sat at the other table in the front of the room. Walter, who had missed the first day of the hearing, was seated with Peter, Eleanor, and Benny in the front row behind the table with Bill Fresno and Betty. Walter leaned with both hands on the crook of his cane. There were no windows in the courtroom, the light a constant soothing glow from the ceiling fixtures. Judge Maria Jackson had not yet entered the courtroom, and Bill Fresno kept looking anxiously to the doors in the rear. The witness he had pushed so hard to be heard, was not there. Betty was in high spirits. Eugene had told her today would be the last day of this nonsense, and she believed him.

Peter was sure that Eleanor had not told him the truth about what she had said to Fresno on Monday. So, Peter was anxious to see what was going to happen. Eleanor sat confidently, sure of what was to happen. She, too, believed Eugene. The only thing Peter believed was that he was going round the bend with all that had happened, with Sherlock Holmes for god's sake solving the murder, with Elaine Singleton killing people and nearly killing him, with smug Eugene refusing to tell Betty anything directly. Always the innuendo, the shaded meaning, the cryptic message. He must have been an aggravating tease when he was alive. God, even Peter was talking about Eugene. Peter shook his head in despair. He needed a vacation, someplace quiet and sane. He winced as he unconsciously leaned back in the chair, and the wound on his back complained.

"All rise," the bailiff said, and Judge Maria Jackson rushed in like a black storm, and took her seat at the bench.

"Sit," she said.

Everyone returned to their seats.

"Good afternoon, everyone. Glad to see we're all here, including your star witness, Mr. Fresno." She nodded her head toward Walter. "Let's get through this quickly, if you don't mind. I'm pressed for time."

"Yes, your Honor." Bill Fresno stood hesitantly, his eyes on the doors at the rear of the courtroom. "Well, your Honor, there are things that must be said first about the guidelines by which we judge a person to be incompetent. They boil down to one simple question: Can a person, in this case Elizabeth Jablonski, make sound rational decisions in their dealings in everyday life. The terms sound clear and reasonable, until we ask ourselves what they mean? What is a sound, rational decision? Could there be more than one sound rational decision for any given set of circumstances? What are the boundaries . . . ?"

"Mr. Fresno"—Judge Jackson's voice was firm—"are you stalling here? Is that your so important witness?" She indicated Walter.

Bill Fresno turned slowly around to look at Walter, taking in the rear doors as he turned. "Well, your Honor, not exactly," he said, as he stared at the rear doors desperately trying to will them open.

"Mr. Fresno!" Anger now, clear and loud, in Judge Maria Jackson's voice. And when Bill Fresno turned to face her, clearly carved in her expression. "Is your witness here?"

Bill Fresno took a deep breath. "No, your Honor. But he . . ."

"No buts, Mr. Fresno. I am paid by the People to keep the wheels of justice moving. I have no more time for your stalling." Then to Betty, "Mrs. Jablonski I have given your case serious consideration. Some people would classify you as eccentric. Which on the outside isn't a serious classification.

What does concern me, however, is that you rely solely on the voices of the . . .''

''Not voices,'' Betty said. ''I talk with Eugene on the Ouija board.''

Bill Fresno kept looking back at the doors.

Maria Jackson nodded her head. ''On the sole advice offered by your dead husband. I feel that such reliance can only cloud your judgment, and prevent you from always making the sound rational decisions required in everyday life. Therefore, for your own protection, I must award guardianship of your person and your assets to Mr. Andrew Jablonski, to be effective immediately.''

''That's not right, your Honor,'' Betty said. ''Eugene said you would not do that.''

''So much for Eugene's accuracy. That was what I was talking about, Mrs. Jablonski. You can't rely on this ethereal advice to guide you. We live in a complex world, requiring us to deal with complex problems for which we must reach rational decisions.''

''But, you don't understand.'' Betty was insistent. ''Eugene is never wrong.''

''Mrs. Jablonski, he is wrong now. I have ruled in this case without the help of voices from beyond to guide me.''

''Not voices . . .''

''Yes, yes, I know. Well, I have not had to seek advice from any sources beyond my own logical mind and the guidance of the law. I'm sorry, Mrs. Jablonski.''

''Your Honor,'' Bill Fresno said, ''full guardianship means that Mr. Jablonski can remove Elizabeth from the home and friends she's known for so many years. Couldn't you reconsider at least letting her stay where she is?''

''I leave the decisions on Mrs. Jablonski's welfare to her son. I'm sure he has her best interests at heart, and will make the decisions that will only be for her own good.''

Judge Maria Jackson stood.

''All rise,'' the Bailiff said.

She turned and stepped down from the bench. It was then the rear doors of the courtroom burst open and a man stumbled frantically into the room.

''Your Honor!'' Bill Fresno called after Judge Jackson.

Judge Jackson had already opened the door to her chambers. She said over her shoulder, "Too late, Mr. Fresno."

"We're talking about a woman's life here!" Fresno shouted as Judge Jackson entered her chambers and closed the door behind her. "Damn," Fresno said.

Andrew Jablonski and Attenboro exchanged satisfied smiles. Attenboro started collecting the papers from the table and putting them in his briefcase.

Panting, sweating, out of breath, the man came up to Bill Fresno. "Are you Mr. Fresno?" The words coming out between pants for air.

"Yes. But it looks like you're too late to help."

"I'm sorry. Had an accident with the car coming over here. Right now it's bleeding all over the road four blocks from here. I exchanged insurance info. with the other driver, pushed the car to the curb and ran over here as fast as I could." He was holding his stomach and sucking air as fast as he could. "Hope I don't have a heart attack."

The man was in his forties, dressed in a suit that was limp with the sweat pouring off his body, the collar open, the tie pulled down. He had a small leather attaché case with him.

The man looked over at Betty who was still seated at the table. She was stunned. This couldn't happen. Eugene was never wrong.

"I'm sorry, Mrs. . . ."

"All rise!" the bailiff called.

Judge Maria Jackson entered the courtroom and marched quickly up to the bench. "Sit, everyone," she said. Then to Bill Fresno, "Let's hear your witness, Mr. Fresno. And this better be good."

Attenboro was on his feet. "But your Honor! You have already ruled in this case!"

"Mr. Attenboro, this hearing isn't over until I say it's over. And I say it isn't over. Now sit down."

Attenboro sat down, but he made it clear by his actions and facial expressions that he was pissed. He and Andrew engaged in intense whispering.

Judge Jackson turned to Bill Fresno. "Well, Mr. Fresno, let's hear from your witness."

Bill Fresno directed the man to the witness chair. The man

seemed unsure of what he was supposed to do.

"It is all right, sir," Judge Jackson said. "Just sit down."

The man sat, and put the attaché case on his lap.

Judge Jackson leaned over toward the man. "Now, who are you?"

The man looked at the judge. "My name is Andersen Brookes."

Fresno jumped in. "And what do you do for a living?"

"I work for Dean Witter in Sarasota. I'm a stockbroker."

"How long have you worked there?"

"Almost ten years now."

"And you know Mrs. Jablonski?" Bill Fresno pointed to Betty.

"Yes, sir." Then to Betty, "I'm sorry to hear about your husband. I mean, I didn't know. I just heard."

"What didn't you know?" Fresno asked.

"I didn't know her husband was, well, dead."

"When did you first learn that Mr. Jablonski was deceased?"

"Yesterday, when you and I talked."

"You handle Mrs. Jablonski's investments?"

"Yes."

Peter looked at Eleanor and grinned. She smiled and nodded.

"When did she first start investing with you?"

He opened his briefcase, extracted a folder, and opened it. He examined the papers. "April 27, 1989."

Bill Fresno looked at the judge. "Your, Honor, that was two months after Eugene Jablonski died." Then to Andersen Brookes, "Tell us how she opened the investment account."

The man shrugged. "Well, she came in with a cashier's check for two hundred thousand dollars, and told me her husband said to invest that money."

"Her husband told her?"

"So help me, that's what she said. I didn't know he was . . . er, not alive then."

"And then you set up her investment account, recommended some stock and . . ."

"No. I didn't recommend any stocks. She had a list of stocks to invest in. She said her husband gave her the list."

"So, the purchases were directed by her husband?"

"That's what she said. But I didn't know that . . ."

"Yes, you've said that. Tell us how those investments faired."

"Pretty good."

Judge Jackson said, "What do you mean by 'pretty good?' "

Andersen Brookes turned to the judge. "Well, a good investment portfolio, say an aggressive portfolio will double its value every five to six years. Mrs. Jablonski's portfolio doubled every three. That's pretty darn good."

"Doubled every three years?" Judge Jackson said aloud, but to herself.

"Yes, your Honor."

"Does she still have those same stocks in her account?" Bill Fresno said.

"Oh, no. She would stop in every so often with instructions . . . from her husband, to sell some company and buy some others. After I saw the performance of this man's recommendations . . . well, truthfully, I set up my own account to emulate hers. And I must say, I've done very well, thanks to . . . to Mr. Jablonski."

"Just a minute," Judge Jackson said. "You said that her portfolio doubled every three years?"

"Yes, your Honor," Andersen said.

"Then she should have over a million dollars in her account?"

Andersen flipped through the papers before him and pulled out one. Looking at it, he read, "$1,385,492 as of close of business yesterday."

Maria Jackson sat back in her chair.

Bill Fresno continued, "In your opinion, how astute is Mrs. Jablonski in regards to the stock market?"

"If you had asked me that the other day, I would have said she knew nothing about it. Now, I don't know."

"How about explaining why you thought she knew nothing about the stock market?"

"Well, she used to come in with a slip of paper on which were written the stock market abbreviations for the company stocks to buy. When I asked her about them, she had no idea what companies the abbreviations were for. Her husband had given her the information on what to buy and sell. That's what she said. She had no concept of what capital gain and loss was. Or selling short. Things like that."

"Did she ever sell any stocks short?"

"Oh yes. Some really nice maneuvers there."

"You would have to admit, wouldn't you, from all you've told us, that Mrs. Jablonski made some shrewd rational decisions in her investments?"

"Shrewd is the best word for it. Never made any mistakes. I wish I knew what methods her husband, I mean, she uses. I just hope she doesn't move her account someplace else until I'm ready to retire. By following her lead, I've made a lot of money."

Bill Fresno then turned to Judge Jackson. "Your Honor, this woman's only fault has been that she seeks the advice of her dead husband. Nothing has been shown here that would indicate that is a bad thing, that it impairs her judgment. On the contrary, using that advice, she has achieved what all of us would like to achieve. She has exercised excellent judgment in her investments, and made herself a millionaire.

"We may not agree with all the decisions she has made—for example, giving twenty dollars to beggars as a matter of course—but then, everyday we disagree with a lot of decisions made by what we consider rational people.

"She is living in good surroundings with people who make no demands on her except to seek her friendship. She takes care of her medical and health needs, feeds herself, clothes herself, and generally enjoys a pleasant life. There is no reason for the court to declare this woman incompetent. On the contrary, we might all want to seek the advice of Eugene at one point or another. I contend that this hearing is simply an attempt by her son to get control of her money. Nothing more, nothing less. And, as we've seen, there is a lot of money at stake here.

"I implore the court not to ruin this woman's life because she is different. And not to give in to the greed of her son."

"Are you through with Mr. Brookes?" Judge Jackson asked.

"Yes, your Honor." Bill Fresno went back to the table and sat down next to Betty.

"Mr. Attenboro, any questions?"

Attenboro let out a sigh and stood. "No your Honor. But I think it is a mistake to accept some luck in the stock market as proof that Mrs. Jablonski is competent to handle her day-to-day affairs. The stock market is nothing more than a gambling arena and a success at gambling does not mean a success in life. Remember, the bottom line here is *she talks to her dead husband.* That is not normal nor rational behavior. And that's what we are here to judge—Mrs. Jablonski's ability to exercise normal rational behavior. That is all I wish to say, your Honor." Attenboro sat down.

Judge Maria Jackson sat upright in her chair and leaned over toward Andersen Brookes. "You may step down, Mr. Brookes."

Andersen Brookes gathered the papers in his lap, shoved them into the attaché case, stood, and walked back to sit in a chair behind Peter.

Maria Jackson then turned to face the two attorneys, and clasped her hands on the bench before her. "The recommendations given me by the committee unequivocally stated that Mrs. Jablonski's judgment is impaired. The question I was asked to consider is: To what extent Mrs. Jablonski is impaired in handling her own affairs? Can she effectively understand and deal with the complexities of everyday life? Can she make rational, sound judgments in her own interests?

"Mr. Fresno has said that the ability to invest successfully is reason enough to consider that her judgment is not impaired at all.

"On the other hand, Mr. Attenboro says the stock market is a gambling arena. And Mrs. Jablonski's luck at gambling should not be construed as evidence of her competence.

"Investing in the stock market can be a gamble. It depends on the investor. I can say that a shrewd investor has to take into account the complexities of the economy, the national political arena, the international economic pressures, and the position of the companies that would best thrive in that situation at that time. Those are complex issues far above those faced in everyday living. Mrs. Jablonski's astounding accomplishments in that arena prove to me she is more than capable of handling the more mundane problems of everyday life.

"I find no evidence to support Mr. Andrew Jablonski's bid for guardianship of Mrs. Jablonski on the basis of her incompetence. *Now*, this hearing is over, Mr. Attenboro." She banged the gavel.

Bill Fresno smiled, let out the breath he was holding and hung his head in relief. Betty smiled knowingly. Eugene was never wrong. Peter and Eleanor hugged each other tightly, Peter wincing with the pain in his back, but not resisting the hug. Walter was nodding in satisfaction until Benny, laughing, clapped him on the back, causing him to lose his grip on the cane, and nearly fall off the chair to the floor. No one paid any attention to Andrew Jablonski and Attenboro as they left the courtroom.

"Mr. Brookes," Judge Maria Jackson beckoned from the bench.

Andersen Brookes left his chair and approached the bench. Maria Jackson leaned over, and said in a confidential tone, "I would like to discuss my investments with you, if you have a moment?"

Peter got up, went over to Bill Fresno, and shook his hand. "I said from the beginning that Betty needed a miracle. I must congratulate you on pulling one off."

"Thanks." Fresno smiled. "But it was really Eugene." He nodded in Eleanor's direction. "She told me that Eugene had said Betty's investments would get her off. And he was right."

When they were outside and had piled into Benny's car, Benny turned to Peter, who was in the backseat with Eleanor and Betty, and said, "Slick, since it's such a beautiful day, and what happened today calls for a celebration, we're going to take you to the beach."

Eleanor grinned. "Your first time since you're in Florida."

"Where do you intend to take us?" Walter asked.

"Thought that place on Manatee Beach. We can sit outside, have coffee and watch all the tourists splashing around in the water."

"Oh, good," Betty said. "Let's go."

When they arrived at the beach twenty minutes later, Peter was sound asleep in the backseat. They left him there and went to the patio of Café on the Beach for coffee.